CATERING TO LOVE

Departments of Love Series
Book One

Joshua Ian

ARE YOU SIGNED UP FOR DRAGONBLADE'S BLOG?

You'll get the latest news and information on exclusive giveaways, exclusive excerpts, coming releases, sales, free books, cover reveals and more.

Check out our complete list of authors, too!

No spam, no junk. That's a promise!

Sign Up Here

www.dragonbladepublishing.com

Dearest Reader;

Thank you for your support of a small press. At Dragonblade Publishing, we strive to bring you the highest quality Historical Romance from some of the best authors in the business. Without your support, there is no 'us', so we sincerely hope you adore these stories and find some new favorite authors along the way.

Happy Reading!

CEO, Dragonblade Publishing

"But in the deep shadows there was mystery enough to feed the
burning impatience of seeing all in the light of day."

—J.P. Mahaffy ["On Arriving in Athens: The Acropolis"]

CHAPTER ONE

London, Summer, 1908

HENRI PAUSED ACROSS the street and waited for the bus, with its twisting staircase on the rear, to move past. He lifted his hat and patted his forehead with his handkerchief. He wore a herringbone tweed Norfolk jacket and a bowtie, and wondered if he might have chosen lighter dress. Though this had been a mild summer so far, July had finally started to act like July this morning and the bright sun had shone down on him as he walked. He often took the tube and possibly a bus to work, but today he had decided he had the time to spare to enjoy the rare rays. He gazed up at his destination, his work place, the place which had been described as "the tiara of the shopping district" on its opening earlier this year: Hartridge & Casas Department Store.

The front of the building was decorated with Corinthian columns throughout its façade, interspersed at various points with carved figures, all classical in nature, mostly women in the national garb of various countries. It had been a nod to all the various products one could find within. Above the main entrance to the store, the grandest entrance of many smaller, there were two towering statues fashioned like two great Atlantes, each one facing towards either end of the city block, which the department store spread the length of. Above their heads, instead of globes or rocks, they held up giant flowers, wrought in polished stone like themselves, that looked at once both soft and impenetrable.

Fanny Clay, one of the telephonists who worked in the main switchboard room, had explained to Henri one day while visiting the Royal Tea Room that the two carved giants were meant to represent Lord Hartridge and Señor Casas, the co-founders of the store, and that the flowers carved into the tops of their ornate column tops were lilies. "White lilies, they say," she had added with a giggle before being dismissed by Mrs. Plaistow and allowing Henri no illumination on the meaning behind this language of flowers.

Entering Hartridge & Casas often felt, to Henri, in those early hours before opening, like entering a cathedral. He had no other reference for the quiet reverence he felt. The sparkling tile work, the mirror-like polish of the wood, the air filled with the various scents that changed from floor to floor. At one level sweet floral perfumes, the next the scent of the polished wood furniture, the crisp linens of homewares, the savory tang of the food hall, the library-like smell of stationery with the musky smell of ink at its edges and so on. His mother had taken him to Le Bon Marché when he was a child, and while it was dazzling, it now felt archaic in comparison. The overly ornate stairwells, the grandiose mantle, all seemed to recede into a dusty past when he looked over Hartridge & Casas with its lifts and moving escalators, its gleaming surfaces and wide open spaces with more colors and textures than the mind could imagine. It felt like the very moment of modernity, and, yet somehow, like the future too. These hours early in the morning, these pre-opening hours, felt like entering into the vestibule of a church of the future, just before the service began, silence and calm, but a calm centered in the knowledge that a rush of humanity would soon flood in.

As Henri neared the central lift, which would take him to the Royal Tea Room where he worked, he let his fingers glide along a display of fine kid gloves laid out on a mahogany table. Only months before, this particular display had been piled high with the cashmere shawls and muffs of the cooler months. Now, a disembodied, faceless mannequin head sat in the center of the stacked table, a lively summer hat, tilted at a fashionable angle, on her head. All around her, pairs of porcelain hands sprung up from the table showing off the newest in gloves, for day, for evening, for special events.

"Good morning, monsieur," said the lift attendant.

"Good morning, Merrill."

Henri leaned back against the wall of the lift and sighed. He felt comforted being in the store, and, more than any other place before, it felt like a fit, as if he had landed in a space where he was only waiting for the next great turn in his life. It gave him a sense of purpose, even if he had to fight daily with the impatience of his want for that turn to reveal itself. He hopped off the lift on the top floor, home of the Royal Tea Room, and headed straight for the kitchens there.

The entire dining room and beyond was filled with the divine smell of baking breads. The bakers arrived before him, and before anyone else for that matter, and even though he knew they could make laminated pastry in their sleep, he liked to arrive early to keep a sharp eye on quality. At least, that was what he told himself. Arriving before opening and staying many evenings past dinner service, and sometimes even until closing, he displayed to everyone who looked upon him, and even to himself, as a gourmand obsessed with his job. Devoted to the task, his eyes only for his work. And while he was that, the hours spent in the store also helped him to check the overwhelming sense of loneliness he felt constantly in his life. So he filled himself up, instead, with the pride of his work. To inhale the deep buttery smell of the croissants, the yeastiness of the rolls, press the tips of his fingers against the rich spring of the brioche, every morning these things fulfilled him. He found in them the passion he lacked elsewhere, the sensuality and the satisfaction.

He greeted the bakers cheerfully and they welcomed him in

equal measure. They finished their shifts before the great chaos of the service day really began, and they had begun to count him as one of their own. They welcomed his inspection and feedback, and exchanged ideas with him regularly.

"H and C came looking for you a bit earlier," said one of the bakers as he nodded a greeting.

"Both of them?" asked Henri.

"Not together as such. But first Hartridge, and then a little later, Casas. Said they would come back later. Nothing that couldn't wait a bit, they said."

"Are you sure? It is not usual for them both to visit the kitchen."

The young man shrugged. "Didn't seem vexed. Said they just had something to ask you."

"I shall wait for their arrival. In the meantime, is there any coffee yet?"

"I'll never know how you can drink that," Mrs. Crombie said from the kitchen entrance. "I know it's become all the fashion amongst the well-heeled but I can never take it over my tea."

"Je suis français, madam. Coffee for me is not fashion, but fortitude."

Mrs. Crombie winked at him and beamed. Henri was always glad to see her, but he couldn't help notice, as she shifted the empty basket to her hip and took a step forward, the stiffness of her gait. Her hip must be bothering her again.

"Mademoiselle Crombie, you needn't come all the way up every morning if it troubles you. I can always send a boy down with the breads."

The employee canteen was located on the basement level of the store, and they supplied Mrs. Crombie's kitchen with all the leftover breads and pastries from the previous day's custom for use downstairs.

"No, no. No trouble in the least. What with those lifts they have, I barely notice. When I think back on my days as a young tweenie, climbing up and down those stairs till my back ached and my knees almost gone, it's a wonder I survived. No, no trouble. It gives me a break from the breakfast rush, at any rate."

"Is it very busy?"

"It will be just. Most of the employees take their morning meal here now. They don't have to fuss about at home of a morning. Even those that live-in in the dormitories tell me it's cheaper than any they can find outside."

"And more delicious too, I am sure."

Mrs. Crombie smiled and dipped her head. "I'm just a plain cook, monsieur. Not so grand as you."

"Nonsense," said Henri. "I may be a trained chef, but I learned my most important skills at the knee of my grand-mère in her country kitchen. She was the best cook I've ever known."

Henri relieved her of her basket and began to fill it with the leftover baked goods.

"You may have too much choice today. I have an excess of sandwich bread. Most of it stale, or nearly so, I'm afraid. And rolls and croissants, at least a day out."

"That's all right then," Mrs. Crombie reassured him. "I've got too many apples on hand so I can use the bread for a Jenny Lind pudding. And we'll be doing an almond soup today—they always want plenty of rolls and such for that."

"Idéal."

"Did Mrs. Plaistow tell you about the new lot for the Tea Room?"

Mrs. Plaistow was the manageress of the Royal Tea Room for which Henri's kitchen mainly worked. In addition, Henri and his staff also supplied the petit fours, chocolates, and sweets for the food halls located a few floors down.

"New lot?"

"Yes, there's some new wait staff starting. Today, I believe."

"Ah, that must be why the messieurs were looking for me before."

Mrs. Crombie nodded. "One young lady and three young men, all good-looking. But, then, they always are, aren't they?

Lord Hartridge has a good eye for that. Sprats to the mackerel, I say. He knows the ladies like to see a handsome face serving them tea."

Henri smiled and gave Mrs. Crombie a look. "I didn't think most English ladies noticed their waiters."

"You'd be surprised how much they notice in not-noticing. I've worked around ladies and gentlemen all my life. And there's one thing I have learned: when it comes to a pretty face, social standing is quickly forgotten. Until sunrise, at least."

Henri grinned broadly. "Mademoiselle, you shock me."

"Not likely." She gave him a wink. "One of the boys is Tommy, a good sort; I knew his father from my days as cook at the Hartridge estate. His father were head gardener and him just a bothy boy, but he didn't have the heart for it. Disappointing for his pa, of course, but he'll earn a good wage. And it's nice to see someone connected to the old house."

"Do you miss working there?"

"Not that I can say, really." Henri noticed her hand fall against her bad hip. "But I do sometimes miss the people." She covered the basket of bread with a towel. "The other young men seem fine. Both Mediterranean fellows, I believe—from Italy or some such—only Tommy, he'll be an undertaking."

"Oh?"

"I haven't seen him since he was a boy, but Mrs. Plaistow says the sharpest thing on him are his front teeth. We shall pray he can manage."

Henri smiled at that. Mrs. Plaistow and Mrs. Crombie were the closest of friends, and had, in fact, decided to live together. Between the two of them not one bit of gossip or information escaped noting.

"Mrs. Plaistow does have her standards," Henri said.

"She does have to be stern, a woman with male staff under her. She must have a firm hand."

"Oui. Elle est redoutable."

"That's right," Mrs. Crombie agreed, vaguely.

Henri grimaced as he picked up a stack of tea sandwiches from amongst the breads.

"Fish paste sandwiches," he declared with disdain.

"I'll take those," said Mrs. Crombie. "Colonel Ambrose will love them."

"I can't believe you keep that dirty animal in your kitchens."

"He's a cat," protested Mrs. Crombie. "They're the cleanest animals around. Besides, he helps catch the mice, doesn't he?"

Henri shook his head. "It is a shame. This building is too new for mice."

"It's London, my duck. You're lucky mice are all that worries us." She chuckled. "I expect I ought to head back. I look forward to hearing your assessment on the new lads." She patted the basket. "Ta as always. Have a very good day, monsieur."

"And you too, mademoiselle."

NICO HAD HEARD stories as a young boy about English soldiers and how they lined up to be inspected just before war, spit-polished and creased, immaculate before the threat of death and glory. But he imagined that none of those poor, brave souls had ever faced a general quite so formidable as Mrs. Elizabeth Plaistow, manageress of the Royal Tea Room. She stood before them, looking over the top of her rimless pince nez, examining them inch by inch, silently, a stern expression on her face. She wore quite a fashionable hat, Nico could tell, that only covered the width of her hair, the side decorated with a burst of raven feathers that spread out from an ebony glass jewel at their center. Her dress was black to match, and instead of reminding one of mourning, it gave much more the impression of a uniform, a suit of silken armor.

As she began to speak to them, she withdrew the hat pin, and removed her hat. Her great mass of dark hair was swept up and away from her face and the rounded coiffure ended with a bun on top. Like the woman herself, tall and strong-limbed as she was, it was grand and impressive. Nico bit back a smile as he wondered if the wire that might have outlined her pince nez had been used for a pompadour frame. He could tell she was far too sober to entertain humor.

If the H&C building was the tiara of the shopping district, then the Royal Tea Room was its central jewel. It took up the fourth floor and the roof patio level above. On the fourth floor was the indoor tea room with nine-foot-high ceilings, with glass windows that ran almost the entire length so that the place was filled with light. There were crystal chandeliers, electric, hung high so that evening patrons were bathed in a glow of light as if the stars had come too close, fallen from the firmament. It was filled with foliage, big leafy green things, large potted palms, ferns and all types of lush exotic plants whose leaves gave color but were sturdy and didn't fall to crumble or give off too much scent. There was an alcove to one side, near the stairwell, which housed a piano and room enough for a violinist or cellist or both. There was an occasional vocalist, mostly reserved for specialist events, and a harpist for the more somber occasions like Sunday afternoons or holidays.

The twisting iron staircase led to the Roof Garden, which was as spacious as the fourth floor, if not more so, save for a center hull which housed machinery, water, and electricals for the building, called The Closet. This area had a smaller separate boiler which vented out so that the tables nearest the wall could have warm air pumped onto them on colder days. Also en-sconced against these walls were great awnings which could be drawn out to at least a dozen feet in length and propped up to offer shade from the sun or protection from the rain. Around the perimeter of these center tables were more tables that could not be reached, but umbrellas were stored in the closet that could be brought out to protect these seating areas. To the other end of the square U-shape was a small area fenced off, as it were, by large potted ferns. This area, referred to by the staff as The Jungle, was a prep and staging area. Spare chairs and tables were stashed here, along with all the cutlery, napkins, and water pitchers needed for service on the deck. This area also led to the staff stairwell, which conveyed the waiters down to just behind the kitchens so they could bring food and appear at service without having to meet patrons on the main stairwell.

Nico had admired the shining jewel from afar since it had been constructed, and it spoke to him as the height of luxury and sumptuousness. Imagine having the time in your day to sit leisurely enjoying tea and cakes or even a multi-course lunch. He could hardly believe that not only had he been given the chance to visit the Tea Room, he would now be seeing it daily.

"Now," Mrs. Plaistow said pointing at the staff standing before her with her hat pin and then sinking it into the felt of the hat on the table like a pin cushion, "you all shall be working the Tea Room under my supervision."

Nico and the rest nodded. Mrs. Plaistow lifted a short type-written sheet from the table.

"Nikolaos Kavafis?" she called out like a schoolteacher.

"Yes, madam," answered Nico.

She looked at him and he thought he could see her eyes soften.

"Ma'am will suffice. Or Mrs. Plaistow, if you will. I have no noble blood; I am but a mere floor supervisor. But do remember," she paused, to let her gaze scan the line of them, "I am *your* floor supervisor."

She named the other new waitstaff besides Nico, including Thomas Ainsley, Mario Lombardi, and a red-headed young woman called Lily Ramsay. Lily appealed very much to Nico, and he hoped he could befriend her without giving the wrong impression of interest. Lily seemed all spunk and action, and he admired her energy. Both young men were handsome enough, if of completely different styles. Mario's young face had an impish quality about it, although his pointed, bushy eyebrows gave his visage a sinister cast at times. But in the brief conversations they had managed earlier that morning, he seemed nothing but sweet and soft-mannered. Tommy, on the other hand, had burst into the waiting room like a bull let loose, and seemed to have about as much intellectual capacity. But, Nico imagined, his rough edges were often forgiven because of his looks. Sparkling blue eyes, straw-colored hair, and the fresh blush of country living on his cheeks—he was not at all Nico's type, but he could see the general appeal.

"And, although I am manageress," Mrs. Plaistow continued her introductory speech, "You shall also be at the disposal of Monsieur Henri, the head chef whose kitchens are attached to the Tea Room. He can, at times, be impetuous, as the French are wont to be, but he is a kind man whose direction you should heed. We are lucky to have him here at Hartridge & Casas, as he trained under Escoffier himself."

"Under a what?" Tommy blurted out.

She gave him a steely look.

"Mister Ainsley, if you intend to succeed at all in this profession, you would do well to educate yourself on *who* Monsieur Auguste Escoffier is, not what."

Tommy dipped his head, abashed. "Yes, miss."

"Ma'am, as I have explained. Ma'am as in ham, not m'm as mum. I am not, nor will I ever be your mother, though I pray for her, whatever unfortunate soul she may be."

"Yes miss—Ma'am, I mean. Yes, ma'am."

"Shall we make our way to the Tea Room then?" Her voice posed a question but her tone was a command.

THE REST OF the staff had begun arriving when Henri returned from the employee common room where he had stashed his jacket, waistcoat, and bowtie and donned his chef's whites. He wore a long-sleeved, double-breasted white jacket and tied an apron around his waist over his dark brown trousers. He finished his uniform with a neckerchief, as all in the kitchen did, but instead of the typical white he preferred colored scarves—his favorite, and most often worn, being an indigo blue. It was his way of asserting an aesthetic individuality, but he had noticed that it also made him stand out from the rest of the staff, signaling his position and presence. He was just coming into the kitchen when he spied Señor Casas entering from the dining room.

Rumors had swirled in all strata of society about Lord Hartridge and Señor Casas for the decade Henri had been in London. Even before they'd joined as business partners, they were esteemed guests at the properties of Ritz and Escoffier; bosom friends, both attractive single men who seemed to much prefer their own company, traveling the world together. It did not take much deep thought, even in those more socially stern later days of Victoria's rule, to suspect a context of friendship not matching the usual mode. Still they thrived and escaped scandal—so much so that they were able to find investors and create this shopping paradise with hardly an eviscerating word said against them—in public, at least. Henri had admired them from afar as a young man at the Carlton, and was beyond flattered when they'd sought him out in consideration of their plan to open a restaurant in their new palace of commerce.

He had not expected a department store to offer the rich mix of the bohemian, the extravagant, and the political that the hotel had been immersed in, but he admired their enterprising spirit and thought he could learn much at Hartridge & Casas. They inspired him, too. He told no one, could tell no one, not even Michel, but he thought if they could achieve such greatness with the open secret of their lives, then maybe he, too, on a much humbler scale might. He had to be more careful than either of them; he did not have the security of money or status to untangle any ensnarement that being a man, like the type of man he was, might visit upon him. But, still, here, and hopefully one day on his own, he reckoned he might create his own universe, orbiting outside all the nonsense of society and its specious morality.

Señor Casas wore one of his signature dark suits with a flower in the lapel—one burst of color in the muted tones of his wardrobe that seemed to signal the mysterious nature of his personality. In all the time he had known him, Henri had never seen Señor Casas in a hat.

If Lord Hartridge was the father figure of the store, Casas was more like the mysterious uncle. One wouldn't see him for days and days and then he would appear, suddenly, all friendly smiles and warm words. It became a joke amongst the staff that one always had to be on one's toes, otherwise the magical Casas might materialize without warning and catch one off-guard. But he was never a frightening genie, no matter what bottle he popped up from. He was always welcome, and while the staff, of course, were conscious of their appearance, behavior, and the general state of their department when he was near, they never worried much about disappointing him. Despite the lapses in his being seen, he always knew all the latest news—birthdays, children, weddings, promotions, all of it—and his main duty, it seemed, was to congratulate people on their achievements; he never failed to win them over. His was a rule of enchantment not discipline.

Henri suspected that Casas was around far more than he seemed to be, as more than once he had caught Señor Casas in a corner of a department, or sitting, ostensibly reading a newspaper on a bench or buffet, but watching everything going on around him with a proud smirk on his face. He courted an air of mystery, intentionally, and it worked. While he and Hartridge both had the looks for an oil painting, Casas was, in Henri's estimation, the more enticing one—the one for whom young ladies might devolve into a titter of giggles as their mothers hurried to usher them absent from his presence.

His good looks had been enhanced of late by his growing a trim beard, dark like the rest of him, with only the first hints of grey at his temples and below his lip betraying the sun-tempered complexion which kept him always youthful and healthy. The new beard slightly gave the appearance of a New York robber-baron but the twinkle in his eye displaced any real association.

"Good morning, señor."

"Good morning, Monsieur Henri. Ah, Michel, perfect timing."

Michel Mauté, Henri's sous chef, with his trimmed little moustache, approached carrying two demitasse cups and saucers to fill. It was custom for Henri to meet with Michel prior to the start of the day to discuss any kitchen issues, decide on daily specials, and plan the menus for the week.

"I am not sure if Mrs. Plaistow has had the chance to tell you that we have new staff starting today," said Casas.

"Mrs. Crombie informed me, monsieur."

"Of course she did," said Casas with a smile. "I hope it won't be too crowded with them shadowing the senior waitstaff."

"No, monsieur. It shall be quite fine. We are glad to have the new staff."

"Yes," added Michel, "our daily seating has swelled of late."

"Yes," agreed Casas. "Of this, we are very appreciative. H&C is becoming quite talked about, I am told, by friends and enemies alike. And so much of it thanks to our impeccable kitchen staff and the talented leadership of Monsieur Henri."

"You flatter me, señor."

"I only speak the truth. Escoffier and Ritz might very well be cursing our names for snatching so bright a star from their night sky of chiffon and silver. But, while I have you flattered, I must ask of you a favor. Lord Hartridge and I will be entertaining a private guest for lunch today. Lord Ockley, an old friend of the family, that sort of thing, who may be working with us on an enticing prospect. It is an exciting summer, is it not? With all the swirl of events around."

"Indeed."

"I wondered, could you have something sent to the office for lunchtime? Lord Ockley has rather staid taste, I'm told, so nothing too Continental for the main."

"Shall I do a jugged hare and oatmeal?"

Casas smiled and cut his eye at the chef. "No, monsieur. I was thinking something with a bit of flair, only not too much. Steak perhaps?"

"Oui, señor. I can do that with pommes frites. And possibly a carrot and swede puree?"

"Utterly boring and absolutely perfect for the occasion. But, please, monsieur, one of your grand desserts, if you will. I cannot bear thinking you have stifled yourself for an entire meal. And I always adore them."

"We have just got some marvelous peaches. I can do Pêche Aiglon?"

"His glace au vanille is perfection, señor. And the ice newly stocked," added Michel.

Casas smacked his hands together. "The famous Escoffier peaches? Oh, that would be delightful."

"Mais un peu plus discret. I shall omit the crystallized violets."

"Yes, don't let's shock the aristocratic palate. They frighten so easily," Casas joked. "Perfect, as always, monsieur. Gentlemen, I thank you."

With a nod, Señor Casas took his exit.

"You were there that night at the Carlton, weren't you?" asked Michel. "With Bernhardt."

"Yes, Michel. You have reminded me many times."

"What a night to have off! I had forgotten that I am still supposed to have not forgiven you for that."

"It was a magical night. She was dressed all in white when she arrived—cloak and veil—like some divine Reine des Neiges. Quite a show. Señor Casas was there that night too—and Lord Hartridge, of course—though I doubt they saw."

"These facts do not compel me to forgive you."

"But you must. Tu ne souviens pas? I gave you my ticket to Cyrano, despite my desire to see Madame Bernhardt on stage, so that you could have two and take Edith instead."

"Bien sûr. Our first real night together. If not for you, I may never have become a married man."

"Ah, oui. In that case, I see why you do not want to forgive me."

"Here now," interrupted a stroppy voice. It was David, the junior chef, who came up beside them, tucking a towel into the side of his apron. "I don't think I've ever seen Mrs. Hartridge come to the kitchen this early in the day."

"That wasn't Hartridge," Michel corrected. "It was Señor Casas."

"Like I said. The Missus Hartridge himself. I wonder if he fetches Lord Hache's slippers at night and all."

David laughed at his joke, but Henri and Michel only exchanged a tired glance.

"Did you need something, David?" asked Michel.

"No, Chef. Just curious why you and Mister Casas don't speak French together is all."

"Why would we?" asked Henri.

"Mister Casas is Spanish, not French," offered Michel.

"So you can't speak his language, then?"

"He speaks Spanish; we speak French," said Henri tartly.

"Yeah, but it's all foreign though, ain't it? Can't be all that different to my mind."

"Parce que vous avez le cerveau d'un poulet," snapped Henri.

David looked at Michel. "Here, what did he say?"

"Le poulet," said Michel. "The cutlets. Have you prepared them?"

"Not yet."

"Alors, faites-le! Et là!" commanded Henri.

David's limited French was overcome by the tone of Henri's command, and he scuttled off.

"Come, Michel, let us plan the menus."

Henri made his way into the dining room through the swinging doors; Michel a few paces behind, having grabbed the two demitasse cups.

"Monsieur, ton café."

"Ah, merci. Turc?"

"Biên sur."

Henri was very glad to have his friend Michel with him here at Hartridge & Casas. Michel was the only person, besides Mrs. Crombie, Henri ever felt comfortable enough around to let his guard down. Henri had recruited him—"stolen him" as the staff had framed it—from the Carlton when he'd left to work for H&C. He and Michel had been in the same cohort when entering the Carlton under the training of Monsieur Escoffier and they had become quick friends, the best of friends, in fact. Michel had been a chef de partie just like Henri—Michel a chef saucier and Henri a chef patisserie—the marvelous assembly line that was the Escoffier style. Henri had moved up, during his time at the infamous hotel, to chef de cuisine. Many talked of his one day possibly being sous chef at the Carlton itself or some other grand hotel. But, for Henri, this was not enough.

His ambitions stretched beyond a mere kitchen position, however grand it might be, and he longed to create something wholly his own. A fire burned within him, a want for something more, something beyond his skills. He still thrilled to execute a dish, but it did not bring him the deep soul satisfaction it once had. There was a chasm in him that needed filling, and he knew it must be achievement on a great scale. Something he could point at and call his own.

In this, he felt fully supported by Michel, as Michel himself didn't have such lofty goals. He wanted to be a good chef, just like Henri, but his main aim in life was to make a good living, have a home and family and live comfortably. And, too, as fiery and bull-headed as Henri could be, Michel was the exact opposite, quietly calming and always composed. Their styles complimented one another to perfection and created what Henri deemed a balanced kitchen. When they worked together, there was an unspoken understanding, almost a connection of the mind, that required little speech to execute dishes perfectly.

Michel would be the perfect person to take over at H&C when Henri finally left, if he didn't desire to follow him into a lesser venture. But, for now, all of that was just a daydream. He still had so far to go to achieve that goal.

They took a seat at a small table for two near the corner of the Tea Room. They shared a moment of silence, savoring their beloved coffee.

"How is Edith doing?" asked Henri.

"She is well. Even with Michael at her skirts still, she manages to flourish. She is expanding her clientele every day. She has just taken on two new ladies, both from Russell Square. Maybe she will take on your grandmother as a client."

"My grandmother doesn't live in Russell Square."

"Close enough to count."

"Hardly. Besides, I doubt my grandmother has had any new clothes since the Queen took up all black."

"Mourning in commiseration?"

"I believe my grandmother has only ever mourned her bank balance. But I will kindly spread the word of Edith's services."

"Merci. She has just allied with a wonderful seamstress."

"Better than Edith herself?"

"Likely not. But she wishes to concentrate more on design and with the work she already takes—alterations and the ordinary things—to make a little coin, it helps to have another pair of hands to craft the bespoke orders."

"Before you know it, your wife will have her own design house. She may be the next Charles Worth."

Michel smiled proudly.

"There is much time to go before that, but it would surprise me not at all. Speaking of the family, you must come over for dinner soon. It will be Michael's birthday soon."

"Another birthday? Did he not just have one some months ago?"

"Yes, Henri. Twelve months ago, in fact. That is rather how

these things work."

"Soon he will be old enough to apprentice in the kitchens."

"He is only turning eight. And I plan to keep him far away from any kitchen."

"Yes, he should aspire to be more like his mother anyway. Of course I shall come. I will make him a cake."

"That would be lovely. Although, usually I am the one to make his cake."

"You deserve a day off. Also, my baking is better than yours."

Michel gave a small roll of the eyes and took a sip of coffee.

"Let us hope my son also aspires to have the confidence of his parrain, Henri."

Henri lifted his cup in toast. "We can only hope."

"Ah, Monsieur Newbold, good morning."

Henri and Michel looked up to see Mrs. Plaistow heading towards them, followed by a group of wait staff in sharply pressed livery.

"And Monsieur Mauté as well." She nodded at Michel. "I am glad to find you together. I only wanted to give you a quick introduction to the new staff who will be starting today."

"Yes, word has quite gotten around," Henri said. "It's very exciting."

Henri held his saucer in one hand and sipped from his demi-tasse as Plaistow gave the introductions. Henri gave each waiter, and the one waitress, a regal nod, with a "bonjour" or "welcome" until the last, who stepped out from behind the rest.

The demitasse stopped between the saucer and his lips and Henri felt his whole body flush.

"Mister Nikolaos Kavafis," he heard Mrs. Plaistow say.

But it did not immediately register as there seemed to be a rush of wind all around him, whooshing through his ears. As his eyes met those of Mister Kavafis, he felt the hairs all over his face and neck stand on end. The room seemed to expand and contract all in one gasp. He felt an urging thrust as if his body were compelled forward, as if shoved by some invisible force, and he tensed, trying to quiet the need to leap out of his chair. Whether it was to tackle the exquisite creature he stared at or to gallop out of the room, fleeing, he could not be sure. Instead he was still, staring.

The exquisite creature, Mister Nikolaos Kavafis, gave a small, nervous smile. Henri was sure that his lack of greeting, and the silence it thus produced, had endured for hours. But he could not bring himself to form words.

"Monsieur," Mister Kavafis said with a small nod.

Michel moved his own cup and saucer, producing a small rattling noise that Henri took as a cue to check himself. Still, he was frozen.

"Yes, well," began Michel. "We are very pleased to meet you all. As I'm sure Mrs. Plaistow has explained, we hold our staff to the highest standards. But we also cherish those who cherish their positions. Please feel free to approach myself or Monsieur Newbold for any questions or needs that might arise." Michel glanced quizzically at Henri before adding, "Except during the luncheon rush, eh, monsieur?"

The group chuckled politely, and finally Henri returned his cup and saucer to the table. He cleared his throat, ignoring Mister Kavafis.

"Monsieur Henri," he said. "To the patrons I am Monsieur Newbold, and on formal events, of course, but please feel free to address me as Monsieur Henri on a daily basis."

"The same for me," said Michel with a nod.

"We're to call you Monsieur Henri as well?" asked the blond, Thomas.

Henri noticed Mister Kavafis stifle a laugh but when he looked to the chef to share in the mirth, Henri found he could grimace. Mister Kavafis dropped his eyes.

Mrs. Plaistow gave Thomas a very pointed look.

"Yes, well, Messiers Henri and Michel, we've taken up enough of your time. We should get on with the business of the day. So much to learn."

The quintet headed off. Mister Kavafis turned slightly before crossing the room, and nodded at Henri. Henri dipped his head in reply. His throat felt parched.

"A good lot they seem," Michel said when they had gone.

"Yes," said Henri vaguely.

"That Thomas seems quite something. Still has the whiff of the farm about him. That last fellow—Kavafis, I believe—was very striking."

"Was he? I hadn't noticed."

"No?" Michel narrowed his eyes. "Anyone could see it. I imagine he will be quite popular among our lady clientele."

"Yes. Well. How very nice for the ladies then."

Henri stood and began gathering his things.

"Are we done?" asked Michel, surprised. "But we haven't finished the week's menus."

"We can finish them later," said Henri flatly as he headed off. "Do you mind clearing my cup for me?"

Henri headed quickly for the staff washroom. Dashing into the gents', he snapped the door closed and leaned against it. He felt lightheaded and discomfited. What had come over him? He moved to the sink and splashed some cold water on his face. Over the years, his position at the Carlton had put him in contact with some of the most handsome, interesting men in Europe. Yet never before had he reacted so singularly to a person. Had he lost control of his faculties? Was this what getting older meant? Only just thirty years old and already blithering like a dotty old spinster. He was acutely aware of how foolish he must have looked. What could Michel be thinking? Even amongst the glittering personalities and luminaries who frequented the Carlton, he had never lost his composure so completely.

Despite his anxiety and embarrassment, in his mind's eye, he kept seeing his face. That beautiful face. All angles and soft eyes, as if constructed by the gods as ultimate temptation.

Nikolaos Kavafis.

The name rolled through his mind like a refrain of music.

That face.
That man.
Nikolaos Kavafis.
That man.
Who must be avoided at all costs.

HENRI DUFRESNE NEWBOLD.

Nico saw the words in his mind. Fanciful, gilt letters that might adorn a calling card or a menu.

Chef Henri

Monsieur Henri.

Henri.

Stormy eyes locked on him over the fine china of the demitasse cup. The hard line of his jaw, the strong nose, and those eyes. Those intense eyes. That had looked at him as if he were once an intruder and prey at the same time. Those eyes that had made him feel stripped bare and wanting. That penetrating glower that had made him giggle like a nervous child.

That man.

"Monsieur Henri."

Nico snapped out of his reverie.

"I'm sorry, what was that?" he asked.

"Report to Monsieur Henri," repeated Mrs. Plaistow, her annoyance sounding in her voice. "The kitchen has a task that needs completing."

"By me, ma'am?"

Plaistow sighed heavily.

"I do not find myself speaking to anyone else, do I? Really, Mister Kavafis, if this is how you mean to go on, perhaps this job is not the right fit for you."

"Oh, no, ma'am, my apologies. I was only momentarily overwhelmed. It's all so exciting, as you said."

His supervisor dipped her head in acknowledgment.

"Very well. But tarry no further. To the kitchens."

On his way, Nico thought again about the moment shared with Monsieur Henri. How the room had seemed to shift, shudder, like the bough of a tree in a strong wind. It was shocking, the feeling, and all too new to know exactly what it meant. He had never denied himself the appreciation of a handsome form, but this was a reaction before unknown.

In the kitchen, Nico found a cart waiting with three covered dishes on it. Behind the cart stood Monsieur Henri, his back to Nico, and Nico started when he realized they were meeting again. He caught his breath, silently waiting, yet Henri turned as if Nico had spoken his name out loud. His eyes burned into Nico.

"You," said Monsieur Henri, his voice dark.

"Monsieur." Nico swallowed hard. "Mrs. Plaistow said I was to attend here for a task."

The monsieur stared at him as he spoke and Nico was sure he was watching his lips move. He stopped speaking and put his hands behind his back. Monsieur Henri looked at him, for a moment longer than one normally would, and Nico thought that his expression seemed to soften momentarily. The hard set of his jaw, the piercing quality of his eyes, all seemed to mellow for an instant.

"Monsieur?"

The stone and ice returned to his countenance.

"Take this cart," Henri commanded. "To the main offices."

"Of Mister Hartridge and Mister Casas?"

"You know where they are, I assume?"

"Of course, sir. I interviewed there."

"Good. Then you shall have no trouble finding it."

"No, sir."

"One of their assistants will be expecting you. And take the main lift, not the staff. No one will complain in this instance."

"Yes, monsieur."

Nico placed his hands on the cart. He paused, steeling his

nerves. Now might be his best chance.

"Well?" prompted Monsieur Henri.

"I wanted to say I am honored to be working alongside you, Monsieur Henri."

"What?" The man looked panicked.

"Only Mrs. Plaistow told us of your training and achievements."

The panic seemed to flash to terror and then anger.

"You shall not be working with me," snapped Monsieur Henri.

"Pardon?"

"You are a waiter. I am the chef. Likely we shall hardly ever interact at all. You carry plates and fold napkins. I cook."

Nico felt as if he had been punched in the stomach.

"Of-of course, monsieur. I only meant—"

"Please. Go. I do not want my work to get cold."

Monsieur Henri turned sharply on his heels and stalked off.

As Nico rode the lift down, he stewed in a mix of emotions. Embarrassment and hurt boiled over into annoyance and anger. How dare Monsieur Henri speak to him in such a manner? He had done nothing to deserve such acid words. Was Monsieur simply that much of a snob? That was not the reputation that had preceded him during Nico's first days of his training before floorwork. He had heard how easygoing Monsieur Henri was, how he and his sous chef enjoyed a light banter with the staff, and his temper only flared occasionally. This did not seem the usual man he had heard talked about. Somehow he knew there was something amiss.

Nico knew what he had felt in the dining room. That jolt, that energy that seemed to flow between the two of them. The invisible current which felt as if it might wrap around them and pull them tight together. That was no ordinary moment, no usual occurrence.

Nico left the lift, nodding to the attendant, and pushed the cart swiftly across the ground level, heading for the lift opposite, which took one to the administrative offices. The confusion of colors and light and conversation on the sales floor did a bit to lift his mood as he moved. He passed the Book and Library Department and gave a wave to Hosea, who was on duty.

"Hark, a gentleman among us!" Hosea cried out, dramatically, thoroughly perplexing his current customer.

Nico laughed, grateful for that bit of mirth. He had known Hosea as a customer himself—he was extremely fond of books— and Hosea had, in fact, been the person who had alerted him to the job becoming available in the Tea Room. Hosea was a character and Nico appreciated him.

The administrative lift had no attendant and, riding up, Nico leaned against the wall, crossing his arms, lost again in his thoughts, and fretting. He was no fool. Every relationship of this sort he had thought of forging in his adult life had been forged on a battlefield. Circumstance—life, even—demanded it. He would not be deterred by flashes of temper or sharp words. He would not let eyes like cauldrons of boiling ink deter him from making a friendship if he wanted one. Monsieur Henri seemed so rigid, standing there in his perfectly ironed, supremely crisp whites. His nostrils may have flared in a show of impatience, but his eyes gave him away. Nico had been looked at too many times by too many men not to be a good judge of the unsaid. He knew that underneath that frigid exterior seethed a fire, and Nico was determined to mine those flames and discover the real passion that fueled them.

It felt like a duty bestowed upon him and he was hell-bound to fulfill it.

"Putain!"

Henri raised his finger to his mouth and sucked it, easing the pain. That was the second time he had burned himself in as many hours. He never burned himself, not since his days as a commis, and he was frustrated to be so distracted.

He emptied the leeks he had been browning in butter into a dish and pulled the nearest sauce to him. He stuck his pinky finger in, tasting. He pushed it roughly aside.

"Who made this?" he demanded.

"I did, Chef," said David, as he approached.

"What do you call this?"

"It's Sauce Gribiche—for the fish, Chef."

"I see no resemblance. It is a paltry mayonnaise at best, little more. Where did you train at that you cannot manage a simple sauce?"

"I trained at the National Training School for Cookery. Chef."

"I thought they only admitted women."

"And some men too."

"Did you attend via correspondence? Or perhaps you were distracted by your fellow pupils. You seemed to have missed some basic skills."

David puffed out his chest. "I was top of me bloody class. That's how I got on here."

"I was absent from the interview, évidemment. Take it away and do it again."

"Now, look here—"

"Look here nothing, monsieur! Do it again. And correctly this time, or you can move your duties to mis en place for today's service."

"What?"

"Need I repeat myself in French—or perhaps Spanish—or can you manage to comprehend English?"

David was clearly furious, but bit his tongue.

"Yes, Chef," he snapped and turned to go.

"Merde alors! Do not forget this." Henri shoved the dish of sauce across the worktop in David's direction. "Take it from my sight."

David snatched the dish and returned to his station, muttering.

Michel came up. "That was harsh," he said. "Even for you."

Henri glared at him. "It was necessary."

"Was it? I checked the sauce myself and it was fine."

"Am I now not allowed an opinion in my own kitchen?"

Michel stepped closer. "Tout va bien?"

Henri closed his eyes for a moment but all he could see was that beautiful face—that beautiful face falling for a moment, crushed by his terrible words from before.

"I'm fine," he replied, intentionally, in English. "Luncheon is upon us, Monsieur Mauté. No time for idle chat."

"À vos ordres mon capitaine."

Henri ignored the sarcasm.

He tried to shake the feeling at the pit of his stomach. Why had he been so entirely awful to Mister Kavafis? As the words left his mouth he regretted them. But he had turned away without an apology, willing himself not to turn back for fear his guilt might leave him undone and he might shatter on the spot, like Lot's wife.

He had been so awful because Kavafis was a threat to all he had constructed for himself. He had created his shield from the impossible distractions, like love and comradeship; he only had time in his life for tangible dreams. The last thing he needed was temptation. It had never done him well to be distracted in this way. He thought he had made himself safe here, up in this pretty nest on the fourth floor, his main interactions with debutants and matrons. But now this magnificent creature had appeared—one he felt drawn to, and one he felt was drawn to him, he was sure of it. The way he looked at Henri, the unspoken in his eyes.

Those eyes.

Like the color of café au lait. Dreamy, soft.

He smacked the table and shook his head.

This was not the place for such thoughts. This was his job, his life's work, he had to be only invested here, in these walls. Indulging in those other thoughts would bring him down. He intended, in no uncertain terms, to let this new fellow, this Mister Kavafis, know that nothing could or would distract him, that no moment, like the one they had prior, would progress into anything more.

CHAPTER TWO

THE EMPLOYEE CANTEEN was an enormous space.

On his first visit, Nico had thought the long, open room, flush with windows and sunlight, looked like one endless restaurant. It offered Breakfast, Elevenses, Lunch, Tea, Supper, and Late Supper so that something was available to accommodate all shifts. The "basic meals" were free to all employees though the canteen did supply a number of a-la-carte items one could buy, as well as the food halls being open to all for purchase throughout the day. Perhaps most appealing was the social camaraderie the canteen offered, a refreshing break from the polite formality of the work floor, aided by the long communal tables at which employees of all position, sexes, and departments ate together.

The kitchens were the domain of Mrs. Crombie and her staff, who served the food in a smorgasbord-type style. Trays were provided—a nod, Mrs. Plaistow had explained to Nico, to the Childs Restaurant in New York which Lord Hartridge had visited—so that each person could cobble together whatever meal they preferred and then seek out a perch.

Nico looked at his tray and back up to the menu:

CAULIFLOWERS, ALA SAUCE BLANCHE W/ CHEESE

ROAST BEEF – OR ASSORTED COLD MEATS

*STEWED CABBAGE * ASSORTED BREADS * PUDDING*

The pudding was unnamed and Nico could see why. He pushed the small dish next to his plate to the edge of his tray, eyeing the pale mound covered in yellowish custard and frowning.

"It's included with the luncheon, pet," said the older lady server who was replenishing the meal plates. "But you needn't eat it."

"Yes, of course," said Nico. "Only I hate to waste food."

"I'll gladly take it."

Nico turned to find a very handsome fellow behind him. The tall, solidly built, young man smiled, displaying a gorgeous set of perfectly white, perfectly straight teeth. They were almost dazzling in their brilliance.

"I've always had a sweet tooth," the fellow continued. "Canary Pudding isn't my favorite, if I'm honest, but I wouldn't turn it down. I prefer a caramel or a chocolate myself."

There was a lovely lilt to his vowels. Though it was only subtle and an entirely different accent, it somehow reminded Nico of Henri's pronunciation. Thinking of Henri made him smile.

"So do I," said Nico.

"They've got some lovely ones in the food hall," the man continued, stepping closer and warming to his subject. "Have you tried them?"

"I have indeed. In fact, I watched the H&C chef make them one morning."

The man with the lovely teeth guffawed. "Now I am proper jealous! I would kill to see that. Did you get to sample any of the mishaps?"

Nico was about to answer but they were interrupted.

"Oi, Eddie!"

Two equally tall and equally strapping young men bounded up beside him, carrying their own trays. The tallest one, who had called out, bumped against Nico's new friend.

"We've barely got time to get this down our gullets and here you stand gossiping like a fishwife."

"Nobody's gossiping, Norman. Me and this gentleman—Sorry, what's your name again?"

"Nico."

"Nico. Pleasure to meet you, I'm Edwin. Me and Nico here were just discussing the finer points of the canteen cuisine."

"Are there finer points?" asked Norman.

"Only at the top of your head," teased Edwin and all three laughed.

The other two started pushing Edwin off and he nodded his goodbye to Nico.

"Don't forget this," said Nico, and he transferred his dish of pudding to Edwin's tray.

"Oi!" cried both the other fellows, reaching for the dish. Edwin stepped quickly to the side, avoiding them.

"Back off, you great empty tree trunks. This is all mine! Thanks again, Nico!"

He set off at a jog, the other two close behind, calling out playful insults. Nico shook his head, laughing, and surveyed the employee lunchroom. He saw Tommy waving at him from a nearby table. Nico approached and sat across from him. They had the communal table to themselves except for two young ladies sitting a little further down.

"I see you met the delivery chaps," said Tommy, grinning. "Quite a bunch, aren't they? Only interested in their own kind from what I've seen. They remind me of the stable boys back at the house."

"The certainly seemed to keep tightly together."

Tommy nodded. "That was Eddie you were talking to. We've taken the same bus a time or two, so I've seen him about. Do you know, he was the first Black fellow I ever met, was Eddie."

"You haven't been in London long then, I take it," said Nico.

"No, I haven't. Not until this job." Tommy seemed thoughtful. "Didn't mean anything by that though, I was only saying.

Eddie seems a lovely chap."

"He's the best of the lot," interjected the dark-haired girl who sat a little further down from them. Her curly hair was pulled back into a bun at the back, which was held in place by a braid woven round it, decorated with small combs. "Most respectful at least. Most of those delivery chaps will just leer at you and grin as much as say hello. But he's a polite sort."

Nico and Tommy did not have a chance to respond before her friend spoke.

"You're from the Tea Room, aren't you?" asked the other, straw-colored hair piled on top of her head.

"Yes, we are," answered Nico. "I'm Nico and this is Tommy."

"Nice to meet you." The straw-haired girl pointed at herself and then her friend. "I'm Jenny and this is Mara. We work in the ladies' fashion department."

"We've been wanting to go to the Tea Room for ages," said Mara. "Ever since we first started here. Is it very grand?"

"The people are, at least," said Tommy. "But it's a nice place to do one's time. Beats trimming shrubbery."

Jenny gave him a bemused smirk.

"I like it quite a lot," said Nico. "Best job I've ever had."

"I imagine the food here isn't half of what they serve," said Jenny. "I'm surprised you even come to the employee cafe."

"It is amazing food, beautiful as well as delicious," said Nico. "I envy their skill. But meals aren't included and it is a bit pricey."

"A lot of frou-frou higgledy-piggledy, if you ask me," said Tommy. "Butter on bacon, I'd call it. The plates look a picture, of course, but couldn't keep a schoolgirl fed on what they dole out. No offense, I mean." Mara and Jenny exchanged a smile. "I'd just as soon eat every meal here. Mrs. Crombie worked at the house too, you know. I was practically raised on her cooking, so it feels like home."

"You know Mrs. Crumble personally?" asked Mara, surprised. "Mrs. Crumble?"

"That's what everyone calls Crombie," explained Jenny.

"She's not a relative like," said Tommy. "But my pa worked at Lord Hache's estate as a gardener, and he and Crombie were good friends." He grabbed the spoon on his tray and sunk it into the warm mound of squidgy cake. "I have missed her Canary Pudding—best I ever had. Just how I remember it. Custard and all."

Jenny eyed Nico's tray. "No pud for you then?"

Nico shrugged.

"Too bland for him, I expect," said Tommy, chewing a mouthful of dessert.

"Is it?" asked Nico.

Tommy nodded, swallowing.

"I reckon you're used to all those exotic spices, ain't you? Like from Turkey, where you're from."

"Are you really from Turkey?" asked Mara. "I have distant relatives there, though I've never met them."

Nico shook his head. "No, I am from Greece. But, that's neither here nor there when it comes to good food. I am fond of Mrs. Crombie's cooking. Besides I've been in England most of my life. Just never much liked boiled puddings."

"Did you arrive as a child?" asked Jenny.

"Yes, just before I was ten."

"Your parents moved here for better jobs and that, I reckon?" asked Tommy, stuffing his mouth with another heaping spoonful of pudding.

"No, my parents died," said Nico. "I came here to London to live with my aunt."

Tommy stopped chewing and grabbed his napkin, wiping his mouth.

"Say, I'm sorry, chap. I didn't mean to intrude like that."

"I don't mind," Nico assured him. "Besides, we all have a story, don't we?"

"That's true," said Jenny. "My ma and pa are dead too. My ma had a time of it. My pa was a mean old sod, drank and treated her rough. He ran off, when I was five, leaving her with four of us and never to be heard from again. She struggled till she found another husband. He was a decent sort, but three years later, he was dead with diphtheria. She went to Homerton Infirmary then, the hospital, what with not being able to cope. She never came back neither and they sent us to the workhouse. Grew up there, didn't I."

"The workhouse? You never," said Tommy.

"I did," said Jenny, proudly. "Don't bother me to mention it. They hired me out to service, didn't they, but I quickly saw that wasn't how my cloth was cut. Went from house to house for a bit. Then I become a shop-girl. Well, we both did, didn't we?"

Mara nodded. "We met in service, you see. Both maids at the same house. And then we decided to strike out for London together."

"And do you have a story?" Nico asked Mara. "Before service, I mean?"

"Oh, you'll have to find that out later," said Mara with a coy smile.

"Are you in the dorms then?" asked Jenny.

"Not me," said Nico. "I still live with my aunt."

"Lucky," said Tommy. "I'm in the dorms. You girls too?"

"Yes," said Jenny. "Stuck with Old Mother Shambles."

Mara giggled and Nico raised a brow.

"Mrs. Hambleston. Our dormitory supervisor. A proper old dust-covered spinster she is."

"She's not that bad," said Mara.

"No, it's true. She's a nice old duck, just a bit dotty is all and thinks we're all her children. Still she's not half as bad as those what ran the Salvation Army school."

"Can't be worse than Johnston in the gents' dorm either," said Tommy.

"Oh no?"

"They say you've got to watch yourself around him."

"What do you mean?" asked Nico.

"They said he's only here cos he got caught out. Up North

somewhere—Manchester or the like. Used to be a solicitor or a barrister or something like that. But then they were found in the throes, as it were, begging your pardons, ladies."

Jenny and Mara exchanged a look.

"Got himself in heaps of trouble," Tommy continued. "With a constable of all people. Almost had to do hard labor, I heard, like his—well, like his constable ended up doing. But luckily, so's the story was told, he had friends in good places. So he only had to hop it and give up the law for good instead of getting prison behind it. They say he was a friend of Lord Hache's family, so he gave him a position here."

"And the constable?" asked Nico.

"Who can say? All day at the capstan, I expect, if he's still living. I reckon the law enforcement don't take well to one of their own being a bugger. Begging your pardon again, ladies."

"Well, it takes sorts, I expect," said Jenny.

"It shouldn't take some sorts, if you ask me," declared Tommy.

"You say the boys keep their distance," said Jenny. "Has he ever tried it on with any of the fellows in the dorms?"

"Not that I know of. He keeps himself to himself for the most part. His rooms are on the first floor and he seems to spend most of his time behind a newspaper or a bottle of sherry. I can hear him play a little violin of a Sunday. He don't give us much guff really."

"Sounds dastardly threatening," said Nico.

Mara giggled.

"What about your Monsieur Henri," Jenny said suddenly, changing the subject and throwing Nico.

"*My* Mister Henri?" asked Nico.

"You hear as much mysterious as you do good about him," Jenny said. "They claim he's got quite the temper."

"One of the fellows told me," said Tommy, "that he threw a cake out of a window. An entire wedding cake, right from the fourth floor. Smashed right onto the sidewalk below."

"Oh no, that's not true," said Mara. "I remember that cake. He didn't throw it anywhere. He actually brought it to the employee canteen here and let us all have it. No charge. He said he was dissatisfied with his work and had to start all over."

"You'll find certain stories take wing in a place like this," added Jenny.

"I'm not surprised there's two versions of the story," said Nico. "Monsieur Henri seems rather hot and cold. His emotions seem to slip suddenly."

"The French are like that, aren't they?" Tommy asked. "Leastways, that's what I've heard."

"I doubt it has anything to do with his being French," said Nico. "He is an artist, after all."

"An artist? For making roast meat and veg?"

"You just told us how the best pudding you remember made you feel at home. That's an art, don't you think? Like a piece of music that takes you right back to a memory every time you hear it."

"Hark at that!" Tommy said. "Next thing you know they'll have old Crumbles at the National Gallery."

Nico sighed. "I only meant artist—creative types—tend to be temperamental."

"You sound like you know him well," said Jenny.

"Oh, no. Not at all. We've hardly spoken really. Just things I've noticed over the last few days."

"He just stands there looking grim is all," Tommy said. "I haven't noticed anything like what you've said."

"Yeah, well, some's not born for noticing things, are they," supplied Jenny.

"Oi, Nico," a voice called from near the exit. It was Edwin with his crew. "Let me know if you've any other spare puds going in future, and I'll help you out."

"Don't feel you have to favor this church-bell," called his mate Norman. "We all gladly accept donations!"

Edwin laughed and shoved Norman out of the door, throwing a wave to Nico who, laughing, returned it.

"Well, the boys certainly seem to like you then," said Jenny.

"I imagine they usually do," said Mara quietly.

Nico looked back and forth between the two friends.

"Well, they're good lads," he said.

"I wouldn't mind an extra pud or two, you know," said Tommy with a slight pout.

"I shall speak to Mr. Johnston about it immediately then," replied Nico.

Tommy's mouth fell open and he grabbed his spoon as if to toss it at Nico.

"Why, you!"

But all three other broke into laughter and Tommy dropped his spoon and joined in.

⫸⫷

HENRI CHECKED HIS reflection in the mirrored glass by the maître d'hôtel station in the Tea Room. He thought he had done rather well today; a sack coat suit in grey herringbone tweed with matching waistcoat and a black tie. He tucked his hair behind his ears and reminded himself that he needed a haircut. Henri always took pride in his appearance, but the last week or so he had made special effort. Even Mrs. Plaistow had commented on how dapper he appeared. He wanted to make more of an effort to be seen in the dining room, he explained to her. He typically made rounds during lunch-time and dinner service—a custom he had taken from seeing Monsieur Escoffier himself practice—putting a face to the haute cuisine which impressed the customers and encouraged word of mouth.

Mrs. Plaistow highly approved, and there was no need to mention to her that he secretly hoped to spy a certain new waiter and maybe right the wrongs of their last few frosty interactions. No need to mention because, of course, that wasn't the reason.

That would make him a silly, desperate man. He retrieved the pocket watch, attached to a button of his waistcoat and tucked into a small pocket, checked the hour. Just about time for the next shift to begin. He glanced around the room and saw the lady manageress at a nearby table. Mrs. Plaistow gave him a slight nod and an almost imperceptible look of implore. Taking his cue, Henri moved swiftly to the table.

"I assure you, grandmama," he overheard the younger of the two ladies say as he approached, "I have never danced the can-can. And, as for looking like a fallen woman, I don't believe you've ever once in your life been close enough to a bordello, French or otherwise, to know what one looks like."

The older woman lifted her head proudly and gave a slight shrug.

"I have been to Paris many times. I cannot help that your modern fashion conjures the association in my mind."

"Speaking of French bordellos," interrupted Mrs. Plaistow, "here is Monsieur Henri Newbold himself. He is our chef du cuisine."

"I have been called many things in my life, madame," Henri replied with a smirk, "but never a bordello."

Mrs. Plaistow held her hand to her mouth briefly saying, "Oh, do forgive me."

"Not at all."

"May I introduce The Right Honorable Countess of Covington and The Honorable Eugenia Whiston."

"But I go by Clementine," said the younger lady. "Do call me Clementine, please. I can't be doing with all that fussiness."

"Yes, no matter what I teach her," added Lady Covington, throwing a captious glance at her granddaughter's clothing, "she insists on being 'forward thinking.'"

Lady Covington was elegantly dressed in an ensemble that might have sprung from the pages of *La Mode Pratique* fully formed. She wore a rose-colored dress with a square bodice cut that was simply adorned with embroidery at the chest and the waist. Underneath she wore a ruched under-bodice, in a soft grey color, the fabric of which came high on her neck and extended down to her wrists. Her hat reminded Henri of an enormous mixing bowl turned upside down. Its large dome shape was dyed to match her dress, and across the front it was decorated with one enormous plume, also rose-colored, which wrapped around the front of the hat and flared on the side.

Her granddaughter wore a pneumonia blouse, with a chemise underneath, and a matching walking skirt and gloves in a lettuce-green color. Her stylish Watteau hat was Castor grey with a burst of pink and green flowers just above where its brim turned up in a saucy curve.

Henri gave a small bow. "Good afternoon, ladies."

Lady Covington looked up with an expression of sincere disinterest as she removed her matching rose-colored leather gloves.

"Monsieur Newbold. It is not a name that sounds particularly French. Is your accent affected?"

"No, mademoiselle, I am French born and raised. But my father was an Englishman."

"Very sensible of you," said Lady Covington. "And you may call me Madame, I have not been a mademoiselle in ages."

"But I assumed you were sisters, non?"

Lady Covington pursed her lips and gave her head a little shake.

"Don't be absurd, monsieur. Your flattery is well-intentioned but verging on fantasy. This is my granddaughter."

"How do you do, monsieur?" said Clementine. "Grandmama was just telling us of her time in France, in fact."

"In fact, I was only just telling my granddaughter how her sartorial choices, in following the new fashions, remind one of Le Moulin Rouge and its questionable clientele."

"So you have spent much time in France?" asked Henri.

"Yes," said Lady Covington with a regal nod. "My parents took me several times when I was a young girl to see the sights of

Paris."

"And how did you find it?"

"Terribly French."

Henri raised a brow.

"Yes, well, here is your waiter now," added Mrs. Plaistow, anxious to make her escape. "Good day, Lady Covington, Miss Clementine."

Henri glanced up to see Nikolaos suddenly beside the table. He felt his heart skip a beat at seeing his handsome face. He nodded at Nikolaos, who smiled back warmly, and Henri hoped the blush he felt on his cheeks did not show.

"Madame, mademoiselle, this is Nikolaos," Henri managed to say. "He is one of our newest and brightest servers."

Nikolaos looked at him in surprise but quickly recovered. Henri was delighted to have surprised him and also saddened that a mere moment of him not being a horrible monster had been a shock.

"I should say," replied Clementine, her eyes shining. "This tea room is certainly staffed by many handsome faces."

"Clementine," said Lady Covington in a chastising tone, "don't be vulgar." She glanced at the waiter. "Nikolaos? An original name. Are you French as well?"

Nikolaos gave a small bow. "Not at all, Madame. But I can always aspire."

"Yes, very droll."

Nikolaos handed the ladies a menu with the day's special written on it.

"Do you know," said Miss Clementine, "that my brother went on a tour of Greece!"

"Did he, miss?"

"Yes, just last year. After he left school. He and his closest friends spent months and months there. He said they wanted to explore the idea of Greek fraternity. Apparently university is just swimming with Greek ideals."

Her grandmother cleared her throat loudly, but the young

woman went on undeterred.

"Though I do find it odd. They spent most of their time on the island of Capri. They shared a house with some fellows they knew from back home, and I expect some locals as well. Greek poets and artists and the like—to get a feel of things. He said they held great salons—parties that went on all night—no girls allowed, that sort of thing. You know how boys will be."

"Yes, miss," said Nikolaos with a polite nod.

"I do believe, however," added Henri, "that Capri is an Italian island, not part of Greece."

"Is it? Is Italy very far from Greece then?"

"Yes, yes, that's quite enough, Clementine," her grandmother interrupted. "We did not come here to share our family history." She studied the menu and tutted. "There they are again. Those large, hulking women that greeted us near the entrance."

"'Large hulking women'? Do you mean the two ladies by the parfumerie counter?" asked Clementine. "I don't think they were hulking—only Scottish."

"No, no. I mean those women in statuary, plastered onto the sides of the building. There are illustrations of them in the corners of the menu."

"The caryatids," offered Nikolaos.

Lady Covington looked at him suspiciously.

"Have times gotten so hard," she asked, "that architects must now take secondary employ as tea room servants?"

"No, madam, of course not. I am no architect. Only Greek. You find them in many places in my country."

Lady Covington gave him a once-over. "Yes, I daresay."

"The caryatids are in honor of the many female staff who support our store," explained Henri. "Lord Hartridge asked for them in the design as he believed shopgirls had built the shopping experience in London."

"Fascinating, monsieur," Lady Covington replied dryly. "A historian and an architect in our midst. Who would have thought? But I suppose we ought not to tarry and should supply the builder of temples with our selections, oughtn't we?"

Taking his implied dismissal, Henri exchanged a small nod with Nikolaos. "Good afternoon, ladies."

"I only want a cup of chocolate, nothing more," Henri heard Clementine declare as he turned to leave.

"Don't be ridiculous, dear, you must have some proper food. We'll have the afternoon tea. One must keep one's energy afloat for the rest of the day's shopping."

"Oh, but I haven't anything more to purchase. Only a new handbag for Mama."

"A handbag?" The Lady's tone conveyed her disdain heartily.

Henri glanced back to the table and found that Nikolaos was watching him walk away. He turned back quickly but he couldn't help the smile which sprang to his lips.

The tweed he wore suddenly seemed to weigh a hundred pounds and his skin flushed. He shook his head, silently admonishing himself for his reaction. He was far too old to be driven to distraction simply because a man watched him walk away. But there was something about the way Mister Kavafis looked at him—not a word was spoken and yet his looks seemed to drench Henri in a torrent of unspoken words. As if his looks were music and only Henri could distinguish the notes being played. He admonished himself again. Attempting to turn mere gestures into poetry. What a fool he had become. He ran a finger along the inside of his collar desperate for a breath of fresh air on his skin.

He saw Michel lean out from the kitchen door. Locating Henri, he gave an urgent wave, which usually indicated some sort of small catastrophe. Henri breathed out in relief and moved quickly towards the kitchen, grateful for the distraction of disaster.

CHAPTER THREE

WHEREAS MANY OTHER shops on the high streets of cities, even those with electric lighting, succumbed easily to gloom, Hartridge & Casas overcame the weight of dark paneling by means of a vast number of hanging globes. Through most of the departments, the walls were light colors—they were bright, encouraging, and, even, as some might say (mainly those enamored of frivolous expressions), they were downright cheerful. Instead of making the process of shopping seem like something to be done in hushed tones and quiet corners, coming to Hartridge & Casas rather felt like a day out: walking in a park, or taking a train to the sea. Bright, open, and full of ebullient charm.

Air and light, those were the most wonderful things about Hartridge & Casas, Nico thought. In a city known for its soot and dark alleyways, H&C had made every effort to fight against the closed-in feeling of urban life. Coming through the doors and into the wide-open spaces of the store, one could stretch one's gaze from the hues and texture of fabrics to the regal bindings of the book department and beyond to the forms and patterns made by furnishings and garden, all without a break in one's eye line. It was not an escape into the modernity of London but an escape into a landscape of the future—all the newest innovations and myriad glimpses into what might come. From an instrument to make a cook's job half as long to a crème or rouge that would make even the plainest face flush with beauty and health.

Despite its luxury, H&C did not cater solely to the Tiara Triangle. Men and women from throughout the city flocked to see the marvels that made them feel younger, wealthier, and grand. Especially women. No more susceptible to vanity or awe than their male counterparts, in Hartridge & Casas the women of London, of all classes, found a refuge. One needn't worry about rustling up an escort, or even to worry of having enough pennies in one's pocket to make a purchase—browsing, "window-shopping," all were encouraged and respected. There were resting rooms where one could sit and escape the bustle not only of shopping but of the day, of life, places to take a refreshing drink or fortifying snack without need of reservation or company, and, most luxurious of all, toilets for women, open to all classes, regardless of purchase or purpose. Seldom before had the women of London been afforded such a luxury of wander and such a freedom of disregard.

An oasis.

That was what Nico had thought of the Books and Library Department, most especially, on his very first visit to H&C. He still remembered the day perfectly. He had dipped into his savings for a much needed day out, all to himself. It was his first visit to Hartridge and Casas and he had spent the entire day in the store, as one might spend a day at the seaside. He spent the morning wandering the different departments, marveling at all the different items on offer and then lunched at the Royal Tea Room. The prix fixe meal he had ordered was rather dear, but he had decided he owed himself an indulgence. His lunch had consisted of bouchées à la reine aux champignons to start, followed by sole grillée with asparagus and finished with sorbet au cassis with langues de chat biscuits and Turkish coffee. Though he did not see Monsieur Henri, or even Monsieur Michel, on that visit, he felt drawn to both the place and the food. He marveled at each item on the menu and, at one point, felt rather embarrassed by how long he lingered over his setting, savoring each flavor. It was as if he belonged here, worlds away from the cramped, dark, odoriferous restaurants he had cut his teeth working in.

After lunch, he had come to the Books and Library Department. It was done in the style of a private library, as one might find in a stately home, and felt like a pocket of escape from even the wonderful, vibrant store it sat in. The room wore dark-paneled wood walls, polished to a sheen, and was adorned with sumptuous leather chairs for sitting and perusing reading material, or just resting. The interior was divided into distinct spaces, all of which were lit with lamps on the desks and side tables, some giving a plain light, and some filtering through their Tiffany glass. Nico thought it was a place one ought to like a cigar and take a glass of port in.

The walls were lined with shelves, filled with books, and though they were cared for and arranged as one might a personal library, these were for sale. Sometimes up to a dozen copies of the same title, all standing neatly like soldiers. There was a separate area for book-lending, a much smaller selection but beautifully arranged in equal measure. Like many public libraries, the department was divided into separate spaces, the central reading room, the magazine room, and the "news" room, filled with newspapers and other reference materials. But, unlike most public libraries, these spaces were not limited by gender and class here, and women could as easily browse the news room as they could the magazine room, while working-class men sat next to middle-class in the reading room.

During his visit, he had decided to treat himself to a brand new book—a rare extravagance for him, but he could not resist the temptation of all the glowing covers and hitherto unread pages. He chose *The Blotting Book*, a mystery novel, a genre which he was repeatedly drawn to, and ran his finger along the tight spine. It was simply bound in green cloth with gilt lettering, but its simplicity made it all the more beautiful. And, of course, this was the day he had first met Hosea, the lead floor supervisor of the department. Dear eccentric, loquacious Hosea whose never-ending good-natured chatter betrayed any idea one might have of a stiff, officious librarian type.

"Ah, Nikolaos, my fine-feathered friend. Welcome back!" cried Hosea.

"'Fine-feathered'?"

"Better than fair weather, I should think. I was wondering if I might see you thusly." Hosea dashed behind the main counter and came back carrying a fine-looking book. He studied the spine. "Your book arrived just yesterday so well-timed, I must say. *The Red Thumb Mark*? But isn't this the one you just read?"

"That was *The Red Triangle*. A different author but still a mystery."

"'A good book is an event in my life.'" Hosea held the book aloft. "Stendhal, *Le Rouge et le noir* since we've established a theme. You do care greatly for a mystery don't you?"

"I do."

"Then you are entirely well-placed with your Monsieur Henri and your shared passion."

"Pardon?"

"Ah, Le Monsieur is quite fond of mysteries, himself. Didn't you know?"

"Is he?"

"Indeed." Hosea ran his finger down the spine of the book, tracing the title. "Have you tackled him yet?"

Nico inclined his head and gave the bookseller a look.

"Tackled whom, Hosea?"

"The author, I mean, of course. Have you read him before?"

"No, it's my first time."

"Always the most exciting time."

"Excuse me, hate to interrupt," said a middle-aged gentleman with a formidable beard who approached the counter.

"Not at all, sir," said Hosea, giving him full attention. "This gentleman is not only a friend but a colleague and, of course, customers come first. How may I help you?"

"Much obliged," said the man, with a nod to Nico. "I was looking at this *Book of Common Prayer*—"

"Oh, yes. Isn't it quite something? Velveteen covered and gilt titled. Hartridge & Casas worked closely with M.B. Fann Books Limited to create this edition, especially for sale here in the store. You'll find one like it nowhere else."

"That would explain the price, then, I assume."

Hosea straightened his spine and lifted his chin, a signal, Nico knew from experience, that he had been piqued.

"My great Aunt Matilda—God rest her soul—attended church at least three times weekly—quite a fan of Evensong she was— and sometimes four visits during Michaelmas. During which holiday, I might add, she always cooked a lovely roast goose and the most delicious blackberry pie for us all. Quite divine, both in the ethereal and corporal sense, if I do say so on her behalf. But my Aunt Matilda said she that the price of sin is never too highly paid."

"I doubt anyone ever asked her to pay an entire shilling for a prayer book," countered the man.

"If no worry for the price of your own soul, sir, it makes a terrific gift. We all must have an Aunt Matilda, or one similarly devout, hidden away in a corner of life, mustn't we."

"I did, in fact, intend it as a gift for our new governess. She might wonder at her salary, however, if I were to give her such an extravagant book."

"Just there, behind the large illuminated globe, you shall find we have some more simply-bound editions. If you would like to highlight your frugality as an employer."

The man eyed the shelves indicated and chewed his lip.

"I shall peruse them, but maybe I ought to settle on this one. After all, we don't want her to think me miserly."

"How she could fathom the notion, I'm not sure, sir."

The man gave Hosea a look that suggested he was unsure but he nodded just the same. He moved off towards the globe.

Hosea turned back to Nico.

"So sorry for that. But as Lord Hartridge always reminds us, 'Without the customer we are nothing'. Which I imagine to be only a step below a governess in a miserly home, but never mind. Back to the passion you share with Monsieur Henri."

Nico laughed. "You have the tongue of a candied viper, Hosea."

"The tongue of a sweet kitten, dear sir; don't offend me thus with such aspersions. Now, mystery books. Your monsieur orders books with French titles—quite a pretty bob, I would say, after the cost import and such. Though, of course, Hartridge & Casas has quite the best connections when it comes to commerce so there's no issue of obtaining them in a speedy manner. I'm afraid my French, as the octogenarian said to his young wife, just ain't up for the job, me duckie. But monsieur has extraordinary patience with me as I muddle through. A trait, which I have heard, by the whispers of those who clatter most—namely the telephonists, of course—is not a one he necessarily shows in his kitchen of late."

"On the contrary, I don't find him that way."

"No? What way do you find him?"

"I admit he was a bit frosty at first—"

"Like the first morning of winter."

Nico rolled his eyes. "But now I find him rather charming."

"You must be a devotee to mysteries indeed in that case. Monsieur is an enigma in a well-cut suit. Even more a closed book than our own heralded Señor Casas. What do you think of his new beard? I rather think it makes him look an adventurous monk, locked away behind the walls of the monastery and yearning for the blade and the blood. I imagine the two of them, sometimes, Monsieur and Señor, locked away in a secret room somewhere in the store, the lights dim, the air heavy, plotting away at schemes mystic and arcane."

"Hosea, I think you yourself must be a complete fantasist."

"My dear boy, any single man of a certain age living in a one-room flat in the heart of Londontown cannot help but be anything other than a fantasist. Shall I wrap your *Red Thumb Mark?*"

"No, thank you, I'll take it as-is."

"Wise move. The miserly walrus seems to have moved on from the prayer book. Any minute he'll be asking me for a discounted atlas for his dear governess, poor woman."

"Now, now, Hosea." Nico wagged his finger, teasing. "Without the customer we are nothing."

"I shall remember that this evening when I stop for my usual supper of a ha'penny of beer and a boiled egg. More anon, fine feathers, more anon."

➤➤➤◄◄◄

AS HENRI PUSHED open the glass door at the top of the spiral stairwell, he squinted against the sunshine that poured in. It was a surprising but welcome change; this summer had been a stormy one, and though no English summer promised long bouts of warmth, this one had been unusually turbulent. He stood for a moment, basking in the warmth of the rays, happy for the escape from the store below. He often took his midday meal break on the grand patio no matter the weather or season, but it was lovely to not huddle in his coat, pretending to be accepting of the chill. He lifted his hand and used the book he clutched to shield his eyes as he looked out over the patio/seating area. There were more patrons at the tables today, as befitted the weather, and a handful of staff waited on them. He was glad for this as he would be even less noticeable in his camouflaged corner. He headed towards "The Jungle," as the staff called it. The small corner had become a bit of a storage and staging area for the staff when waiting the tables, and large potted ferns had been placed in front of the tables to further disguise them from view. The plant-shrouded tables were where Henri went to escape. Like today, he often brought a novel to absorb his attention, and he was refreshing his memory of where he'd last left off in the story when he heard someone call out.

"Hullo, Monsieur Henri, is that you?"

When Henri turned towards the female voice, he at first only saw a small violet-colored bird. It was a small stuffed sparrow dyed, no doubt, to match the material of the enormous hat it sat upon, with peacock feathers planted behind it to give the illusion of a miniature of the grander bird. The bird was also nestled in a nest of silk flowers and leaves which ran around the crown of the hat. The glass-eyed creature bobbed a little as the wearer tilted her head, and Henri caught by the sight, almost did not realize it was Lady Covington.

"Yes, indeed, it is," said Lady Covington. "Come, monsieur, and greet my guests."

Surprised by her familiar tone, Henri did as he was bidden.

Lady Covington sat at the table, with seats enough for five, with two ladies. Though they both seemed extremely respectable and self-possessed, Henri was surprised to see them in the company of one such as Lady Covington. They were clearly not of her class, and he didn't expect she often associated with anyone not of her own class.

"Monsieur Henri, I would like you to meet Miss Sybil Fenton Newall—"

"Call me Queenie," the woman addressed interjected.

"And Miss Charlotte Dodd."

"Lottie, please," said the second lady. She too was a hand-some, strong woman.

Lottie wore a shirtwaist and a skirt that corresponded even if didn't match. Over which she had a bicycle jacket and atop her hair, pulled back in a serviceable if not elaborate bun, was pinned a straw boater. She struck Henri as something like a picture-perfect advertisement for the Rational Dress Reform movement, though its founders might disagree. Queenie was dressed in a skirt, bound with leather at the hem, and a Norfolk-style jacket, over a blouse with a high collar and a tie. The skirt and jacket were drab of color, and served with very little adornment or embellishment, making it all look suspiciously like a golfing costume. The only splash of color in her ensemble being the costume brooch she wore pinned on her lapel, that of a heron done in sparkling blue and teal glass. She carried a dark-colored stiff felt which she had removed and tossed into the free chair beside her. Neither of them wore gloves, he noticed, quite the contrast to Lady Covington whose arms were swathed in silk. Her ladyship wore an elaborate day dress the color of which matched her hat perfectly. Its lace bodice and cuffs were heavily decorated with beadwork and button and her skirts so full she practically perched rather than sat on the chair.

"They have accepted my invitation off the back of an enormous achievement," explained Lady Covington. "They both took the highest ranks in Women's Archery at the Olympic Games just days ago."

"Oh, yes," said Henri. "On Friday and Saturday, non? In Shepherd's Bush? I heard some of the men in the kitchen talking of it."

"Yes, you see, Monsieur Henri is the Head Chef here at Hartridge and Casas," said Lady Covington. "He oversees all the kitchens, food halls, and this lovely tea room."

"Well, I don't actually—"

"Now, don't be modest, monsieur. The French so often are interminably so. Monsieur Henri trained with Escoffier himself. At the Ritz, or was it the Carlton?"

"Who's that?" asked Lottie before Henri could respond.

"Auguste Escoffier?" said Lady Covington. *"Le roi des cuisiniers et cuisinier des rois?* Surely you have eaten at one of his restaurants?"

Both women athletes looked confounded.

"I didn't realize before," said Henri, hoping to change the subject. "That women were participating in the archery."

"Weren't many," said Queenie. "We were the only nation to send any females."

"My brother Willy competed in the men's tournament," said Lottie. "And took gold."

"Then the talent runs in the family," Henri said graciously with a nod.

"Do they have archery in France, monsieur?" asked Lady Covington. "I don't know that I've ever seen a Frenchman shoot an arrow."

"Only when provoked, madam," said Henri and the two ladies of the bow laughed.

"Have I been usurped?" asked a voice from behind.

Henri turned to see Mister Hawthorne sidle up beside him. Mister Hawthorne was a frequent face around H&C, and though Henri did not know him very well, his reputation preceded him. He often appeared in various departments in search of props or costumes or various other accoutrements of a theatrical nature for his productions. He was always, as today, impeccably dressed in a perfectly tailored suit of the latest mode, though its finish and accessorizing might lend towards the prim in appearance. Despite the fact that age had streaked his brown hair with mentions of silver and grey, he had kept his youthful trim. He had an ear for gossip and a word for all, especially, so Henri had heard, the better-looking male employees of the store.

"I do realize he is younger and far more handsome than I, so I can't say that I blame you. Nevertheless," he said, turning to the table, "it is quite lovely to see you all."

"Are you quite sure Mister Hawthorne?" asked Lady Covington. "Your tone seems rather strained."

"Only the effects of too little rest, I assure you."

"When one's days start in the evening, I shouldn't wonder. I never know how you lead your life embroiled in theater as you do."

"I am merely a producer. And, my dear lady, the theater ends at a respectable eleven o'clock as you well know."

"Just because the stage lights dim doesn't mean the players stop their machinations. There's always some boy to train up, isn't there?"

"I beg your pardon?" Hawthorne interjected with a sniff.

"Playing some page attendant to some king—or whatever young man who must be shown the proper way to put on his tights?"

Hawthorne lifted his chin. "I'm sure we have dressers for that sort of thing, madam."

"Yes, I'm sure you must do. But I thought your wife would be joining us. It really is too sad how seldom we see you two together."

"Oh, my dear wife is terribly busy, as always." He placed his hand on Henri's arm and gave him a grave look. "She is very invested in what are popularly called the social causes."

"Charity, one assumes," Lady Covington offered, giving Hawthorne an appraising once-over.

Hawthorne pursed his lips and gave her a gimlet-eyed look. "Among other pursuits." He moved to take his seat at the table. "She has become most recently preoccupied with the question of suffrage."

"Oh," said Lady Covington, "I do hope she won't go chaining herself to things."

"I believe she plays a more administrative role," replied Hawthorne as he spread his napkin across his lap with a great flourish. "Besides, why shouldn't women have the vote, after all?"

"Hear, hear," said Queenie.

"Well, we cannot have the world going all topsy-turvy, can we," declared Lady Covington.

"It has been my experience, Lady Covington," said Hawthorne, "that the world rather turns whichever way it needs to turn in the end."

"Possibly. But we must make sure we don't go toppling off the end when it does."

"I am in full support of the vote," said Queenie.

"Yes, but you are a woman of athletics," countered Lady Covington. "And those are often the types of woman unconcerned with the typical duties of man and wife."

"Quite," said Lottie Dod. "And all the better. I, for one, never plan to marry."

"Oh, don't condemn yourself to such a fate," said Lady Covington. "You're still young—comparatively speaking—and there is time still to find a husband."

"I should never hope I do," said Lottie with a huff. "I find a husband a particularly useless thing."

"Yes, well," said Lady Covington, dipping her head. "On that I cannot entirely disagree."

"Ladies, Hawthorne," Henri interrupted. "I find myself entirely out of my depth on this topic, so I should retreat and allow you to enjoy your luncheon."

"Very nice to meet you, sir," said Queenie, and Lottie nodded in agreement.

Henri settled into his table and opened his novel, but found it hard to concentrate as he unintentionally eavesdropped on the nearby Olympic table. He stared at the printed page but the amusing words floated across the patio rather than from the writer's pen.

"Mrs. Hill-Lowe, the bronze medalist, was also meant to join us," Lady Covington was explaining to Hawthorne, "but could not be located this morning."

"Probably on a train to Shropshire as we speak," Lottie said. "Beatrice is always very apt to forget social engagements."

"She is Irish," explained Lady Covington.

Mister Hawthorne nodded, knowingly. "So," he said to Miss Newall, "you are the gold medalist and you go by the nickname Queenie. How apropos! Almost as if it were your destiny."

"Yes, well, I like to think—" began Queenie.

"Yes, she took first," interrupted Lottie. "But we'll see. In just a few days she'll be up against Legh at the National Championships."

"What of it?" asked Queenie.

"Legh?" asked Hawthorne.

"Alice Blanche Legh," explained Lottie. "Greatest woman going, they say, as relates to archery, at least. She surely would have won this week had she competed. I, myself, am actually rather more fond of tennis—"

"Yet she did not," interjected Queenie. "Compete, I mean. So there is no benefit to speculation. After all, I might have been the Queen of Sheba had I been born in the right time."

"Unlikely, dear," said Lady Covington. "Jerusalem is a very sandy place. Not at all the environs in which an Englishwoman might thrive.

Queenie looked at her in confusion before continuing. "And as for the nationals, if I took the gold, why shouldn't I win the nationals?"

"Yes, well," said Lottie, "London isn't Cheltenham, at least."

"And, too," said Mister Hawthorne, "you might not have the wind and the rain against that day."

"No matter if I do," said Queenie. "I thrive in challenging circumstances."

"As do I, dear lady," agreed Lady Covington.

They all turned to her in astonishment.

"I've never taken up the archery bow myself but I love a good hunt," said Lady Covington. "Quite the shot I used to be. In fact, when my husband had a post in India, I accompanied the men on a tiger hunt more than once."

"My word," said Lottie, leaning forward. "And did you bag a tiger?"

"Indeed we did," the countess said proudly. "You know the natives had never seen a woman hunt. But I showed them I could command well. I told them all exactly what to do and how to do. I have always felt that the servant classes need strong guidance to blossom. They were so impressed they began to call me The Great Saali Kutti."

Hawthorne choked on his sip of tea.

"What does that mean?" asked Queenie.

"I never spoke much Hindi myself but my husband told me

that it meant The Great Huntress."

Hawthorne cleared his throat loudly and his mustache twitched as he poured himself a new cup of tea.

"You speak Hindi, don't you, Hawthorne?"

"Only a little, my lady. And I'm sure your husband would know much better than I."

Eventually the conversation became more mundane and Henri's attention fell again to his novel. He was just getting himself again involved in the mystery contained within when a shadow fell across the pages and distracted him. He looked up, slightly annoyed, to find Nico standing on the other side of the potted fern. Framed by the broad leaves of the palm and the summer sun burnishing his golden complexion, he seemed to Henri, in that moment, to resemble the hero of one of the adventure novels that had so consumed his imagination as a youth come to life. His mouth fell open as he stared at Nikolaos, briefly imagining him to be the dashing protagonist of a Robert Louis Stevenson story or some such.

"Am I disturbing you, monsieur?" asked Nikolaos, the cloud of Henri's fantasy dissipating.

"Not at all," Henri replied shortly, quickly snapping the book shut and covering it with his arm.

"Only I was bringing up fresh cutlery for the Jungle and Monsieur Michel mentioned you would likely be here for your lunchtime break. He was concerned you had forgotten your meal and asked me to bring this to you."

Nikolaos nodded to indicate a small packet wrapped in wax paper and string, but he did not hand it over immediately, instead taking the cutlery to the neighboring table and depositing it beside the carafes of drinking water waiting there.

"Michel shares a little too much," Henri said, his tone gruffer than he intended. "And he sometimes thinks himself my mother. I don't need looking after."

Nikolaos turned and handed Henri the small packet.

"Everyone needs looking after occasionally, monsieur." He

gave a small shrug, adding, "Besides it is only a sandwich. A shooter's sandwich."

Henri gave a small embarrassed smile and murmured his thanks. Nikolaos turned back to the table to fill a glass of water.

"And you'll need some water as well, naturally."

"Are you my mother now too?"

Nikolaos chuckled.

"No, monsieur. I would never imagine myself anyone's mother. A wife, perhaps—or, I suppose I mean husband, don't I?" He deposited the water on Henri's table and smiled. "Well, I'll leave you to it, monsieur."

"You needn't go," Henri blurted out. Then added more calmly, "Besides, this enormous sandwich is too much for one man. Won't you join me? That is, if you haven't already had your lunch?"

"No, I haven't eaten yet today," said Nikolaos. "But Mrs. Plaistow is expecting me to start my shift soon."

"We're not so busy as that. Besides you can tell her I kept you. She won't argue with me."

"Very well, monsieur," Nikolaos said. Henri wondered if he saw him give a little bounce on the balls of his feet. "If you insist." Nikolaos gestured to the water. "May I?"

"Of course."

Nikolaos filled a glass for himself and sat across from Henri. Henri unwrapped the sandwich, neatly cut in half, courtesy of Michel, and passed a portion to Nikolaos. They smiled at one another politely as they enjoyed the first few bites, chewing in silence.

Nikolaos took a sip of water and inclined his head.

"Your book," he said. "Is it a mystery novel?"

"Yes," Henri said.

"Hosea mentioned you often ordered French mysteries."

Henri was shocked.

"Did he? It seems I am mentioned quite often. First my lunch spot, now my reading taste."

Nikolaos picked at the tablecloth and smiled shyly.

"Hosea didn't mean to talk out of turn, I assure." He looked up at Henri. "He only meant to say we share a passion."

"Do we indeed?"

Henri felt a rush of nervousness envelop him and he bit into the sandwich, chewing slowly so that he would not be forced to speak further.

"Those were his words. Hosea likes to talk quite a bit."

Henri took a sip of water, nodding. "He is quite the character."

"You don't mind Hosea then?"

"He is himself, and I appreciate that. He is not one to worry what people think of him or his manners. He is brave, really, and I admire that. It is a rare thing.

"Don't you think of yourself as brave, monsieur?"

"Perhaps not enough so."

Nikolaos nodded and looked at him thoughtfully. Henri wished he would say more but he was silent, only studying. Finally, he took a bite of the sandwich and they both ate quietly for a moment.

"I love mystery novels," Nikolaos said after a bit. "When we first came to England, my sister would read to me out loud and then later I to her, to improve our English. I always returned to the mysteries. Sherlock and the American Butterworth lady were my favorites then."

"I, too, like Sherlock. He featured in some stories I read with a French detective, Monsieur Lupin. My aunt knows I like mystery stories so she used to send me clippings from *Je sais tout* and *L'Illustration*. That is where I got the first book by this man, Gaston Lerounx. I read the clippings until they crumbled in my hands."

"And now she has sent you this new book from France?"

"Yes."

Nikolaos put his elbows on the table and leaned forward. Henri felt himself flush from the closeness.

"You have a good aunt then,"

"I do, oui."

For a moment, neither of them spoke, they just stared into one another's eyes. Henri felt the urge to run his tongue along the bottom lip of that beautiful mouth, and clenched his fist to still the rush of blood that pulsed through him.

"Maybe I should read it too?" said Nikolaos finally. "We can compare opinions of the story."

Henri sat back, feeling slightly aswim. He shook his head and chastised himself silently.

"Only if you read French," he said shortly, gazing out at the patio. "It hasn't been published elsewhere yet. And I doubt you speak French."

Nikolaos sat back.

"Alas, no. Only English and Greek, of course."

Henri looked at him. "You are Greek then?"

"Yes," Nikolaos nodded, fingering the rim of his water glass. "I, too, am from elsewhere. Just like you."

Henri smoothed the white tablecloth. *Just like you.*

"But France is not Greece," he said stonily. "They are entirely different places."

Nikolaos slid back in his chair. "Not so very different, monsieur. Most people still feel very much the same things, even if their scenery is different."

He stood and turned as if to leave.

"Thank you," Henri muttered softly. "For the sandwich, I mean."

Nikolaos turned back. "Sometimes, monsieur, I get the feeling that you do not like me very much. In fact, you sometimes give the impression that I repulse you."

Henri blanched. Perhaps his plan had worked too well. But wasn't that for the best? He knew he must keep this man at an emotional distance. But still it hurt him deeply, in an unidentifiable way, to think that this gorgeous boy thought himself repulsive to anyone.

"No, no, that is not true," he stammered.

"No?" asked Nikolaos, his eyes suddenly bright.

"No, not at all." Henri made direct eye contact. "In fact… well, in fact."

He wanted to admit the truth then and there. He wanted to say that no one had ever been more captivating; that he wandered around the Tea Room like a lost soul sometimes, only hoping for a glance. That every moment of every day since they had met, he wanted Nikolaos near him, close to him, but that he couldn't stand the thought of where that might lead, what it might mean.

That he was a fool. A stone-hearted, cowardly fool.

He saw a smile dance across Nikolaos's lips. He nodded.

"I know, monsieur," he said. And again he gave a little bounce as Henri had noticed before. "I know you do not really dislike me. I only wanted to make you convince me of it."

Nikolaos turned to leave.

"Wait," Henri blurted out.

Nikolaos paused on the other side of the fern and peered through its fronds.

"That is not a very nice game to play," Henri said, cringing at his own voice, which sounded thin and whiney.

"I do not mean to play games, monsieur. Only I hope that one day, very soon, I will make you like me very much."

He moved away, swiftly, and left Henri sitting, shocked. He thumbed the pages of his book. What a shocking way to behave, he thought; what boldness. And as he raked his thumb across the rough edges of the cut pages, he smiled.

What boldness, indeed. And how thrilling it felt.

CHAPTER FOUR

THE WAIT STAFF stood in front of them, in a neat queue, both the men and the women. They all looked pinpoint neat and they all wore expectant expressions. They reminded Henri of the servant body at a grand house on Boxing Day, all waiting to see what paltry gift would be bestowed them. Still, Henri was proud of them. They made an impressive front, and he was happy that Hartridge and Casas was not run like some manor house, and that all the staff felt free to express themselves and their needs, in a fashion. Of course, some, like the pug-face Jamie, were a little free in their expression.

"Thank you all for arriving earlier than usual this morning," said Mrs. Plaistow, getting things going. "I'm sure you all are wondering why we asked you, but you needn't worry, it isn't a thing at all troubling."

Henri scanned the line of faces, which seemed to relax *en masse*, and landed on Nikolaos. Nikolaos was watching him and for a brief moment their eyes met. Henri could swear he felt a small blush come to his cheeks and he schooled his expression, hoping to keep his reaction well hidden.

"Yes," he added, looking away quickly from Nikolaos and nodding to Mrs. Plaistow. "We are most appreciative."

"Now," Mrs. Plaistow continued, "we simply would like to ask if there is anyone who might be interested in working an extra shift in the Tea Room this evening. Misters Hartridge and Casas will be hosting a party of acquaintances as they so often do, and they have volunteered the Tea Room for the occasion. Monsieur Henri has already pulled together his kitchen staff for the evening, but we will need at least two wait staff to assist."

"It will be a less formal occasion than normal," added Michel. "More relaxed, especially as it will be rather late at night."

"But we still expect up you to uphold our usual standards nevertheless," Mrs. Plaistow said firmly. "It will, as Monsieur Michel said, be a late evening affair. So anyone wishing to assist will be allowed early dismissal after this afternoon's service in order to return later."

There was a hushed murmur amongst the staff as some wondered what could be happening at night in a tea room, and others made firm their dislike of coming back later.

"I will happily assist," said a voice Henri had come to recognize well.

He looked over and Nikolaos had stepped forward, his chin held up, and a grand smile. My God, thought Henri, but he was like something out of a painting—some divine creature captured in oil and light.

"Parfait," Michel whispered with a small chuckle.

This pricked Henri's feeling somehow and he shrugged.

"We shall need more than one pair of hands," Henri said, perhaps a bit too loudly. "You there, Mister Thomas, what about you? You have seemed eager to learn the way of things, and this will be a grand chance."

Tommy glanced about nervously. "Yes, of course, m'sieur. Only of a Saturday I do often try to—"

"We'll pay you double," interrupted Henri.

He felt Mrs. Plaistow bristle beside him and both Nikolaos and Tommy seemed surprised. Tommy nodded eagerly.

"Oh yes, sir, m'sieur. That would be all right then."

"Donc du coup, in that case," began Henri, starting to walk off.

"If you'll be needing a girl in attendance, I'm free," said the small red-headed waitress Lily, raising her hand.

"Do you have any worry for the lateness of the hour?" asked Mrs. Plaistow. "Will it cause you any problems at home, or for your reputation?"

"I wasn't aware I had a reputation, Mrs. Plaistow," said Lily innocently to scattered chuckles. "But I live in the H&C dormitories, so I reckon it shouldn't be hard to arrange."

"Of course," said Mrs. Plaistow with a nod. "I shall send word to the dormitory mistress that you will be working this evening and therefore excused from curfew. Thank you very much, Miss Ramsay."

"Of course, Mrs. Plaistow."

"Now let's get back to work in readying for the afternoon." Mrs. Plaistow addressed the assembly. "Thank you all."

And with that the troops were dismissed.

Henri and Michel headed for the kitchen.

"Why did you laugh?" whispered Henri, but before Michel could respond, Mrs. Plaistow called his name.

"Monsieur, I am shocked at the mention of double pay. Mister Casas did not mention this when he approached us about organizing this."

"Not to worry, madam. Les Messieurs do not worry so much about cost when they host these petites fetes of theirs. We can incorporate it into the expense."

"I do worry of a precedent begun," said the ever-pragmatic Plaistow. "I wouldn't want to give the expression that salaries are so easily raised, nor give any young women the idea that they ought to compromise themselves for an extra shilling or two."

Michel ducked his head, smiling.

"You are wise to entertain such worries," said Henri. "I do apologize for not consulting you first. I think we can be assured the ladies here at H&C will be well-looked after. And I have seen Miss Ramsay handle the male clientele that sometimes visit the café; she is quite capable. In fact, she reminds me very much of you, Mrs. Plaistow."

Mrs. Plaistow rolled her eyes heavily behind her pince nez. "I am immune to flattery, monsieur. Especially that which is so transparent. But I appreciate your consideration in consulting me in future. And you are right, Miss Ramsay is quite capable. As are all my girls."

"Indeed, madam."

They nodded at one another and Mrs. Plaistow returned to her station by the door. As they entered the kitchen, Michel sniggered.

"She made it sound as if we were introducing the poor child to prostitution," he said.

Henri slapped his shoulder. "You and your jokes! Why were you laughing just now?"

Michel feigned a countenance of extreme innocence. "What do you mean, monsieur? Laughing when?"

"When Mister Kavafis volunteered."

"Was I laughing?" Michel raised his brows comically high.

"You whispered and chuckled; do not play the fool with me."

Michel gave him a look. "I only thought him a marvelous choice. He is quite professional, Mister Kavafis, and the best-looking chap in the place. Which always goes a long way with the friends of H&C. Surely you have noticed how handsome he is?"

Henri narrowed his eyes at his friend. "Have we finalized the menu?" he asked, ignoring Michel's question.

"I assumed we would do your usual arsenal, all the impressive things they like most." Michel batted his eyes at Henri, teasing. "Unless, of course, monsieur is inspired to try a more Mediterranean palate?"

"Michel, you are terrible and I am not sure why we remain friends."

Michel's grin widened.

"Oh, monsieur, how you wound me," he countered, theatrically.

"Fetch me a knife and I just might."

Michel burst into laughter then and moved swiftly off.

"You'll let me know, monsieur, when you need me to begin this evening's prep."

"Jamais!" Henri called after him.

He gathered his apron and began to tie it about himself, getting ready for the lunch prep. He allowed himself a little smile. He ought to be more worried that his feelings for Nikolaos were so obvious, but Michel knew him much better than most and discerned things others did not. Michel could sense even the smallest diverting of his emotions, and often knew the source before Henri himself. And, it seemed, Michel was quite fond of the idea of Henri's interest in Nikolaos, which was most encouraging. His friend was a very precise judge of character, even if Henri had chosen to ignore his wise warnings in the past.

"Bâtard insolent." Henri whispered to himself as he tied the knot on his apron. But, still, he smiled again, knowing his friend's teasing was a good omen.

EVEN THOUGH NICO had arrived earlier than need be, and was in no particular rush, he felt breathless. It was a feeling akin to his excitement as a youngster whenever his aunt would take them to the seaside or a visiting circus or, on the rare occasion, a pantomime on Boxing Day. He felt that same sense that something wonderful and exciting was about to happen. As he made his way through H&C he should have been sobered, he thought, given the scene. But he wasn't. As he passed the night workers, he smiled despite the stoic faces of many of them as they set about their afterhours tasks of cleaning and polishing. Stock boys reshelved the items sold during the day and some young ladies, even, were there to organize displays and lay out the silk scarves and gloves and other accoutrements fresh for the new sales day approaching. Nico half expected the store to be swathed in darkness, but although the lights near the entrance had been dimmed at closing, the store still pulsed with light and life, though of a quieter variety.

He took the staff lift at the back of the floor, hidden away from the view of customers, which put him just off beside the kitchens upstairs. It was his usual departure point when coming to work, but he was met with quite a different sight. The Royal Tea Room after dark felt magical. Even though the summer sun had not long set, the city outside was a nighttime landscape. From this vantage point, the lights of London looked like a second sky, their streetlamp stars and flares of light bumping against and blending into those of nature. Like competing heavens, Nico thought. The overhead electrical chandeliers of the dining room had been dimmed and only the table lamps and the odd wall sconce light were lit. It had turned the gilded glass box of the daytime dining room, all candescent with sunrays and color, into a cushy sultry lair kept cordoned in by the dark skies that wrapped around it like the sides of a Bedouin tent. It was seductive, a feeling Nico never thought he would associate with his place of work. Across the room he saw Monsieur Michel chatting with two under cooks. Michel caught sight of him and gave a little wave.

"You're early," cried Michel. "Still setting up but make yourself comfortable for now. Have a drink or something. In the kitchen if you like."

Nico nodded but lingered for a moment, taking in the atmosphere. He stashed his jacket and cap in the common room closet, and, straightening his livery, headed towards the back larder, nearest the ice room, where they kept the beverages. As he moved into the larder, he stopped, surprised. At the large table in the center of the larder, Monsieur Henri was bent over the table, deep in focus. Piping bag in one hand, Monsieur Henri traced it slowly, as if writing something in the air. Nico saw that he was applying a design to rows of chocolate bonbons. Like a musician over blank sheet music, Henri seemed to compose his embellishments as inspiration struck. Nico was mesmerized watching his handsome face, deep in study, as his eyes traced the lines of chocolate. He felt he ought to speak, to announce his presence, but to do so would disturb the magic he was witnessing. Monsieur Henri finished one row and shifted his bag to the next, his wrist turning in quick strokes and then moving the bag up and down as a ballerina might prance across a stage. When he finished the last chocolate, he lifted the bag placing his fingertip at the tip to catch any excess. Nico watched as he brought the fingertip to his lips and licked away the sweet liquid. That breathless feeling overcame Nico again, and he felt a rush go through him; he pressed his hands down his chest and below, smoothing the fronts of his livery, trying to quell the shivers rippling across his skin. Monsieur Henri looked up then and their eyes met. Nico felt caught, accused, and he froze, his hands resting just above his waist. He saw Henri's gaze move down his body, stopping where Nico's hands rested. Nico swore he saw the smallest lift of one brow as Henri, hand still at his mouth, sucked the tip of his finger again before turning his head sharply away.

"Mister Kavafis," he said, his voice ringing across the silent space.

Nico cleared his throat and steadied himself. "Monsieur."

"I didn't see you there," said Henri as he busied himself with putting away his chocolate-making tools.

"N-n-no, sir," Nico stammered. "I didn't want to interrupt your work."

"That is appreciated."

Still Monsieur Henri would not look in his direction.

"Frankly, monsieur," said Nico, even as he himself wondered why his mouth still formed words, "I was fairly mesmerized."

Henri turned to him.

"Have you never seen chocolate before?"

"Yes, of course." Nico stepped closer to the table. "A bar of Fry's, even a Cadbury's Fancy Box. But nothing so fine as your technique. Nothing so beautiful as this."

"'Beautiful'?"

"Very beautiful, monsieur. So exquisite, so perfect. Every detail your eye lingers."

But Nico was not interested in the sweets as he said this, instead he studied Henri's face, so that he noticed the small blush on the chef's cheeks as he ducked his head.

"You are too kind, Mister Kavafis. I am no master chocolatier. No. Simply I make the bonbons and the petit fours for the food halls. There are much finer craftsmen about, but Messieurs H&C like presenting a specially made product."

"I can't imagine that anyone's could be finer than yours."

A flash of something that Nico could not interpret went across Monsieur Henri's ruddled face.

"Would you like to try one?" he asked.

"Very much indeed."

Nico moved around the table and came to stand by Monsieur Henri, far closer than need be.

"Which one can I have?" he asked.

"Whichever you like best."

Nico couldn't help but smile at that.

"But you must be careful not to muss your livery."

"Then perhaps, Chef, you ought to place it in my mouth?"

Monsieur Henri guffawed loudly then, his cheeks pure crimson. Nico felt he was surely pushing his luck but it thrilled him when he could elicit these unguarded responses. For someone so stoic and hard-lined, Monsieur Henri was easily flabbergasted.

"I am sure Monsieur can feed himself."

Nico glanced over the chocolates and chose the least perfect one—hardly imperfect, but the line had gone just slightly askew towards the edge. He lifted it to his mouth and bit into it. The smooth and mildly bitter chocolate gave way to a salty and creamy caramel center. Nico gave a small hum of pleasure.

"Even more exquisite-tasting than looking," Nico said, popping the other half into his mouth.

"I can only hope so," replied Monsieur Henri, a queer note in his voice. Nico looked at him, but he dropped his eyes to the table. "Tell me, why did you choose that particular bonbon?"

"The line was off a bit. Only a very minor imperfection, of course."

"You noticed that? Most people, given the chance, would have chosen the flawless one."

"But I wanted to leave you with all the perfect ones to sell in the food stalls."

"Because without the customer we are nothing."

"No. Because I want people buying them to admire you, the magician who crafted them. Thinking of it somehow made me feel proud."

Monsieur seemed unable to reply. Nico let his tongue linger over his fingertips as he pretended to lick the residual chocolate from them, hoping Henri's eyes followed his tongue. He gave a little shrug.

"Besides, slightly flawed is usually better," he said. "Don't you think? Always more satisfying than perfection. What could be more boring than a perfect thing?"

Monsieur Henri's face was once again a mask. Nico could sense the energy between them, and his lips felt hot, so great was his need to take Monsieur Henri's mouth to his. But still something held him back. The whites of his uniform suddenly seemed like a suit of armor around the chef and Nico was not certain he would be able to break through it. But he wanted to try.

Nico took a step closer to him.

"Monsieur."

"Oui," Monsieur Henri whispered, his voice husky.

Nico stepped closer still. "Monsieur?"

"Oui." Monsieur Henri nodded.

Nico stepped closer, lifting his hands.

"Mon dieu! There you are!"

Michel burst into the room and Nico spun away, moving quickly to the end of the table, grabbing onto the corner and steadying himself, trying to hide his face.

"I should have known you were in here. Freezing yourself over chocolate," said Michel.

Michel halted, looking back and forth between the two men; his brows knitted.

"Désolé, je t'ai interrompu," he said.

"Non, non, non," Monsieur waved his hand, seemingly aggravated. "What is it Michel? Why have you to hunt me down?"

"You must begin getting ready soon. But why have you only brought the trainee cook and that David tonight?"

"He needs the experience."

"He needs une casserole to the back of the head, if you ask me."

"He will do. Have you come only to complain to me of David?"

"No, actually, I have come to beg off."

"Excuse moi?"

"It is my wife. Well, my son actually. She has sent word by the neighbor. The boy has been sick with the croup for two nights now and she has gotten no sleep. Now her mother is also unwell, and she is staying with us. If I leave Edith to be nursemaid another evening, I am afraid she may have left me when I return in the early hours."

"Of course, of course, go. I can handle it."

"But with David? Are you sure? Shall I send word to one of the other chefs and have them return?"

"I can assist." Nico turned to face them.

"You?" asked Monsieur Henri.

"I grew up in a restaurant, monsieur. Where my aunt has always worked. I don't have Monsieur Michel's training, of course, but I do have skills."

"Which is more than one can say for David, really," said Michel. "Already I am more confident in Monsieur Kavafis and I have even seen him boil a kettle."

"Yes, yes, yes. The point is made. Go, Michel, tend to your

family."

Michel grabbed Monsieur Henri and kissed him on both cheeks as Monsieur rolled his eyes and pushed him away.

"Monsieur Kavafis," Michel declared. "I owe you a great debt. Ah, the other wait staff have arrived, by the way. They are waiting in the dining room."

As Michel rushed out, Monsieur Henri eyed Nico from across the table.

"Do you really have skills?" he asked. "Or were you trying to be helpful for Michel's sake?"

"I do not confess to any heights of Escoffier, monsieur. But, yes, I do have some skills."

Monsieur Henri furrowed his brow. Nico found it irresistibly enticing.

"We shall. Come, Mister Kavafis, we must begin the night."

"Yes, Monsieur. I am at your disposal."

THE WAIT STAFF were just putting the finishing touches to the dining room when there was a burst of noise from the lift as it opened. Nico turned and watched the entourage enter. Far too many bodies were crammed inside the contraption and they began to tumble out, laughing and cajoling one another. Slim-hipped men in coats and tails, followed by young ladies in what appeared to be tea gowns, bursting masses of muslin and lace, some without hats, all of which seemed most refreshing for such a summer night. The young men and ladies alike pointed all around the Tea Room, offering loud exclamations of commentary. A duo of burly fellows emerged, as well as one or two smaller ones who seemed to have forgotten to remove their stage makeup, their arms laden with overcoats, furs, and hats, and then Nico could see the tall, elegant Señor Casas revealed in his tuxedo. He stepped forward and extended his arm, and out walked one of the prettiest women Nico had seen of late. She was flocked by a trio of ladies, dressed equally as elegant, in the middle of whom walked Mister Kenneth Hawthorne, wearing a tuxedo and opera hat, with a lady on each arm.

"Oh my! That's Gabrielle Ray," said Lily.

"Who's that?" asked Tommy.

"She's an actress," said Lily. "I saw her in *Lady Madcap* when I was younger. She was so beautiful up there on stage. I'll never forget it. My cousin and I spent weeks trying to do her dance in the show, the Maxixe. We never could get it right."

Miss Ray had a massive head of curls, which she wore lifted around her head, in the latest fashion, like a crown. Her skin, Nico noticed, was smooth and clear, shining even in the dim light of the transformed dining room. She looked fresh and her pale skin went unbroken and unblemished down her neck and shoulders and finally her décolletage. She wore a dress that emphasized, a silvery rose, in layers of lace and chiffon which gathered at the center of her chest where there was adorned a great silk rose to match. On her head she wore a Juliet cap like a net of woven sparkling silver stars. She seemed to glide into the room on her Cuban heels, as if she were being lifted on either side by invisible arms and carried forward.

Gabrielle separated herself from Casas and stood in the middle of the foyer space, perfectly positioned under an electric chandelier which dappled her with light. Standing there, she threw up her arms, took a deep breath and began to sing, in a clear, resonant soprano.

"Gentlemen, you really are too good to me you are!" she sang. "I haven't been in Paris long," she continued, stepping forward, and caressing Henri on the cheek, "And when I meet a man, I'm always saying something wrong!"

Señor Casas took in her beaming audience and offered her his arm, escorting her to the table in the center of the room. Nico saw Monsieur Henri emerge from the kitchen and move towards the table. Mister Hawthorne settled into the table just beside them. He collapsed his Gibus opera hat, by way of its button mechanism, and stowed it beside him on the table. Pressing another button on his Oxford walking stick, a mechanism opened a compartment on the top from which he extracted two cigarettes and a matchbox.

"Oh, Housey, it's even more lovely than I remember," she said to Casas. "There's something special in here tonight."

"We find you in good spirits this evening, madam," said Henri as he approached the table and gave a small bow.

"Oh, Monsieur Henri, I haven't a complaint in the world, really. The show is doing marvelously well. And after a number of tragedy pieces—abandoned wives, East End beginnings, you know the sort—I was simply ecstatic to be in something comedic again. I was thrilled to find that Monsieur Lehar had a sense of humor—even if it is a German one."

"He's Austrian, I believe, my dear," offered Hawthorne, leaning over from his table.

"Is he? I'm afraid I never know the difference really. So long as he's not Russian, I don't mind. I did a bit of that Chekhov fellow once. The one where the lead shoots himself at the end of the play? And, I must say, after performing it multiple nights a week, I was quite sure I wanted to join him." She looked up as Nico approached her table. "My goodness, Housey. You really have made many improvements since my last visit."

Casas smirked and gave Nico a nod. Monsieur Henri, too, gave him a nod and headed back to the kitchen.

"Champagne, madam?" offered Nico.

"Is there any other drink?" she replied.

"There was a Chekhov play not too many years ago where a wife lamented that her husband died of drinking too much champagne," said Casas.

"Oh, but he sounds like a most sensible man," Gabrielle said. "Maybe I should revisit my feelings on the playwright. Housey, you really are too cultured for your own good."

"Perhaps you ought not call our esteemed host by that nickname in mixed company," offered Hawthorne.

"Not to worry," said Señor Casas. "This is select staff."

"Of that I'm sure," said Gabrielle, giving Nico a once-over. "I call Señor Casas 'Housey' because of his surname, of course. I once remarked on how accurate it was because he was as tall and sturdy and as handsome as any townhouse in Belgravia."

Nico filled Casas' glass in turn. "And I told her that she flattered me in excess."

"Possibly so, but what can I do? It's in my nature. Besides, a woman in my position in society can never admire too many men. One always needs allies. And Harty and Housey are two of the best. Where is our dear Harty tonight anyway?"

"He's in America this week. Business matters."

"The man never stops working. But I suppose that is how he creates things such as this marvelous place."

Miss Ray looked around and sighed.

"And I suppose neither of you has seen my show yet? Despite it being an enormous success and playing for a year now."

"With apologies; I'm afraid this last year or so has been rather busy for us," said Casas. "What with creating this marvelous place and so on."

"Of course, dearest, how insensitive of me."

"I'll have Patrick in the Theater Booking department set aside two tickets for you," said Mister Hawthorne. "You can have my box. Any night you like. I have seen the show more times than one ought to have."

Miss Ray tutted at him.

"Much obliged," replied Casas.

Nico moved to refill Gabrielle's glass, which had quickly been emptied, just as Tommy appeared with a tray of hors d'oeuvres. Gabrielle picked up a small savory and sighed.

"These are delightful, of course, but I was rather hoping for something new."

She popped it into her mouth and chewed vigorously nonetheless.

"Is the food not to your liking, señorita?"

"No, of course it is, Housey. It's delicious always. Only I'm in the mood for something exotic." She pointed at Nico. "You there, do you know where Monsieur Henri has gone to?"

"Yes, miss. He has gone to the kitchen to prepare the main meal."

"Take me there, won't you?"

Nico looked to Casas for guidance and his employer nodded. "Right this way, Miss Ray."

"DAVID, WHERE IS the cream? I need the cream, tout suite!"

Henri was carefully piping the mousse de jambon on the small squares of toast, his hand steady despite the fraught expression on his face. "Merde! Must I do everything myself? Crème! I need cream!"

Both David and James, the junior cook whose name Michel could never remember, appeared, carrying bowls of whipped cream.

"Putain," exclaimed Henri as they finished the last toast. "Leave the cream, James, and start arranging the quail for the Cailles Souvaroff. We shall begin roasting them momentarily. David, begin the pommes de terre, if there is enough cream."

"Blimey, Chef," said David. "How are we expected to serve all that number of people out there?"

"We are expected to do it quickly, eh?" shot back Henri. "If you want to work properly, you must learn. It will not always be finger sandwiches and china cups. Maintenant, les pommes!"

David scuttled off and left Henri to spoon a shallow dollop of cream onto each mousse, topping it with a shard of Roquette leaf. He glanced up briefly when he heard the door open and noted Nikolaos entering with a companion.

"Mister Kavafis, dieu merci! Please, come assist me, I need—"

"Goodness, but it is marvelous, isn't it?" gasped a female voice.

Henri looked up to see Gabrielle Ray, and stifled a groan.

"Mademoiselle Ray. In my kitchen. To what do I owe this pleasure?"

"Monsieur Henri, I've told you to call me Gabs, all my friends do. I've never been back here before, you. It's like the engine room of some great ship. Guts of steel and machinery." She laid her hand on Nikolaos's arm. "I've been on a liner or two, you know. In fact, just before *Merry Widow* I was asked to provide entertainment, main billing, on one of Reginald Churchen's brand new ships—a sort of maiden voyage, if you will."

"And was it a success?" asked Nikolaos.

"Well, we didn't sink. Which I suppose is something."

"Is the food not to your liking?" asked Henri impatiently.

"That's what I mean to ask about."

"Oh?" Henri put his utensils on the table and crossed his arms behind his back. Better to keep away the temptation to throw anything. "You do not like the hors d'oeuvres?"

"Oh, the little savories are just divine. I feel as if I might be at the Ritz."

"But?"

"But it's all so terribly British, isn't it?"

"Au contraire, mademoiselle, it is all so terribly French."

"Yes, of course. But you know what I mean, don't you? Every time I come to H&C I feel as if I'm making a discovery—a new scent, a new pattern, a new gadget—something from some corner of the world I never thought about. I would love if you could entertain us tonight with something like that—in the culinary sense, I mean. Something far-flung."

"And the rest won't mind?"

"This lot? They wouldn't know a jellied eel from a joconde sponge. So long as it's not tough as old boots and half as tasty as the leather, they won't complain."

"And where does mademoiselle suggest I travel on this adventure?"

"Oh, Henri, you're the chef, darling." She stared at Nikolaos. "Maybe somewhere hot—sultry, you know—and a little spicy. I'm sure you can find inspiration."

"Of course we shall, miss," Nikolaos said as he turned and held the door open for her.

Henri was grateful for this small moment, as he was only just prepared to inform "Gabs" exactly where she might travel herself.

"I never miss my cue," said the actress, dipping out of the door. "I'll leave you to it, then."

Tommy slipped in past Miss Ray as she exited.

"Ainsley!" Henri bellowed, catching the boy off-guard. "Take these hors d'oeuvres."

"Yes, Chef," replied Tommy, stopping just short of a salute. He grabbed the trays and retreated into the dining room.

Henri turned to Nikolaos and gave him a chastising scowl.

"Must you have brought her back into my kitchen?"

He saw Nikolaos bite back a laugh as he began to circle the prep table.

"It is well that I did, monsieur. The idea was hers, not mine, and sanctioned by Señor Casas, and by the look on your face, my escort saved the young woman from being jettisoned back through the doors in mid-air."

"Well, what am I to do?"

"Surely you have some exciting ideas as yet unexplored in that haute cuisine mind of yours?"

Henri put his fists on his hips. He should have been furious with this teasing but, though he refused to show it, he was actually enjoying it. Nikolaos's impish grin made him feel like dancing inside. He set his jaw to disguise his feelings, though he suspected he had already betrayed them.

"You are well-traveled, are you not, monsieur?" said Nikolaos, standing just beside him now. "Nothing comes to mind?"

"I know nothing about sultry and spicy."

"Oh, I very much doubt that, monsieur."

"Putain," whispered Henri before he could stop himself.

Nikolaos grinned at this and gave Henri a look that made his stomach flip. Then he lifted his chin, his eyes wide, and snapped his fingers.

"Aubergines," he said. "Do you have any aubergines?"

"It's summer time; of course I do. Newly arrived."

"There is a dish that my aunt used to make back home – my mother's sister, who lived in Smyrna – kolokithakia me to kreas. It is a dish of ground meat cooked in red wine with layers of roasted aubergine on top. It was a favorite when I was a child."

"Yes, I believe I have had something similar when I visited Morocco."

"But Miss Ray did say something special. How to make it special?"

"You heard her. I am sure it will be special to them all. The flavors are not their usual cup of tea. It sounds rather special to me, already."

But Nikolaos did hear him, so absorbed was he in his own thoughts. Again inspiration seemed to hit him.

"Béchamel," said Nikolaos. "Sometimes we would sprinkle kefalotyri on the top. Maybe if we made a béchamel to cook over the aubergine and topped it with a similar cheese. Something salty and nutty."

Henri knew a true cook when he saw one and he thrilled to watch Nikolaos devise a dish like this. A sudden swelling of emotion filled him and he lost all ill feelings. He smiled.

"It sounds delicious. Shall we try it now?"

Nikolaos grabbed the deeply purple vegetable. "Why not? We can only fail."

Henri looked surprised. "'Only'?"

"If we fail, we try again," Nikolaos said shrugging. He was already slicing the aubergines thinly. "Of course, my aunt will say I deserved to fail, defiling her recipe like this."

"We will keep it our little secret then, non?" said Henri.

"A secret? That sounds very sultry and spicy indeed, monsieur."

Nikolaos turned to the cooking range and began to sauté the aubergine, turning his back to Henri, but Henri was sure he must be smiling too.

THE AUBERGINE AND béchamel creation having proved quite a success as a main meal, the party had moved on to the dessert and drinks. More drinks. The drinks never stopped flowing, and Nico wondered if his wrist would survive the evening of pouring and refilling, let alone the champagne vaults of H&C. Luckily, Miss Ray's demand for exoticism did not extend to these last courses, so the cast and crew were happy on chocolates and fruit and cheese and port and claret. And champagne. Dizzy from the late hour and full bellies, many had begun draping themselves over the tables and seating areas when suddenly Gabrielle jumped from her table and cried out.

"Percival! Where are you, dear? Yes, there, there; come now! Do play us something light-hearted so that we might work up a proper appetite for the feast. I feel the need to sing!"

A stout young man with a strong jawline and expressive brows hurried to take a seat behind the piano, now caparisoned by the vibrant shawl which Miss Ray had draped over it, and began to play.

"Oh, darling, no!" cried out Miss Ray, turning to him with her hand on her chest. "Not *Miss Hook*! Nothing from that dreadful show! I wish the lady in question would hook it back to Holland and be done with herself. If I never have to sing another note from that drivel, I shall be forever happy. No, please play the selection from *The Geisha* which I adore—you know the one."

"We all know the one," said Hawthorne, letting out a bored sigh. "Entirely too well."

The piano began a light, bouncy tune and as the notes went

on Miss Ray lifted her skirts just enough to show her ankles. She extended her slippered foot and turned it from side to side as she tapped out the rhythm of the song.

"*A gold fish swam in a big glass bowl, as dear little goldfish do,*" she sang, her voice high and childlike in its sunniness. "*But she lov'd with the whole of her heart and soul, an office from the ocean wave, and she thought that he lov'd her too!*"

As she continued to sing the infectious little number, Gabrielle pranced around the dining room. She lifted her skirts here and there as she twisted into a pose, in order to show off her intricate footwork. She crossed her feet, as a ballerina might, and then, with a little leap, landed into a tip-toed run, letting the sound of the keys carry her. She affected looks of surprise, and here and there innocence, though the latter proved an unconvincing affectation on her sly, smiling face.

She ranged about, touching the faces of her onlookers, or providing them with a wink, and soon the whole cohort was singing along with her.

"*And she thought, it's fit-fit-fitter,*" she continued to sing, her cast members chiming in, "*He should love my glit-glit-glitter, than give his heart away to the butterfly gay, or the birds that twit-twit-twitter!*"

"One wonders if her glit-glit-glitter might sometime be so blinding as to inspire a migraine," commented Hawthorne. He turned to Nico. "To which end, might you have any more champagne on offer? Or even something stronger?"

Nico smiled. "Of course, sir. Only a moment."

Nico retreated to the kitchen where he found Señor Casas and Monsieur Henri standing together, deep in conversation. Nico smiled, remembering Hosea's fantasy of the mystic and arcane. Casas looked up and gave him a warm smile.

"I've only come for champagne," said Nico.

"Yes, of course, of course," said Casas, clasping his hands. "But Monsieur Henri tells me that you have created this evening's star dish."

Nico felt a slight blush stain his cheeks. "I wouldn't say I created it, sir. It is an old dish, I only changed it a little. Incorporated some new tastes I have learned."

"But that is exactly creation, good sir," Casas said with an emphatic nod. "I must dash, but I do regret that I shall not be able to taste this once it has cooled. It is heavenly." Casas moved from around the counter and headed for the door. As he passed Nico, he laid a hand on his shoulder. "I had no idea Monsieur Henri had such talent amongst his ranks. This is precisely the thing we had hoped to find in creating this store. We must encourage you to show us more."

From the dining room the music and laughter, both increasing, pushed their way through the kitchen doors.

"Ah, that is my signal to make my exit," said Casas. "Before I am witness to things a decent proprietor should never be witness to. Again, well done. Both of you."

He patted Nico's shoulder and left.

Monsieur Henri's expression was somewhat inscrutable but he gave Nico a nod. "Monsieur Casas seems genuinely impressed, non?"

"I'm sorry, monsieur. Have I overstepped? I apologize if I have distracted him from your marvelous work."

Monsieur Henri waved his hand. "Not at all, no, no." He smiled then, a sudden bright thing that caught Nico off-guard. "I don't mean to show any jealousy. Quite the contrary. Though I will very much relish letting Monsieur Michel know how little his services were needed after all."

Nico blanched a little, worried that he might have created an uncomfortable rift in his new friendship with Michel. But that worry was dispersed when Monsieur Henri burst into a shout of laughter.

"Oh, Mister Kavafis! I can imagine his face now. The teasing I will give him!"

"Will he be upset?"

"Michel? Never. Michel cannot stay angry with anyone or

anything for very long; it is not in his nature." Henri winked at Nico. "How do you think he has survived all these years being my friend?"

Nico laughed at the joke, but in reality, his laughter was a burst of nervous energy. That small wink, along with the so seldom found smile, from Henri had made his stomach flip. It was not a large gesture, but it felt like an achievement to Nico, and he realized how he had pined for such attention from the handsome man in white standing across from him.

Monsieur Henri cocked his head, and for a breath Nico wondered if his unsaid emotions had been found out. But Monsieur Henri was only listening.

"The music is reaching a pitch," the chef said. "Do take more champagne, then come back to help me serve. Once the floor show has ceased, they will be famished."

The doors to the kitchen swung out suddenly and Tommy burst through.

"Mister Henri," the young man cried out, sweat on his brow and his face red.

"Yes, yes, what is it, Mister Ainsley? You look rather flushed. Have you become ill?"

"No, Monsieur, I'm not sick." Tommy glanced over his shoulder. "Only they're dancing on the tables, sir! And some of the ladies"—He looked between Nico and Henri, embarrassed—"Some of the ladies, sir, have removed their shoes and even their stockings."

Monsieur Henri nodded and although his face had returned to its usual stoic stance, Nico saw the light of laughter in his eyes.

"I understand your shock, monsieur. But, as you know, these are invited guests of the Misters Hartridge and Casas—a select group of friends—and we must try to keep our usual expectations of decorum to ourselves."

"Of course, sir. Only—well, we used to have parties at the house, sir, but never none like this. One girl threw her stockings across the room and they caught on one of the potted ferns, sir!"

Monsieur Henri lifted his chin and swallowed. "Then you must remember to retrieve it for her before she leaves, Mister Ainsley. These are the people from the night side of London, you must remember, who do things just that bit differently from the luncheon crowd."

Tommy nodded emphatically. "Yes, sir."

"Now, please help Mister Kavafis with the champagne, won't you? I imagine all the dancing has left our guests parched."

In the dining room, things were as surprising as Tommy had indicated. The piano was clanging at a raucous pace and some of the folks had begun to clap along loudly, singing a tune Nico did not recognize. He made his way around the few tables of observers still seated, offering drink.

Gabrielle Ray, indeed, was dancing on the tabletops. Several had been pushed together for her, as a makeshift stage of sorts, and she twirled around, punctuating certain moments with high kicks. As Nico approached Mister Hawthorne's table, he saw Miss Ray do a handstand and then flip off the tabletop where she was caught by four men and held high, kicking her legs in time and singing in full voice.

He bent to refill Hawthorne's glass.

"She's doing her Frou Frou number," said the producer, his voice flat.

"You seem unimpressed, sir," offered Nico.

"When you've seen a thing dozens of times, it is hard to remain impressed. No matter how many high kicks she throws in."

"I must say, sir," said Nico. "It does seem a feat. Does she do this every night on stage?"

"She does. And then some. But, of course, I've been in theater for years, so things don't reverberate within me with quite the same resonance as they did when I was younger." He took a sip of his champagne and Nico felt his appraising glance. "Speaking on youth, I imagine a young man like you would have too many admirers to forfeit your evenings for work."

"I am wed to my work, sir."

"Aren't we all, I do say. But it's never healthy to concentrate on only that. You're in your prime, don't squander it for farthings and shillings."

Nico attempted to change the subject.

"I am surprised not to see your friend here this evening."

"My friend?"

"The Lady Covington. I have noticed you taking lunch together."

Hawthorne chuckled into his champagne flute. "Oh, heavens, no. Can you imagine? Imogene Constance Dewsdearn, the Right Honorable Countess of Covington, at a late night soiree? She would be entirely scandalized." Hawthorne giggled and lifted his empty glass to Nico. "I sometimes wonder if she doesn't already think I ought to be doing hard labor somewhere in penitence for my sins, like Mister Wilde."

"Surely she can't judge you so harshly," said Nico, pouring. "You are friends."

"We are society friends. A status which does not necessarily demand the baring of one's soul to another. But, no, you're right, of course—I am being slightly hyperbolic. I'm sure she wouldn't imprison me anywhere. Except, possibly, for that one injustice of having her to dinner when cook served Dover sole. I don't believe she has forgiven me for that yet. But Lady Covington knows that I spend most evenings unlike tonight—at home with my wife, by the fire, and away from all this chaos you see before you."

"I'm sure it makes for a very charming evening."

"It does rather. My wife has taught me embroidery, you see. And many nights the two of us sit, hardly speaking a word, engaged in our petit point."

"Just as I would imagine marriage to be, sir."

"What's this I hear?" Suddenly Miss Ray was upon them. She flopped into the chair next to Hawthorne, resting her feet in the empty one beside and grabbed an empty flute. She fanned herself and Nico noticed how she glowed, whether from the exertion of the dance or the attention paid her, he couldn't say. "I come to get a cooling drink, and I hear talk of marriage!"

"I was only telling this lovely young man how my wife might be wondering as to my whereabouts," said Hawthorne.

"Oh, come now, Kenny. Your wife is the most understanding creature I have ever met. She is more than familiar with your professional habits and still offers naught but smiles and good charm whenever I have met her." She turned to Nico. "He likes to pretend, of course, as if she is some judgmental harpy—as most men do of their wives. He paints a picture of her—do you remember that old advertisement for Ogden's Midnight Flake? The line was, 'Why Jones stays late at the office' or something? And it showed a very stern, very matronly and proper lady staring down her nose at her husband, as if she were judging him for smoking a pipe."

"The one where the man was seated next to his pretty young typist?" asked Nico.

"Yes, that's the one," said Miss Ray. She stole a glance at Hawthorne. "So not entirely realistic, of course. But that is how he likes us to believe his wife to be."

"I beg your pardon," said Hawthorne, huffing. "But never once have I portrayed Mrs. Hawthorne in such a light."

"Not in mixed company, perhaps. But boys do talk, Kenny." She pointedly ignored his sputtering. "Do take a drink with us, won't you, Mister Kavafis?"

"I'm afraid I really couldn't, Miss."

"Can't or won't?"

"Some people do believe honoring their profession, Miss Ray," said Hawthorne.

She winked at Nico. "How do you think, Mister Kavafis, that one honors being born into money?"

Nico bit back a smile and dipped his head. "If you'll excuse me."

AS THE EVENING neared its natural close, the dancing continued, but at a more languorous pace. No further demands were being made of the wait staff, and Henri sent Tommy and Lily off to the kitchen with a bottle of champagne to enjoy with David and James. He could not find Nikolaos at first but he finally spied him in the musicians' corner. Nikolaos stood, half-hidden behind a large potted plant, watching the dancers, captivated. Henri peered out over the crowd and thought he understood.

The pianist played a slow waltz and pairs of people glided around the dining room. Men with women, women with women, and men with men. No matter how many times Henri had been privy to such private parties, no matter how many hidden cabarets he had snuck off to in the dark hours of the night, no matter how many times—though these times had been too few, really—that he himself had held another man close and graced a dancefloor; no matter how many times, when he saw two men dancing together, he always felt thunderstruck.

It was a simple, beautiful moment. A moment that "ordinary" couples took for granted. For seeing it always kicked up the feeling that it was indeed simple and beautiful and natural and correct. Above all, correct. And yet it was so rare. Never seen, never talked of—hidden under cover of night, squirreled away in secret corners, disguised by pretending it fiction, cruelly deeming it imaginary and not real, as real as the touch of one palm against another.

He looked again at Nikolaos, who still watched the dancers. Even half-shadowed by the plant, his beauty shone. The flicker of a nearby sconce made his skin glow like gold beside the dark sky outside. He had shed most of his livery and stood there in his waistcoat, his collar abandoned. His powerful broad shoulders, his square back, the taper to his waist, its tight lines etched against the window behind him. He stood, the light in his amber eyes, so still, so quiet, that Henri thought he might be a painting. An ethereal moment of male beauty, too immense to be real, caught by an artist's brush.

He came up beside Nikolaos and stood there silently. Nikolaos did not take his eyes from the dancers when he spoke.

"I think your evening was a success."

"Hardly my evening. It was for the messieurs."

"No. I think it was only yours, Monsieur Henri."

Henri looked at him, his sculpted profile against the dark green of the great leaf behind him. His lips seemed to call out for kissing and Henri cursed himself for not having the bravery to kiss them.

A couple danced up very close to them, two men. The one man who had rested his head on his partner's shoulder lifted it and smiled at them both before letting himself be guided away.

Nikolaos turned to him. His gaze was powerful, full of want, full of need, full of hope.

"Don't you want to dance, Monsieur Henri?"

Panic slapped Henri across the face. "With you?" he blurted out before he could stop himself.

He stared at his feet, feeling foolish, ashamed. How could he let himself suggest such a thing? Even here, even now, with all this around them. He thought of Tommy and David and Lily in the kitchen. Anyone might see them; anyone might whisper—or worse. It was foolhardy and, worse, dangerous to entertain such fantasies.

"No, of course you didn't mean that. Pardon me."

He tried to pretend a smile. He thought he saw a sadness in Nikolaos's eyes. A sadness he knew, that he could feel, but was not courageous enough to answer, lest they both be caught up in the current of it and swept away.

"A silly thing to say, forgive me," he continued, hating the words as they left his lips. "Just the atmosphere, I suppose.

He waved his hand at the dining room, but Nikolaos simply looked at him, offering no reply.

"Besides, I don't dance anymore," concluded Henri.

"Anymore?"

"I am old."

"Nonsense."

"And I am too busy for such things. I am afforded neither the chance to dance much nor the partners."

"I am quite sure the partners are more than available, should you ask them," said Nikolaos. He returned his gaze to the crowd. "And you have worked in some of the best hotels in London and Paris. Surely you have been afforded many nights with an opportunity for a waltz. Like tonight, for instance."

Henri shrugged. "I cannot say, really."

"You should never stop dancing, monsieur. Even if you have forgotten the steps, you must never let your body forget the joy of feeling the music."

"Monsieur!"

Henri was spared a response by David calling his name from the kitchen door.

"Monsieur, Chef, sir! What shall we do with the quails?"

Henri nodded at Nikolaos although Nikolaos had not broken his study of the dining room.

"My apologies, I must attend to the kitchen."

Nico leaned against the brick wall and inhaled deeply of his cigarette. He buried his hands in his pockets and let the fag dangle from his lips, exhaling. Despite it being a summer night, it was raw. The whole summer had been that way, pelting rain and cold one hour then the sun beating down the next.

Gabrielle left the group gathered nearby and stood by him.

"Any extras about?" she asked, indicating the cigarette.

Nico fished out his pack of Murads from his pocket and lit her a smoke from his own. They were all standing across the street from H&C, the rest of the theater troupe, which Miss Ray had just left, huddled near the line of cabs.

"Why do you linger?" Nico asked.

"We're waiting for my chaperone."

"You don't seem the type to be in need of a chaperone."

Gabrielle chuckled. "I am never in *need* of a chaperone, I assure you. Only in want of one. Besides, a lady can never be too sure at night." She inhaled of her cigarette. "Besides, why are you lingering? Waiting for your chaperone as well?"

"No, miss. Just to make sure all is done in the Tea Room."

"Call me Gabs. And isn't that Monsieur Henri's job?"

Nico shrugged. "I feel a certain loyalty to my job."

"Of course you do."

Nico leaned back again, resting against the wall which was plastered with a faded advertisement poster. He saw that Gabs looked up at it. The illustration was of an army of maids, all in a row, all spotless and pinpoint perfect in their black dresses and white aprons, all reflections of one another, identical and without distinction of person. She ran her hand along the outline of one of the maids' dresses.

"Don't you ever get tired of being a waiter?" she asked.

"Miss?"

"Of waiting on people. Enduring their ridiculous attitudes and snobberies. Doesn't it sicken you to be at the beck and call of these high society types? Had you or I only been born with a different surname or in a different neighborhood, we too might be society. It is all so arbitrary."

"I am not overly concerned with such things."

"How can you not be?"

"I suppose I realize my worth does not come from my coin purse."

"So you'll be happy being a waiter all your life then?"

"Not at all. Not that there is anything wrong in being a waiter, but I have plans for my life."

"Such as?"

"One day I'd like to open a restaurant, or perhaps a tea room like this."

"And will you let only snobbish ladies in silks in?"

"Never. My establishment would be open to all, of course. So long as they can pay the bill."

"And there we are back to money again."

"We cannot survive on bread alone, Gabs."

"Or caviar and champagne for that matter. So you do this work in hopes of owning a restaurant?"

"It's good training. And besides, it pays well. I must save up quite a sum if I am to one day have my own establishment. This is only a stepping stone. We do what we must to earn enough to succeed."

"A fact I am quite keenly aware of." Gabrielle dropped the cigarette on the ground and stubbed it out. "You really are too intelligent and too good-looking to be stuck in a place like this."

"I thank you. Although I'm not sure what my looks have to do with my worthiness."

"Then you know less about the real world than you think." Her disposition suddenly brightened, and the glow Nico had seen earlier, that of the actress in her spotlight, came back. "You know, we're going to a delicious spot—at the Piccadilly end of Regent Street as the lady in feathers once said—called the Purple Rabbit or the Violet Hare or some such. At any rate, the lot of us are going there to drink the midnight hour away, before the boys go wandering the coffee-stalls, as they like to say. You should accompany us."

"I'm afraid I don't care much for drinking."

She took another cigarette from his pack and gave him a look.

"Well, that's not all the night will entail, I assure you." She extended a hand and smoothed his shirt front around the neck. "The drinks are just the excuse. I can offer much more than that for an evening."

Nico smiled politely and lifted her hand from his collarbone.

"I'm afraid the night must end here for me, Miss Ray," he

said, giving her hand a small squeeze before returning it to her side.

She laughed and nodded and took his cigarette to light her own.

"Yes, I was afraid of that. Although, I've never been so soundly rejected so quickly and in so polite a fashion."

"Oh, no offense meant. I think you're quite lovely. But, I—"

She waved her hand, then exhaled a cloud of smoke.

"Not the type of jam you prefer on your toast. I suspected as much, but you can't blame a girl for trying her luck."

Nico gave her a look.

"Oh, you needn't look so terribly shocked, darling! I'm in the theater, after all. An actress. Practically a degenerate in the eyes of society. I know all about the real things of life. And I'm not afraid to speak of them. Even if the lace caps and silk cuffs are." She flicked the ash from the end of her cigarette. "There might be other types of jam available though." She chuckled. "Marmalade even."

Nico heard the side entrance to H&C open then and Monsieur Henri exited, Tommy and David at his side. Nico raised his hand and Monsieur Henri waved back, a polite, if worn, smile on his face. They began to walk towards the waiting crowd.

"There's my chaperone then," said Gabrielle. "At last."

"Monsieur Henri?" Nico exclaimed.

"No, dear, do not worry. The other one. I forget his name. The tall blond."

"Tommy? You were waiting for Tommy?"

"Don't blame me. We both know he's rather easy on the eyes. And as I said, a girl has to try her luck where she finds it."

Nico looked back and watched as Monsieur Henri and Tommy crossed the street, David having gone in a different direction. Despite his obvious exhaustion Monsieur Henri was terribly handsome there in the late night. The soft glow of a street lamp falling on his skin and making his dark hair shine as if trimmed in silver.

"The food was particularly delicious this evening. Inspired, I'd say," said Gabrielle. "You helped Monsieur Henri, didn't you?"

"Yes. In my way, I suppose."

"You make a good team then. You should definitely pursue that."

"Cooking, miss?"

"Well, yes, that too."

She gave Nico a pointed look, a mischievous smile on her lips.

Monsieur Henri and Tommy had reached them. Monsieur Henri stood in front of them, his hands shoved into his jacket, seeming rather uncomfortable.

"Shall we make a leave of it then?" Hawthorne asked, approaching from the waiting carriages. Over his arm was draped a sleek fur coat which he handed to Tommy. "This is for her, dear boy."

Tommy took the fur coat and held it out for Gabrielle to slip into it.

"Isn't it a tad warmish for furs?" asked Hawthorne.

"Opulence is irrelevant to the weather, dear Kenny. Besides the night will have gone colder closer to dawn." She pulled the coat over herself. "Now, handsome Nicky here has already turned me down, but shall you be accompanying us to the Blue Coney, or whatever it's called?"

"I'm afraid I must decline," said Hawthorne.

"Monsieur Henri?"

"Non, mademoiselle. The dawn comes very soon, and I have work to do."

Gabrielle sighed. "What a terrible bore you all are."

"Trust you don't end up dancing on any table tops, Mister Ainsley," Nico teased.

Tommy blushed.

"We can make no promises," said Gabrielle. She turned toward her crowd of theater folk and clapped loudly. "Time, time! Time, darlings!"

Those assembled scrambled for the carriages.

"You manage them well," noted Tommy.

"Yes, I do, don't I? I seem to manage most people well." She bopped Tommy on the nose and he grinned widely. "In fact, perhaps I will one day be a producer myself. What do you say about that, Kenny?

"Everyone has ambitions in life," replied Hawthorne dryly. He turned to Nico and Monsieur Henri. "Well, fellows, my carriage is at the end there. You're welcome to share it, and they'll drop you wherever you need to go."

Nico and Monsieur Henri exchanged a glance and nodded, following Hawthorne.

After Hawthorne climbed in, Nico followed suit and turned to offer Monsieur Henri a hand. The chef hesitated, staring up at him from the curb. Monsieur Henri pushed his hands back into his pockets and took a step back.

"Thank you," Monsieur Henri said. "But I think I'll walk instead."

Nico felt as if he had been punched in the chest. He sat back on the bench, his arm still extended.

"Are you quite sure, old man?" asked Hawthorne. "My driver doesn't mind wherever you might need to go."

"Quite sure. Merci, monsieur. Bon soir."

Hawthorne shrugged and pulled the carriage door shut, prompting Nico to withdraw his hand. As the carriage began to move, he looked out of the window at Monsieur Henri, still standing on the curb. It seemed as if Monsieur Henri thought to lift his hand from his pocket to wave, but seeing Nico's face thought the better of it.

Nico sat back in his seat and was glad of it; a wave would have felt like a slap just then.

CHAPTER FIVE

IT WAS A glorious day and Henri was glad for it. His days off from H&C were few, and most of them he spent resting. It had been so long since he had ventured out with the only intent of diversion, and that the sunshine and temperature had aligned with a proper summer on his one day made him all the gladder.

He followed the crowd as they exited the tube at the Wood Lane entrance, surrounded by cheerful talk and astounded gasps. The crowds had been flocking to Shepherd's Bush since May, and although Henri himself had been in no great hurry to visit, no one could deny the grandeur of the huge swath of land London had converted for the Franco-British Exhibition. There had been created a city within a city—over two dozen structures, all constructed with an eye towards classical beauty and all formidable. And all white. Henri thought, looking out over the acres of buildings, that they appeared as if they were constructed of meringue—as if a strong wind might shake them loose and send their sugar-like forms into the air to blend in with the clouds. Though he could now see it now, he also knew that an enormous stadium, also newly built, encompassed part of the meringue city and had served as home to many of the Olympic Games which had gone on throughout the spring and summer.

He stopped just outside the tube exit and enjoyed the sunshine on his face. A young lady passed by and nodded from under her parasol saying, "Good day, sir."

And indeed it was. He wanted to leave the tension of the last fortnight behind. It had been about ten days since the night of the theater party in the Tea Room. Ten days since that night. Ten rotations of the clock since those moments that had warmed his dreams every night since and fueled the fire of his worry every day. Ten days since the night he had almost lost all good sense and let his body rule over his better judgment. Dim light, slow music, and a beautiful face was all it had taken to make him ignore sensibility and indulge his heart. What he had been willing to risk in those moments, what he had endangered. What a shocking lack of dignity and discipline.

He had chastised himself daily for his foolishness, for so easily letting his guard down. He must stay focused on his ambitions, his plans for a life—a life that could actually be a career, a future—not the fevered fantasies that overtook as he lay in his bed alone, in the dark. Not the thoughts of those lips, those eyes, the line of Nikolaos's strong neck as he massaged it at the end of a day, stiff from hours of perfect posture and polite deference. Spending the last moments, as he did, of every shift standing near the musicians' corner—as if waiting, as if in hope. Henri saw this from his perch near the kitchen door. Not that he made an effort to be there at the end of each shift Nikolaos worked; it was mere coincidence.

And he had not spent the last ten days intentionally ignoring the man whenever they were near each other. He was simply busy; he was only operating with the proper decorum demanded of a coworker. The theater party had been an unusual night, a different state of affairs; the night had been like an actress on stage in costume, indulging imagination. But then the workday retuned them to reality; the daylight brought down the curtain and wiped off the grease paint. A chef and waiter. Both with duties, both with roles, both without the privilege of exploring the delusion of the stage.

The days since the party had been unendurably slow and yet

unusually taxing. Henri felt off-center, as if he were executing to his usual standards and his temper in the kitchen reflected it—the poor young men who worked under him seemingly unable to do anything correctly of late. They must have thought him a monster. So when Michel pressed the invitation to this outing, he tried to shrug off his usual curmudgeonly instincts and accept. He needed a break.

Up ahead he saw Michel waiting with Edith, his wife, and their son, Michael. As he waved and they waved back, he noticed Michel speaking and a man standing just beside them turned towards Henri. Nikolaos. Henri had no idea he would be here today. He ought to be angry with Michel for the ambush, and indeed he was, but, for a moment, as he approached the trio, his anger was forgotten, captivated as he was by how handsome Nikolaos looked. He wore dark trousers, with a white collarless shirt, and suspenders. His light khaki jacket did match the trousers, but was appropriate to the heat of the day, and he wore a baker boy cap which sat a rakish angle atop his curly hair. Usually, at the Tea Room, Nikolaos wore his hair parted on the side with pomade or Macassar oil to keep it under control and neatly flattened. But no such products had been applied today, and his curls, freshly washed Henri imagined, were full and peeked out from underneath his cap. He had only, of course, ever seen Mister Kavafis clean-shaven, his skin smooth and flawless, but today he had elected to avoid the razor and his jawline and cheekbones were highlighted by the beginnings of stubble. Henri was shocked at how the sight of a hint of beard so excited him so deeply. Anyone might have mistaken Nikolaos for a common laborer so relaxed was his style, but Henri had never seen a laborer so neat, so handsome, so unaffected, so casually devastating as this.

As he got closer, Nikolaos put his hands into the pockets of his trousers, pushing his jacket back at the waist, and Henri gritted his teeth against the urge this inspired to grab Nikolaos by the suspenders and pull him in roughly for a kiss. Or more.

"Mister Kavafis," his voice came out a rough bark. "I had no idea I'd see you here."

He saw Nikolaos's sunny smile falter slightly but he quickly righted it, turning to Michel.

"Yes, Monsieur Michel invited me."

"Oh, hadn't I mentioned it?" Michel said, affecting all innocence. "I thought we all could use a day in the sun."

"Yes," agreed Edith, "you have both grown awfully pale of late."

"Thank you for noticing, ma chérie," answered Michel with a wink.

The party wandered down the path which ran parallel to Wood Lane. None of them spoke for a bit, all looking around taking in the sights, and Henri wondered if they weren't lost. But he said nothing, appreciative of the disconnect from the reality of the moment. He had been more shaken than he'd like to admit seeing Nikolaos—especially here, outside of work, and especially with this company. Michel and Edith had become like a second family to him, and he wasn't sure he liked the odd currents of his tentative friendship with Nikolaos crossing over into his pseudo-family. Michel was to blame, of course, but Henri could never truly be upset with him.

Michel had pegged the truth about Henri early on in their relationship and had let him know, in his smooth and subtle way, how accepting he was of it. Henri had been cautious, of course, even given this acceptance, but eventually he could not help but notice that Michel had made it one of his ways of mothering in trying to connect Henri with other young men like himself whom Michel approved of as a match. He had only seriously attempted this two or three times, and the last attempt had been many years ago when Henri had chastised him hotly in private for his meddling. Michel had sagely accepted his scolding, but he never stopped trying to encourage Henri to break through the icy exterior he showed the world and let companionship in.

And now, he had inserted himself yet again in inviting Nikolaos to join their close-knit group for an afternoon at the Exhibition. In truth, Henri appreciated his friend's concern, and he could not, even to himself, communicate how deeply touched he was by Michel's acceptance of him as a whole person. But this time, with this man, this Nikolaos Kavafis. This time, for some reason, it felt different. Never before had he been this nervous as a result of Michel's machinations, and never before had he felt like such a bumbling schoolboy. In truth, he fought the urge to flee, to dip into one of the white-painted alleyways of the Exhibition and run back home.

Henri jumped as Michael squealed. Two motor launches darted ahead of them in the walkway, barely missing one another, it seemed to Henri, as they sped by.

Michel laughed.

"He is fascinated by anything with wheels," Michel said. "He could watch the buses up and down our lane all day if we let him"

"As was I as a boy," said Nikolaos. "I always begged to ride in my father's carriage no matter where he was headed." He turned to Henri. "Were you the same, Monsieur?"

"*Non*," answered Henri curtly.

He instantly felt bad for his coldness, but could not force himself to say more.

"This one?" Michel laughed. "When we first arrived in London, I could barely drag him onto the tube. He did not countenance a train that ran under the ground, he told me. Who's to say if at any minute we might be crushed to death!"

Henri tried not to give his friend a piercing look, instead smiling wanly at Nikolaos.

"He exaggerates."

"I understand, monsieur," said Nikolaos. "New things can often be frightening."

"I was not frightened," said Henri. "Only distrustful."

"It is worrying to put your hands in the fate of another," offered Nikolaos.

"Yes. Quite."

Michael squealed again and pointed.

"Oh, Papa," the boy exclaimed, "can we, please?"

"Not now," said Edith. "Come."

Realizing that they wanted the Court of Honour, and had gotten too far off-track, Edith turned the group around and directed them to cut through one of the halls dedicated to Science. They passed through a series of exhibits presented by the Wellcome Chemical Research Laboratories, none of which proved interesting or worthy of commentary, until suddenly Nikolaos stopped.

He stood with his head cocked to the side and Henri wondered if he too was considering escape. Though he told himself it would be a relief, another corner of his mind decidedly hoped not. Nikolaos pointed at a nearby exhibit. In it a collection of leaves along with samples of bark were presented next to a large illustration of a tree whose tall, branchless trunk grew up and to the side until it burst into a great growth of branches and foliage so thick and reaching that it looked like a sculpted topiary. It reminded Henri of a skinny woman with a great bouffant of hair atop her head.

"But it's an olive tree," said Nikolaos.

Henri squinted at the box of text beside the illustration. "So it would appear."

"But they're everywhere in Greece," said Nikolaos. "In many countries, in fact. Is an olive tree really a thing so exotic?"

"My friend," said Michel. "To the English, everything is exotic."

"Now, I take offense, sir," said Edith. "We are not all the same."

"Of course not, ma chérie. But I think you'll find the English man is particularly suspicious of anything unknown."

"If you ask me," countered Edith, "I think that is likely a common trait among men the world round."

"Quite right," said Nikolaos. "I think men of all races are stubborn and scared of anything that might ask them to accept a change in themselves."

Henri looked at him.

"I think you are right," agreed Edith.

"So women are always so welcome? I'm not sure I see that," said Michel. "I don't think anyone supposed Queen Victoria, for instance, to be malleable."

"I think women are more used to change," said Edith. "There are certain women who are stalwarts, of course. Usually worried about losing their security, be it earned or bestowed. Far more often in life they are asked to amend their behavior or change their mode of being to suit other people's rules and perceptions. Men seldom have this thrust upon them."

"Not all men," said Henri. "There are some men who find every day of their lives that, being born into the state in which they were born, they must adjust themselves to fit into someone else's scheme."

Henri glanced at Nikolaos, who simply nodded. Edith and Michel exchanged a brief but poignant glance.

"Of course," said Edith.

"I think," Michel interjected brightly, "that what we have learned from this scrawny little olive tree is that generalizations do us a disservice. All of us. Also, that I have the most brilliant wife in all of England."

"I have only ever doubted Edith's superior intellect once," said Henri.

"Oh? When was that?" asked Edith.

"When you chose Michel to marry, naturellement."

Michel and Edith laughed heartily.

They had come to the northern end of the Court of Honour. Just ahead of them towered the Congress Hall, a magnificent building, white like the rest, flanked on either of its sides by minarets and topped with a crested dome from which jutted some turrets, which gave the structure the look of wearing a crown. The front was decorated with a tiled design which resembled the dome of a mosque centered above the most impressive feature, a broad circular stairway running the width of the Hall. Water was pumped down the stairway and fed into the large lake surrounding the building. The lake fed into two canals, one to the left and one to the right of the Congress Hall, which formed a long circuit through the nearby courts.

The water was navigated by small boats, quite regular in appearance, as well as the contraption which had caught young Michael's attention. The swan boats, small, flat, open-floored vessels affixed with garden seats, were all around. They earned their name from the large carved swan at the back of each boat, astride which sat the driver. They looked like something fantastical, as the oversized, long-necked swan seemed to guide their riders over the water as a mother swan might hurry her team of cygnets.

"Aren't they wonderful," said Nikolaos and Henri had to begrudgingly agree.

"They're only a sixpence each, darling," said Edith. "Shall we?"

Michel smiled. "I think we must."

They hailed an empty boat as they waited at the edge of the lake and, in only a moment, they were flocked by half a dozen other visitors. The empty swan pulled alongside and they loaded in. Michel, Edith, and young Michael took up the back most bench and Henri and Nikolaos filed into the next. Henri was grateful when another young man sat beside them, filling up their bench, so that if his tongue continued to refuse to work, Nikolaos might have someone to chat with. Nikolaos, however, seemed not to notice their neighbor at all, his body half-turned towards Henri. As the swan boat began to move, Nikolaos extended his arm in front of Henri, pointing.

"Do you ever indulge monsieur?" he asked.

Surprised by the question, Henri looked at him.

"Cigarettes, I mean," explained Nikolaos. "Look just there. What a marvelous place to obtain one's tobacco."

Just in the distance was another magnificent structure, its

design matching the front of the Congress Hall decoration like some powder dusted mosque or domed khanqah. *ABDULLA Cigarette Palace* the signage read on the outside. Surrounding it, small clutches of people posed to have their pictures taken by photographers. It was a bizarrely incongruous yet joyful little oddity.

"I don't smoke," said Henri.

"I admit I shouldn't but I have never had much resistance to indulge." Nikolaos bumped his shoulder against Henri's. "But it looks like an exciting place to get lost in, don't you think?"

Henri eased up a bit and allowed the fantasy. "A little too cozy for more than two people, I would imagine."

"All the better then," said Nikolaos with a wink. Henri willed himself not to smile.

"What a marvel," Edith said from the seat behind. "The entire place looks like some grand village made of alabaster. Everything so white and pristine. How do they keep it all clean, I wonder?"

"It they're anything like Monsieur Henri in his kitchen," said Nikolaos, "I imagine they curse at their workers until it is spotless."

Henri's moth fell open but, knowing his reputation in the store kitchens, his shock turned to laughter.

"Now here is a man that pays attention," cried Michel, also laughing.

"You are both terrible," said Henri in mock hurt. "And I am mortally offended."

"The truth is never offensive, monsieur," replied Nikolaos, with a wink. "No matter how much it hurts."

⇥⇥⇥⫷⫷⫷

THEY DISEMBARKED AT the Palace of British Industries. Edith had gotten word of a textiles exhibit contained within that she was very keen to see. As they walked to the Palace they passed the Hall of British Education and marveled at the lively frescoes painted along the walls showing the phases and types of education in a person's life, both urban and rural.

Inside, they found various cases displaying all manner of textiles and fabrics, the machinery and appliances used alongside them, and examples of dress and adornment from the world all over.

"What wonderful garments," said Edith. "I wonder where exactly these Moorish women are from."

"North Africa, I believe," offered Nikolaos.

"North Africa. It must be terribly hot there," said Edith. "What a very sensible style of dress."

"And much cheaper than an Englishwoman's wardrobe," Michel added with a wink.

"Possibly," said Nikolaos. "Among certain classes. Although my father told me stories of some of the women in Tunisia wearing some of the most luxurious silks he had ever seen. He even had some pencil drawings he'd done while there to try to capture the colors, which he showed me."

"Your father was in Tunisia?" asked Henri.

"For a short while, when he was very young," said Nikolaos. "He moved there because of a job. He had aspirations of being a scholar, but he was poor and schools were scarce. But a friend of his uncle worked as a personal secretary for Mustapha Khaznadar. He got my father a position there until Mustapha passed away."

"And did he realize his dream of being a scholar?" asked Henri.

"Somewhat. He did some teaching over the years, and held various diplomatic posts," said Nikolaos. "He liked to say he was a scholar of the world."

"And he does something diplomatic now?"

"No. He passed away when I was young. Both he and my mother."

"I am so sorry." Henri felt a wave of warmth for the man. He wanted to reach out and put a comforting hand on his arm, to embrace him somehow. But he resisted.

"Not to worry. It was a long time ago. My sister and I were well-cared for."

"Is that when you came here?"

"Yes. To live with my aunt—my father's sister. She had married an Englishman and moved here when she was young. Her husband passed before I was born, but she stayed here. And we came to live with her."

"How old were you?" asked Edith.

"My sister was fourteen and I had just turned ten."

"So young," said Edith, with a touch of sadness to her voice. She looked at her son. "Michael is not so far away from ten now and I cannot imagine losing him then, or him losing me. It must change a child profoundly."

"Quite possibly," said Nikolaos. "Of course, I'll never know how I might have otherwise turned out. But I was very lucky to have my sister. It was much easier to bear, not being alone."

"Of course," said Henri quietly. "It is always better that way, to have another there, even if we tell ourselves otherwise."

He and Nikolaos exchanged a glance.

"But, please, please, enough of this reminiscing," said Nikolaos brightly. "This is a happy place and it should be a happy day. Where to next?"

"Well, I do have something on the agenda," said Michel, "that will excite Henri and myself, but may bore the rest of you to weeping. The Palace of Decorative Arts is nearby and they have an exhibition of kitchen ranges and cookers."

"That sounds fascinating," exclaimed Nikolaos.

"Does it?" asked Edith. "I won't say I married a chef to avoid having to do much in the kitchen, but it certainly is a nice benefit nonetheless."

"Your contribution the other night was not simply out of politeness, I take it. You have a sincere interest in things kitchen?" Henri asked Nikolaos.

"Oui, monsieur." Nikolaos touched his cap and gave a cheeky grin. "You don't think I joined the Tea Room simply out of the joy of serving tiny cakes, however beautiful you make them. As I mentioned before, I grew up in restaurants, but I wanted to get a new perspective at H&C."

"How interesting," said Henri. "I hope we have been worth-while instruction."

"It has been… illuminating in many ways," Nikolaos said. "But don't tell Mrs. Plaistow of my motives. I'm not sure she would approve."

"I'm not sure," said Henri dryly, "that Mrs. Plaistow approves of much of anything, despite her charms."

Nikolaos laughed at that and Henri allowed himself a small chuckle.

⇛⫷⫸⇚

THE MEN SPENT a while ogling over stoves and kitchen appliances, most in reverential silence punctuated with the occasional yelp of excitement or astonishment at a technological advance or ease-making device, until Edith returned with Michael in tow.

"Dearest, I thought you had abandoned us," said Michel, kissing her on the cheek.

"I stopped to purchase an Exhibition guidebook and then I took Michael to the see the tableaux of furs in the Palace of French Industries, and he decided to have a small nap on one of the couches there. As I assumed you boys would be enthralled in the rapture of knobs and hot plates, I let him rest a bit."

"Quite sensible."

"Have you decided on how many stoves you shall buy in your daydreams?" asked Edith.

"Yes," answered Henri. "Between the three of us, I think we have completely refitted the kitchens at Hartridge and Casas and then some to spare."

"We should propose our ideas to Lord Hartridge," said Nikolaos. "I've been told he is always interested in having the most modern of all accommodations."

"Oui," said Henri. "However, he is also quite fond of turning a profit. Mon dieu! Is this real?"

Before them stood an entire house, situated on a plot surrounded by a garden complete with privet hedge and dotted throughout with yew and poplar trees. The house was Tudor-style, the sedate colored wattle and daub walls punctuated with half-timbering. The steeply pitched roof was a rich red-brown and, at the end, was a great chimney of brick masonry. Its leaded glass windows were diamond-paned and its recessed front door cozy and welcoming.

"It says it was brought here, in total, from Ipswich," Edith informed them, referring to her guidebook.

"How does it go on so?" asked little Michael. He pointed at the rolling meadow behind the house, through which cut a river crossed by way of a darling stone bridge.

"A little paint and a large canvas, I believe," explained Edith. "The house and the front garden are real and whole, but the rest is an artist's rendering—on a grand scale, of course."

"It seems all very real," said Henri, impressed.

The party wandered the garden, studying the house, peering through the windows and even running their hands on the trunks of the trees. Behind the main building, Nikolaos had found and quickly toured a model cottage with furnishings and decorations.

Michael chattered with glee, and he trounced through the closely cut grass and marveled at the open space filled with green.

"I think Edith might very much like a house like this for her family," said Henri as Nikolaos came up beside him.

"It is quite lovely, almost idyllic," said Nikolaos wistfully. "Who could ever imagine that it might be dropped down here in the middle of London."

"Would you like a country home like this?"

"I like the idea of domesticity, of being sequestered away with the ones you love," Nikolaos said. "But I have so long lived over a restaurant, I don't think I could do with the quiet. I would miss the hustle and bustle terribly; I would miss all the people clamoring around in their warm chaos."

Henri looked at him in surprise. "I thought you grew up in restaurants, not above them."

"Why not both?" asked Nikolaos with a laugh. "My aunt, who took us in, worked for the restaurant Persopoulos, run by the family of the same name—one of the few Greek-run restaurants. She and her husband, in fact, and they took rooms just above the restaurant. When her husband passed away, she remained, and that is where she was living when we joined her."

"Some part of me is very jealous, I must admit. I would have loved to have always been near a restaurant instead of in the countryside as a boy."

"So I take it you would want a grand Tudor house then, monsieur?"

"Henri, please." His voice was unusually soft.

"I'm sorry?" asked Nikolaos, blinking.

"No 'monsieur' here. You must call me Henri, please. That is how friends refer to one another, isn't it?"

"Yes, of course," said Nikolaos. "Friends."

"But, no," continued Henri. "I don't care about a house. I don't mind grand, of course."

"I would have thought no less," interjected Nikolaos with a cheeky grin.

"But what I am concerned with is having a restaurant of my own. I want to create something all my own, something new for the people of London. I am not interested in being a duplicate of Escoffier or any other, I want to create something entirely new."

"Of anyone I have met, I think you are the one to do so."

"That will be my home, that restaurant."

"Maybe I will live above your restaurant then," Nikolaos said cheerfully.

"You have a deft hand in the kitchen. So why not live below

too?”

“But I have so much to learn.”

“Not so much as you think, perhaps. You have already shown your skills.”

“Not hardly. I have many more skills that need to be developed.”

“Perhaps we can explore those skills then.”

“With the utmost pleasure… Henri.”

Henri thrilled at hearing his name on those sumptuous lips.

“Shall we get something to drink?” asked Edith, coming upon them, holding Michael’s hand. “I think the little one has gotten rather flushed. I saw a cart some ways back selling something called Vim Tonic, and peppermint water too. Can you imagine? I haven’t had peppermint water since I was a child.”

“For refreshment, wouldn’t you rather visit the Moët & Chandon Pavilion?” asked Henri. “They may be offering samples.”

“I think Michael is a bit young for that,” Edith said.

“Nonsense. All over Europe children are given wine with a little water from the time they can walk,” argued Henri. “I myself had it and I am sure Mister Kavafis did as well.”

“I’m not sure that argues the point very well,” said Nikolaos.

At that, Henri laughed. “Well, you may be right.”

⇒⇒⇒⟨⟨⟨

SIPPING THEIR DRINKS, they strolled past the walls of the Machinery Halls, relishing the lovely colors and shapes of the flanking beds of trees and vines planted there. Apricot, apple, plum, cherry, pear, currants, gooseberries, and more grew all around, trained in various shapes, umbrella and pyramid, and cordons. In the soil of the beds were planted strawberry plants as well as more whimsical choices like Burning Bush shrubs, tropical palms and ferns, all kissed on their sides and perimeters by a wealth of

English flowers. It was a breathtaking burst of color and fragrance against the white corridors.

Henri paused in his stroll, lifted his head, and listened.

"Louise Farrenc," he said dreamily.

"Who?" asked Nikolaos.

"The composer," Henri said, "they're playing her music. Ecoutez. *Symphonie trois,* I believe. This brings back many memories. Maman and I would go with Tante Rosa and have a picnic by the river near our cottage. The band would sometimes come and play at the kiosk there. Michel, do you remember?"

Michel smiled and pushed the straw boater back on his head.

"I grew up in Paris, remember? The closest I ever came to a picnic was sitting by the Seine and trying to keep pigeons from stealing my sandwich."

"It must be coming from the sunken bandstand," said Edith. "I've been told it's a lovely promenade."

"Let's visit, shall we?" said Nikolaos. "I love music."

Michel looked at Henri. "I suppose you wouldn't rather visit the Machinery Halls?"

"Évidemment pas."

"Then shall we meet at Lyon's in the Grand in half an hour or so?"

"That supposed French restaurant?"

"Supposedly, yes. Only we've promised Michael we would take him to the Machinery Halls. They've a fleet of battleships, all in scale models."

"Mama's book said they have the *Minas Geraes* and the *Ermack* too. And the *Ghurka* too!" added Michael.

"All hail the Gods of War," replied Henri.

"And don't forget the full-size railway carriage on display," Edith reminded them.

"No matter that you arrived on the tube?"

"Uncle Henri," said Edith, "you know that isn't at all the same thing."

"Évidemment pas."

"I see the tube every day," Michael piped up.

"Of course, my dear boy," answered Henri. "Not at all the same thing. I am a fool to think otherwise."

"Évidemment," added Nikolaos, teasing.

Henri lifted a brow at him.

The Family Mauté headed off for the Machinery Halls while Henri and Nikolaos went towards the music. Left alone, they fell again into silence, Henri feeling self-conscious and afraid to broach any subject. Pedestrians of all sorts passed by; ladies in sensible shirtwaists and parasols in tow, and threes and fours, grand couples in top hats and lovely hats adorned with silk flowers and fruit, young boys, running free, laughing and shouting with sticks of rock sugar in their hands, their sisters watching from behind their mothers' skirts.

An older gentleman in top hat with a polished black walking stick passed them. He wore an enormous moustache, whose ends dropped down on either side of his mouth so that they reached his chin, the ends waxed into curled tails. Henri opened his mouth to whisper to Nikolaos about the moustache when a loud shriek stopped them and the top-hatted man in their tracks.

Moving quickly towards them was a man, his face screwed in concentration and sweat beading on his brow, who pulled behind him a contraption like a small bath-chair.

"A rickshaw," offered Nikolaos.

The occupant of the rickshaw let out another hoot and threw her hand up to clutch at her large hat, covered in blossoms and branches, and pressed it to her head.

"Slow down this instant!" she bellowed at the driver, who seemed deaf to her commands. "Take a reasonable pace immediately or you shall be hearing from my solicitor!"

Still the man ran on, whisking her past Nikolaos, Henri, and the mustachioed man who held his walking stick up and brandished it like a weapon as the rickshaw trundled by. The woman, overcome by speed, leaned forward in her seat as she passed the men.

"Fear for your lives, do!"

In a flash she was gone and the older man stuck his stick firmly in the ground, turning to Henri and Nikolaos. The ends of his moustache trembled as he harrumphed.

"And they expect us to give them the vote," he thundered before stalking off.

Henri and Nikolaos burst into laughter. Henri had the sense that the ridiculous situation had broken the tension and they both seemed to laugh loudly and freely. As they stumbled towards the bandstand, holding their sides, their laughter was renewed with each glance at one another. Finally, they fell onto a bench, their sides aching, as the band struck up a new tune. They sat, listening, and sharing no comment except the shared silence of music appreciation. The band performed an upbeat selection and the sun shone high in the afternoon sky. Henri removed his boater hat and began to fan himself, all the while feeling Nikolaos's eyes on him as he did. He turned to look at his neighbor who smiled back at him.

"That breeze is nice," said Nikolaos, nodding at the hat and prompting Henri to fan a little harder.

Nikolaos closed his eyes and tilted his head back slightly, enjoying the air. Henri noted that he had undone the topmost button of his shirt and shed his jacket, which lay in his lap. The shirt revealed a peek of undershirt below, and the base of Nikolaos's neck. The skin there glistened like freshly fallen dew on a spring morning lawn, and Henri studied it, wondering how salty and sweet it might taste if he were to press his lips there and let his tongue caress. He glanced up and Nikolaos's eyes were open again, watching Henri. Henri felt the blush burn across his cheeks and he turned away, staring at the musicians.

"It is rather overly warm," he said.

"It feels perfect to me," Nikolas replied.

The tempo of the music shifted as the band began a more moderate selection, lilting and romantic. Henri watched as a couple here and there got up from their seats and began a little waltz around the lawn. It made him smile to see it, and his hat-fanning slowed. Out of his periphery, he saw Nikolaos move on the bench, angling his body towards Henri. Henri braved a glance at him. Nikolaos had rested his arm against the back of the bench, his head slightly dipped to the side.

"Why is it, monsieur," he asked, his eyes looking particularly soft and warm, "that we always find ourselves among dancing lovers? Do you suppose it is a message of some sort, some kind of heavenly sign?"

Despite himself, Henri let out a small, airy chuckle.

"I'm not dancing with you now either," he said, smiling. "Not here, in front of all these people."

"'Not here, not now'," repeated Nikolaos. "Then later, maybe, elsewhere, when we are alone?"

Henri grinned and shook his head. He dropped his hat onto his lap. He felt heady, breathless, as if the bright sunshine was being absorbed by his body and pushed through his limbs. He meant to say nothing in reply, but found himself speaking nonetheless.

"You make me distrust myself," he admitted, his voice breathy.

Nikolaos scooted a bit closer on the bench.

"Perhaps it is rather that I actually make you trust yourself, what you feel."

Henri studied his face and sighed heavily. He tore his gaze away reluctantly, facing forward, and clasped his hands, resting them on the hat in his lap.

"I think, perhaps, Mister Kavafis, that we should simply enjoy the music."

"As you wish, monsieur."

Nikolaos shifted so that he was facing forward but still as close. Henri could not concentrate on the notes being played, so aware was he of the heat of Nikolaos's body beside him, threatening to overwhelm his senses.

AS THEY APPROACHED the Grand, Henri saw Michel and his family waiting.

"There you are," said Edith brightly. "We thought we might have to send a search party."

"We found ourselves distracted," said Nikolaos. "By the music."

"Sadly we have only stopped to say we must be going," said Michel.

"'Going'?" asked Henri.

"Yes, I'm afraid the heat and excitement has proven a bit much for the boy," said Edith, ruffling her son's hair. "He should get home before he becomes irritable and unmanageable."

"Poor fellow," said Nikolaos. "I do hope he can return soon for more of the Machinery Hall."

"Papa says next time we can ride the Mountain Scenic Railway and maybe the Renard Train too," said Michael, punctuating his sentence with a yawn.

"What a Papa you have."

"Yes, Papa, a moment," said Henri, "before you leave."

Henri guided him some feet away from the rest of the party.

"Perhaps we should all leave and join up another day?"

"No, no. Edith and I want you to stay. Tu devrais diverti ton ami."

"He's not *my* friend."

"Enjoy the afternoon. And try not to think of things to such excess of emotion. Maybe by the end of the day he will be your friend, after all."

"And will you always use your child's moods and illnesses to manipulate situations?" snapped Henri.

Michel laughed. "But of course, monsieur! That is one of the main benefits of having children, non?"

Henri gave him an imploring look. "Michel…"

"Trust me." Michel clasped him on the shoulder. "I have a good feeling about him."

Henri waved his hand dismissively. "He's too young."

"You're barely four years his senior."

"And how do you know this?"

"Because I asked. It is an admirable feature of conversation. Something you may try one day."

"Always looking after me. My grandmother lives in London; I am not in need of another."

Michel scoffed. "I am offended, monsieur. I am not your grand-mère; I have had her cooking and I am far superior."

"Bâtard. Besides, you know she employs a cook."

"She should sack whoever it is."

"Michel," Edith called from nearby.

"Coming, mon amour!" He slapped Henri on the shoulder. "Au revoir, mon frère. Enjoy. I am told the Court of Honour at night is particularly romantic. A scene from a storybook."

"Connard," Henri muttered as his friend strolled off.

Henri rejoined Nikolaos and found him deep in study of the guidebook Edith had left with him.

"So you're staying then?" he asked without looking up.

"Oui."

Nikolaos closed the book and his smile was startling in its brilliance.

"Terrific! Because we must do that!"

He pointed to the enormous machine looming behind the Grand. Its two long arms met at a central mechanism at the bottom of the machine and sprung outwards in a wide V-formation. The two arms reminded Henri of the Eiffel Tower, both of them constructed of crosshatched steel in the mode of "la dame de fer." At the end of each arm of the ride a platform basket was attached, each of these cars holding more than four dozen people. As the electric engine churned, these arms rose from the horizontal into an overlapped vertical so that those inside sat stories above all else, looking out from all sides. The Giant Flip-

Flap, it was called. It was an attraction that had been all the talk since the opening of the Exhibition and one that, despite its behemoth proportions, Henri had pointedly ignored the entire visit thus far.

"Doesn't it look thrilling?" asked Nikolaos. "But, first, come, let's go to the Australian Palace. They're meant to have delicious ices in their special refrigerated section."

"A whiskey might be more in order," replied Henri, eyeing the great steel giant.

"Monsieur Michel," said Nikolaos as they made their way to Australia's corner of the white city. "You are very close?"

"Yes. Michel and Edith are like my family."

"But don't you already have family here?"

"I do. But my English family do not understand me the way that Michel and his wife do. In fact, they understand me better than even my French family, if I am honest. And understanding a person can be the strongest bond, I think. Even stronger than blood oftentimes."

"Like love."

"Yes. I suppose. Like love." Realization hit Henri. "But how did you know about my family?"

"There's a queue forming, monsieur. Come, before it all melts away!"

Nikolaos grabbed his hand and started into a jog. The touch erased any lingering questions Henri had in mind.

THE ICES WERE a triumph. Nico could tell that Henri was delighted in choosing them. He sensed that Henri was beginning to ease somewhat. Michel and Edith, and little Michael, were altogether agreeable company, but in their presence Henri was the overly self-aware creature he so often was. Constantly minding his every move and comment. Nico suspected that

Henri himself was not even aware of how he was, but Nico had seen the glimpses, the moments when Monsieur Henri Newbold, Chef Extraordinaire, fell away and there was only left the soulful, quiet man with the sorrowful eyes that touched Nico to his core. At H&C, even though Henri was just an inch or two taller than him, it felt as if he towered over Nico. But here, watching him lapping the frozen treat and laughing like a schoolboy, he seemed smaller, more manageable, more real. Here Nico felt he could wrap his arms around Henri, pull him close, and kiss away the lines at the corners of his mouth, which formed whenever he frowned, which was often.

The colorful liquid ran down the back of Henri's hand and he ran his tongue after it, trying to catch it. Indecisive, they had both gotten two ices each so that they could try all the flavors on offer.

Nico laughed.

"You'll ruin the sleeves of that suit," he said.

"Here," Henri said, shoving his ices at Nico. "That is easily solved."

As Nico tried to balance four ices in two hands, Henri shed his jacket and threw it over his shoulder. He rolled his sleeves up to the elbows. Nico noticed the lines of his arms, the rounded muscles of his forearms, how they flexed as he moved. A man who worked with his hands. Strong, talented hands. Nico bit off a mouthful of ice to distract his thoughts.

"Ah, ah, hand it over before you eat all of them," said Henri. "I am well-prepared now."

Nico surrendered two of the ices.

"Well, prepared to lick the entire length of your forearm now?"

"Wouldn't you like to see?" replied Henri with a wink.

Nico's mouth fell open. Open flirtation. Who knew that to thaw the man out, one only had to ply him with sweets.

"You must try a bit of the lemon and the blackcurrant together."

Henri looked at his. "But I only have the citron."

"Take a bite," Nico commanded. "Now, here, mine, the blackcurrant."

Nico held his ice up to Henri's mouth and as he leaned in, his mouth open for the treat, their eyes met. The position was awkward yet electric, too. Henri gulped a bit of ice and then began to choke.

"Are you all right?" asked Nico.

Henri shrugged and they both fell into nervous giggles.

"Once we finish these, where to next?" asked Henri.

"I have told you. The Flip-Flap. I must ride it."

"Are you quite sure that monstrosity is meant for entertainment?"

"Yes," Nico laughed. "Look all the people on it now. It is the main reason I wanted to come today. Well, among the main reasons."

"You're like Michel's boy with his love of trains."

Nico shrugged. "One should embrace what gives them joy."

"I distrust it," said Henri.

"Joy?"

"No. That contraption, I mean. No one should be that high in the air."

"Nonsense. It can't be as tall as H&C and we know you love to sit on the roof there. Besides, hundreds of people have ridden it and no one has been injured."

"Yet."

"You can't worry about the possibility of disaster. That is always there. Embrace it—you must to live properly. Come!"

He grabbed Henri's hand again.

"We should wash first. Our hands will stick together," warned Henri.

"I won't mind," Nico assured him.

INSIDE THE CAR was a crush. A great mass of bodies, and all pressing towards the sides, all trying to get the best vantage point as it rose skyward. Henri somehow carved a path to the railing on one side, grabbing Nico and pulling him along. Nico was behind Henri who leaned over the rail, his disdain for the *"monstrosity"* seemingly forgotten. Henri craned his neck, peering out, and Nico, too, enjoyed his vantage point.

The light linen shirt fell against Henri's back, and when the sunlight hit it, Nico could see the shadowed line of his torso underneath, as if teasing him. Henri craned his neck even further and Nico studied it. His usually close-cut hair, dark and thick, had begun to go wavy at the ends from the heat and perspiration. It curled against the creamy ivory of his skin, and the contrast aroused Nico. He imagined kissing the back of Henri's neck as he dragged his eyes down his body daydreaming of all the places he would place his lips, until he settled on the perfect rounds of Henri's arse, pressing against the trouser linen. Nico imagined placing one delicate kiss on each cheek.

"Beautiful, isn't it?" he heard Henri ask.

"Indeed."

"Come, come, you must see." Henri turned, making space for Nico to move closer to the railing. Henri took Nico's jacket and draped it over the rail with his own, leaning down on both with one arm to keep them steady so that when Nico shifted, he was essentially enclosed by Henri's body.

"Look in that direction there."

Henri pointed and stepped forward slightly, his body pressing against Nico's.

"I think that must be where H&C is, far over there."

"I don't see it," said Nico.

Henri leaned in further, stretching his arm.

"There, I think it may be over there."

Nico wondered how far he might take advantage of their closeness, and so he tested the limits. He leaned forward a bit, as if following Henri's direction, and, in doing so, pressed his arse snugly against Henri's crotch. He wanted to see if Henri would pull away, but he did not.

"Ah, I think I see it now," said Nico.

"Yes," said Henri quietly.

Reluctantly Nico straightened.

"Do you think Mrs. Plaistow can see us from here?"

"She never goes out onto the rooftop. She abhors the sunlight."

Nico turned towards Henri.

"Which explains her disposition."

Nico was aware of their closeness, and he knew Henri must be too. That familiar breathless feeling returned. So close it would hardly take a movement for their lips to touch. Why couldn't he kiss the man here and now? Why *shouldn't* he kiss the man here and now? It was the only thing that felt right in the moment. Nico licked his lips.

There was a squeal of excitement as a young woman bumped into Henri, jostling him. He grabbed Nico's hips to steady himself.

"Oh, look," cried the young woman, "we're passing by the other cart!"

"I say, old man," said a large man who looked to be the young woman's father, "all apologies. The little wife gets carried away sometimes."

"Not to worry," said Henri as he pressed closer to Nico to allow the substantial fellow passage.

Nico felt himself getting hard, and with great speed. Henri seemed to notice as well and dropped his hands to his sides, releasing Nico's waist. Still he moved no further back. Nico felt his breath coming heavy. Henri, too, was aroused.

"Maybe you were right, monsieur. Maybe it is dangerous being this high, after all."

"Yes," said Henri. "Very dangerous indeed, I think."

Nico reached up and massaged his own neck.

"But it certainly inspires awe."

Henri returned a hand to Nico's hip and let it rest there.

"Quite," Henri said.

"Oh my!" cried the same young woman from before. "We're moving again."

Clutching her closed parasol, she elbowed her way in beside them. They broke apart and both turned to face out as the car began its descent. Henri handed Nico his jacket and they both held them in front of them, draping them in front of their waists.

"I say," said the young woman. "It's so subtle. If you weren't paying attention, you might entirely miss the motion."

Nico nodded slowly.

"Indeed, miss."

⟫⟫⟫✦⟪⟪⟪

NICO'S SUGGESTION OF their dining together after the Flip-Flap was quickly quashed when he saw the menu at the Grand and balked at the price.

"Feh. Come, we can find better," said Henri as he swaggered off.

"Are you sure?" asked Nico. "We can dine there if you would like. I was only surprised at the cost."

"No, not at all," says Henri. "Their menu was paltry and not worth the charge. What instead? I saw fish and chips just over there."

"Fish and chips?"

"It is British, I am French. That is the idea of the day, *non?*" Henri answered with a smile.

"But I didn't think someone like you would eat fish and chips?"

"Someone like me? A person with taste and good sense? I am a chef, monsieur, but I am not a snob."

Henri purchased two portions from a kiosk, wrapped in greaseproof paper and newsprint. He suggested a stroll in hopes the food would cool enough to save their fingers as they ate.

"You didn't have to pay for me, you know," said Nico.

"N'importe quoi. If I was willing to pay a shilling each for us to experience that sad place at Le Grande, why should I dole out two pennies?"

"I wouldn't have expected you to pay there, at the Grande, most especially."

Henri looked bashful. "I have very much enjoyed this afternoon and simply wanted to show my thanks for your company. Is that disrespectful?"

"Not at all. I am only surprised." Nico straightened the edges of his paper wrapping. "I have very much enjoyed the afternoon as well."

"You were very impressive the other night with Monsieur Casas' theater party."

"Impressive then? But not today?" Nico teased.

He was delighted to see Henri chuckle again.

"What I mean to say is I wonder if you were serious when you said you wanted to learn more? Of cooking and running a kitchen?"

"Why do you think I broached the subject? Simply to spend time with you?"

Henri guffawed. "There could be worse reasons."

"There could be no better reasons. And, yes, I am very serious."

Henri smiled broadly.

"What would you say to my teaching you then? Nothing formal; I don't want you to feel like I'm your tutor. Simply sharing. There are many things I know you know better than I, so it would benefit us both."

Nico raised a brow.

"Professionally, I mean."

"Yes, monsieur, of course. Professionally. Purely professional." Nico batted his eyelashes and feigned innocence.

"You are worse than Michel."

"But prettier I hope?"

Henri bit back a reply and Nico felt emboldened. Henri cleared his throat.

"I am always at H&C late, if not prepping for the food halls then perfecting my own recipes. Why shouldn't you join me?"

"Just the two of us. Alone in the kitchen. At night."

"Well, there will always be the rats, of course."

"You let David work at night as well?"

Henri cackled and Nico felt a surge of lightning run through him.

"You make fun, but I am very serious."

"Of course, I am too. I would very much be open to anything at all you care to teach me, sir."

"Anything?"

"Anything."

"Those are very dangerous words."

"Oh, I hope they are indeed."

Nico saw that beloved blush stain Henri's cheeks and his heart swelled. They walked on, eating their dinner in comfortable silence.

As the sun began to set, they neared the Congress Hall, close to where their day had begun.

"Look at that," Nico exclaimed.

From the top of the stairway on the Congress Hall, a cascade fell down the great stairs, bursting into foaming caps as it tumbled to the lake below. The stairs of moving water were illuminated a host of colored lights, throwing a rainbow onto them, and creating a sparkling effect of magic as it rippled. The area all around the Congress Hall was speckled with the multicolored beams. The Swan Boats, swimming below, changed from white to rose colored to a sunny golden to the palest of violet and back again like so many great magical beasts from a child's fantasy book.

They clutched the railing and watched the lights dance. Nico leaned down so that his elbows rested on the railing and, in the waning light, he moved one hand surreptitiously over Henri's. Henri glanced down at this and then leaned his elbows as well, shifting his arms so that their hands continued to overlap. Their faces were quite close, and Nico had the urge to touch his forehead against Henri's but resisted.

"This is where we started," said Henri.

"Not quite," answered Nico with a smile, "but almost."

Out beyond the Congress Hall, the white city began to spring to life in an entirely new way. The buildings in and around The Court of Honor burst into dazzling splendor. The arches and lines of the different buildings lit up, as if traced by luminous moonlight, the shapes and intertwining curves of the lines, cutting through the darkness as if the edifices were being drawn by a great God of illumination. The bridges, their minarets sparkling, their arches glowing, like constellations sprinkled in a night sky. The canals cutting through the city shimmered in silver, their silky surface reflecting the gleam and glitter all around them.

"There is so much we haven't explored yet," Henri said quietly.

"There is time. Perhaps we can come again? On a next day off."

"Yes. We must."

"And maybe next time your friends will be feeling better than today," said Nico.

"Or maybe we can come alone. Just the two of us."

He looked at Nico then and Nico could see the lights flickering in his eyes.

"Just the two of us. I would like that very much, Henri."

Henri places his hand over Nico's. "I like to hear you call me by my name."

Nico studied their clasped hands; he shifted his fingers slightly so that they became entwined.

"I hope the next time we take that ride together again," said Henri.

Nico could not help but to laugh. "But I thought you objected to it. Have I turned you into a thrill-seeker after all?"

"I believe you have. I think you have very much the power to change my mind about many things, Nico. Do you mind if I call you Nico?"

"I have been waiting for you to do so."

Nico leaned forward so that their shoulders were touching. In the dark, he moved his thumb, caressing the back on Henri's hand.

"You see," said Nico softly. "I promised you that I would make you like me one day. Henri."

Henri gave him such a look that Nico wanted to lean in and kiss him there, taste his mouth and close this glorious day with the ending it ought to have had. But, of course, he could not do that, not here, not with so many people, and the fire of desire and affection burned so hot in his belly he thought he might be ill. Instead, he contented himself with throwing his arms over Henri's shoulders, as any friend might to another, and let it rest there as they both gazed back out over the water, listening to the splashing water and the murmuring voices of the crowds, quelling the words that sat on their lips and in their hearts.

CHAPTER SIX

"WELL DONE WITH those Americans," said Mario, in a rare outburst of verbosity. "You handled them well. Americans seem to think all of Europe is just a shopping excursion."

"Given the setting, that would be accurate, wouldn't it?" asked Nico.

He, Mario, and Tommy were heading towards the kitchen from the Tea Room, en route to the staff common room for their tea break.

"Still," said Mario. "They can be awfully trying, Americans."

Tommy slapped Nico on the shoulder.

"Good old Nick," he said. "He could charm the whiskers off a cat, he could."

"Oh, they weren't so bad, really," said Nico. "You just have to affect a bit of regality, that's all. Americans like to think we're all toffs. It settles their nerves if they think they can look down on us for our airs. As long as you handle their egos with silk gloves, that is."

"Silk gloves all the way to the elbow, rather, don't you know," added Tommy, his vowels suddenly cut glass and elongated to mock a posh accent.

All three laughed as Nico pushed through the kitchen doors and then came to a sudden stop. Standing inside, by the main work station, speaking with Henri were Hartridge, Casas, and another unknown gentleman. Nico was wary. A visit from Hartridge or Casas was not common, especially both together. He wondered if something were wrong, and he was nervous on Henri's behalf.

Nico's worries were mostly dispelled though when Henri looked up, pointed at Nico and smiled. "Just the man I was speaking of," he said.

All three of the other men turned to study him. Nico's nerves returned. "Speaking of me, monsieur?"

"Quite."

Tommy and Mario, glad not to be singled out, scrambled off to the common room.

"Very nice to see you again, Mister Kavafis," said Señor Casas. "You know Lord Hartridge, of course, and may I introduce Lord Ockley."

Looking at Lord Ockley, Nico thought of dusty armchairs and the stale smell of cigar smoke. The man was pressed and put together, even if a touch ridiculous wearing a hunting suit in the middle of the day, the thick, tweed knickers puffing just above his dark boots and his cap still on his head. Something about him emanated decay and called to mind all the poorest traits of what Nico imagined to be the country gentleman type. He imagined for a moment that he would not at all be surprised if the man pulled a dead pheasant from his back pocket and cried, "Tally-Ho!"

Lord Ockley studied Nico too, eyeing him from head to toe. The way his eyes ranged over Nico's form turned his stomach. It was the type of examination he had seen one too many times before when well-clad Englishmen turned up in his neighborhood or the restaurant he lived above leering at any half-handsome, olive-skinned boy that passed by.

"So you're the Greek?" Lord Ockley said bluntly.

"I'm sorry?" replied Nico, blinking.

"His name is Mister Nikolaos Kavafis," corrected Henri, his

eyes bright with fire.

"Mister Kavafis, please forgive our friend's bluntness," said Lord Hartridge. "Monsieur Henri was only just explaining how your background and knowledge made you perfectly suited for the proposal at hand. So it must have been fresh on Lord Ockley's mind."

"The proposal, sir?"

"Yes, Lord Ockley is hosting a Greek delegate who will be visiting London. The delegate is coming to show support for the Greek participants in the Olympic games. He and Lord Ockley have discussed arranging an event, a celebratory dinner of sorts, to congratulate and thank the athletes of Greece who competed in the events here. Knowing me as he does, Lord Ockley suggested Hartridge & Casas as the proposed venue."

"The place has a reputation, you know," said Lord Ockley. "Very en mode, embracing the foreign and all its style. After all, no other store in London boats a Spaniard at its helm."

Casas's gaze fell on Ockley, his expression cloudy and inscrutable.

"You see," Casas picked up where his associate had ended, "we were explaining to Monsieur Henri that although we would like to present the athletes with the best of both French and British cuisine, we also want to make sure there were touches of their home country." He cut his eye at Ockley quickly as he straightened his cuffs. "Not some sort of Greece through a British lens sort of approach, but something more authentic—or at least paying proper homage to the home country. We naturally assumed monsieur would be able to research and incorporate his knowledge into such a task, but then, of course, I remembered your marvelous showing some weeks back. On the night of that wonderful aubergine."

"I explained to them about your experience in the restaurant," said Henri. "That this was no mere chance, but that you were an accomplished cook yourself."

"You flatter me, monsieur, señor. My skills are only at the

beginning stage."

"Not at all," countered Henri.

"I didn't realize there were any Greek restaurants in London," said Ockley. "Must be a local establishment, confined to the Greek quarter of town."

"I suppose so," said Nico.

"Yes, wouldn't find that on the High Street, what. Though, it must be said, I am rather fond of the Greek way of cooking, indeed anything Mediterranean piques my palate. I have done a lot of traveling all over, you see. The Baltics, Egypt, all over North Africa."

"Lord Ockley is an archeologist," supplied Lord Hartridge.

Ockley gave a small laugh and twisted the end of his mustache. "Some have even called me an adventurer."

A culture thief, thought Nico.

"I have worked very closely with the Greek government over the years," continued Ockley, "on a number of projects for the British Museum and several other institutions. You've probably seen my pieces there."

"I haven't much visited the museums, I'm afraid," said Nico.

"Yes, well, each to their own and whatnot," said Ockley. "Besides I expect you've already seen it all anyway."

"On Monsieur Henri's suggestion," said Lord Hartridge. "I would like to propose that you assist him with planning this dinner—work as consultant on the menu and its development. If you would be so amenable."

"Of course, sir," said Nico. "I would be more than happy to assist when my schedule allows. I shouldn't want to shirk my duties to Mrs. Plaistow."

"Of course not," said Casas. "But there is no worry there. We will explain to Mrs. Plaistow that accommodation will be made to your schedule to allow time to work with Monsieur Henri as he needs you."

Nico caught Henri's eye and saw him smiling, silently encouraging Nico to accept.

"And there will be additional compensation," added Hartridge. "As this falls outside of your regular duties."

"Well, sirs, I don't see how I can refuse. It sounds like a terrific opportunity."

Nico saw Henri sigh with some relief.

"Bright boy," declared Ockley. "Smart boy. Good move. I shall look very much forward to working with you." He turned and added a nod to Henri. "With you both, of course."

"Splendid," said Hartridge. "We appreciate you both being so accommodating."

"And we anticipate a great event," added Casas. "Lord Ockley, if you will," he extended his arm towards the doorway, "We shall visit our Oriental department now, per your request."

"Quite, quite." Ockley grabbed his walking stick. As he passed Nico, he surreptitiously gave him another once-over, muttering, "Yes, quite splendid indeed."

Nico looked to Henri as the trio departed the kitchen. Henri have him a slight nod.

"Monsieur Kavafis, a word please?" He jerked his head in the direction of the large larder nearby.

Nico followed him into the larder. Henri's expression was the usual placid front until the door closed behind them, at which point he lit up in a golden smile.

"What do you think?" he asked, the enthusiasm coloring his voice. "This is a terrific opportunity, non?"

"Yes. Terrific." Nico felt nonplussed.

"Nico?" Henri frowned and stepped closer to him. "Are you upset by this? I realize I might have discussed it with you before volunteering you, but it all came on so quickly."

"No, I am not upset."

"But I am confused. You do not look happy."

Nico himself was confused. He wasn't sure what he felt at the moment, so many contradictory thoughts bouncing around his mind. He looked at Henri very seriously, his mouth set in a line.

"Why do you call me Nico now?"

Henri blinked, surprised at the question. "Because you told me I could."

"Yes. But why do you want to call me Nico now?"

"What do you mean?"

"Why am I no longer Mister Kavafis?"

"Because. Because we are friends, of course." Henri reached out and took his hand. "Nico et Henri."

Nico grasped his hand and pulled him closer.

"But, don't you understand, I want to be more than friends, Henri. More than just colleagues."

"I understand this, of course, but I thought this was a chance to spend more time together. Where else we would get the chance? To your home that you share with your aunt and sister? To my home where my grandmother watches over me like a schoolboy and spends all the time I am there trying to arrange social visits with eligible women? All of that you understand that, non?" He brought Nico's hand to his lips and kissed it. "You must understand what I mean."

"Of course I do. And I agree." Nico pressed their clasped hands to his chest for a moment, thinking. "I am sorry. Of course I am thrilled to work with you and to do this job. I suppose I wish this simply wasn't all we had. That this weren't the only place we could be together and regard each other with such familiarity."

Henri ran his fingers through Nico's hair; Nico closed his eyes and leaned into it.

"It is only for one, cher. One day, hopefully soon, we will have somewhere more, something more." Henri spoke quietly, soothingly. "But we both want more in our work. And maybe with that advantage we can build more for each, more security, more space to share."

Nico looked at him. "As Hartridge and Casas have done?"

Henri withdrew.

"Yes. If that is what they have indeed done."

Nico smiled and shook his head.

"Always so circumspect, never admitting the obvious. Even

with me."

"I admit what needs to be admitted," said Henri primly. "When it needs to be admitted."

He leaned in, resting his forehead against Nico's. "We will have our time, Nico. But until then we must wait. Will you wait?"

"For you, I will wait until I am as old as Mrs. Crombie."

"Mon dieu, not that long. I will turn to dust."

Nico laughed and kissed Henri. Henri took Nico's face in his hands and pulled him, deeply kissing back; for a moment, he lost himself in this shared pleasure, forgetting all else.

"Will you do me a favor?" Nico asked, when they broke apart.

"Anything," answered Henri, breathless.

"Come to my home, for dinner."

"Comment?" Henri was taken aback. "With your family?"

"Of course. Come meet them."

"Are you sure?"

"Very much so."

"But will they be upset?"

"That I invited my close friend and colleague to dinner? I have already told my aunt about your delicious sweets and she is intrigued by the mysterious French man with the sugar skills."

"I thought we were meant to be more than friends and colleagues. So quickly you forget."

Nico smiled; he liked it when Henri teased him. "Ah, yes. Should the question arise, I shall admit only what needs to be admitted."

"You are terrible," said Henri, leaning in for a quick kiss. "I will come to dinner, but on one condition only."

"What condition?"

"That you must return the favor and come dine with me and my family as well."

"Will your grandmother try to connect me with an eligible young woman?"

"Oh, yes, quite possibly. And will your aunt demand that I make a mysterious French dessert?"

"Quite possibly."

"Then it is settled. Although I am a skilled chef, you must make one thing clear to your aunt. I have not and will never wash dishes, even if she demands I cook on the spot."

"Oh, that's nothing. Whenever we have a big dinner my aunt always flirts with one of the men downstairs and has our dishes sent to the restaurant to be cleaned."

Henri laughed. "Already I feel like your aunt and I will get along well."

"Besides, why should my aunt demand you cook on the spot? She already lives with a—how did you say? 'A very accomplished cook.' Apparently, I have many skills."

Henri pulled him close, his hands curving around Nico's arse and clutching tightly.

"I do not think I care to discuss your many skills with your aunt. She may be scandalized."

"Chef, such behavior in a larder. You forget yourself," Nico teased, pressing himself against Henri.

"Oui, you always make me forget myself."

"I shall remember you for both of us," Nico said.

Henri kissed him again, even more deeply than before.

>>>><<<<

"DINNER WILL BE ready quite shortly," Nico's sister reminded them.

"Yes, yes, Zetta, I know," replied Nico. "After all I cooked it, didn't I? We only need to discuss something related to work for a moment."

"Nico," Zetta said, a warning in her voice.

"Only a moment."

Nico ushered Henri into his room and pushed the door shut

impatiently.

"I thought you introduced her as Georgia?" asked Henri.

"Yes. Zetta is only a nickname."

Seripha, Nico's aunt, had been warm and welcoming when he first arrived but his sister was another story entirely. She had grimly said her hellos and offered nothing more. As Nico and Seripha had chatted with him about his journey here and showed him the flat, Zetta had stood near the dining table watching silently. Henri felt like a naïve gazelle trouncing through the grass as the lioness watched from the nearby rock, sunning herself.

"I didn't realize you lived so close to Finsbury Circle," said Henri. "Coming here brought back many memories. I was almost late, taking in the lovely park again."

"You've come here much before?"

"Not for years, really. When Michel and I were young and just starting out at the Carlton, he got the idea of touring all the famous markets in the city. He had somewhere read something about a gander who took up residence at Leadenhall Market called Old Tom. The notion tickled him so we visited more than once, strolling around, as Michel imagined the old goose must have done."

"Not the most exciting entertainment."

"Admittedly no. But we had little coin in those days and everything about London fascinated us. When he began to court Edith, we actually spent an afternoon in the park. Michel and Edith, and a friend of hers, Elisabeth, I believe her name was."

"It wasn't an attempt at matchmaking, was it?"

"Not at Edith's insistence. But I was younger then. One of my few failed attempts to toe the line." Henri shook his head. "Anyway, I hadn't been back to Finsbury since. It's still lovely and green though."

"Possibly we can visit some time. Make better memories."

"Yes." Henri smiled. "But you said you wanted to discuss something? About H&C?"

"Not exactly," said Nico, holding up a finger. "Just a moment."

He moved across the room, and sat on the bed, pulling out a small box from underneath.

It wasn't a large room, but Nico had done all he could to make it like his own apartment. Near the door was a small sofa, big enough for two people; the cushions of which did not appear new but well-maintained nonetheless. Their turquoise color stood out brightly against the Turkish carpet in front of the sofa, its deep brick-red warm and strong. Next to the cozy seating area was the bed, neatly made, with three pillows, the waning afternoon summer falling over the bed and cutting it in half diagonally. Opposite the bed, there was a wardrobe with a mirror, and beside it a small writing desk, filled with drawers and topped by a small shelf. The desk was scattered with the accessories of living, a comb, a small bowl with cufflinks and collar pins, a book, with a torn H&C sale paper used for book-mark, and, on the shelf, two yellow vases. One contained a spray of bright, cheery silk flowers and the other a collection of paint brushes and pencils, charcoal and colored wax. Next to the vases were two children's toys, a small mohair elephant with a blue saddlecloth trimmed in yellow over its back and a miniature wooden rocking horse, hand-carved. The whole atmosphere was warm and welcoming, comforting even, with pops of color and unexpected items to surprise one. Just like Nico himself, thought Henri.

Nico crossed back to him and held out his hand.

"I wanted to give you this," he said.

Henri saw that it was a book, with a very lovely binding. He took it from Nico and handled it gently, turning to read the title on the spine: *"Le mystére de la chambre jaune."*

He looked at Nico. "You bought this for me?"

Nico nodded.

"You mentioned that your clippings from the magazine your aunt mailed had fallen to shreds. So I thought you might like a proper copy. You don't already have it, do you?"

"N-no," said Henri, feeling a catch in his throat. "I don't."

"Good," said Nico, nodding. "I also bought an English translation as well. I thought maybe we could read along together?"

Henri felt a flutter in his chest.

"But where did you find it? I didn't think it had been published in England yet."

"No, not yet. But it has in America. Hosea helped me to locate an American edition. After all, English is English, no?"

"I am not sure the English would agree." Henri laughed.

"No, possibly not."

Henri was very touched, so much so that he did not know the words to say. He felt, as usual in such circumstances, that his tongue was too thick, his mind too slow.

"I-I think this is a very grand gift, Nico. Thank you. I would very much like to read along with you. I'm not sure—that is, I mean…"

Nico grabbed the front of his jacket and pulled him close. He kissed Henri deeply, eagerly, moving his hands around his neck and curling his fingers in the dark curls which fell against Henri's neck. He pulled away and Henri, surprised and delighted, caught his breath, feeling slightly lightheaded.

"I could not wait all evening to do that," said Nico breathlessly. "Dinner would have been torture if I had."

"I am quite happy to relieve your torture," said Henri. He pulled Nico in for another, softer kiss. He ran a finger across Nico's cheek. "Your room is beautiful, by the way. It very much reminds me of you."

"It is only modest," Nico said with a bashful shrug.

"As are you," said Henri. He tried to memorize every aspect of the room. He knew later, laying in bed, he would think of this place and remember this kiss and imagine Nico's body pressed against his own.

Nico led him to the bed and they both sat. Henri ran his hand over the thick, soft quilt there.

"I am very happy you came tonight," said Nico.

"I am quite happy to be invited," replied Henri.

They kissed again, exploring, their tongues tracing terrain as a cartographer might, to create a map for future conquest.

Nico nuzzled Henri's neck, kissing it, tracing his lips down to his collar, his tongue brushing against the underside of Henri's chin. Nico caressed Henri's thigh, his strong hands massaging the curve of the muscle, moving in, between his legs, and up. Henri inhaled deeply and pushed Nico's hand away, standing.

"We can't have too much of that, or we'll never make it to dinner," said Henri, pressing his hands below his waist and trying to shift the rising there.

Nico grabbed his hands and pulled him closer. His beautiful eyes gleamed, his lips still wet from kissing. A force of desire ran through Henri, stirring him so strongly that he thought he might go blind from want.

"I don't care if we never make it to dinner," said Nico as he pressed his hand against Henri's crotch, rubbing the bulge there.

Henri shuddered from the blow of desire that wracked him. He closed his eyes, breathing deeply, trying to fight the sudden urge to press Nico to the bed and rip his clothing free, piece by piece, to let his mouth explore that glorious, golden skin.

"Non, non," he said, his voice heavy. "Arrêt, arret." He shook his head, trying to regain his sense. "No, Nico. We mustn't."

He pulled back, freeing himself from Nico's grasp, freeing himself from the overwhelming threat of desire. He stood, clearing his throat and trying to straighten his jacket.

"What would your aunt and sister think if they overheard anything? I think your sister already dislikes me."

Nico smiled. "My sister dislikes everyone. Such is her way."

"Well," Henri sighed, "I think this especially would give her a reason to dislike me."

He turned and leaned on the chair in front of the writing desk. He studied the objects on the shelf, trying to compose himself. He reached up and stroked the head of the small plush elephant on the shelf.

"These were toys of yours as a child?"

Nico got up and came to stand beside him.

"Yes. Do not think me strange for keeping them."

"Of course not. Not at all. I find it very touching. They must have special meaning for you?"

Nico nodded, picking up the rocking horse. "When we first came here, Mister Persopoulos, who runs the restaurant downstairs, carved this for me. He explained to me that all good English boys have a rocking horse, so now that I was going to be a good English boy, I must have one too. I decided then that I must be a good English boy, as he said, so that I would do well here in this new place."

"And did it work?"

Nico looked at him. "Do you think I am a good English boy?"

"I think you are a very good boy; the English I am far less concerned with."

Nico bit his bottom lip, which did nothing to help Henri's situation.

Henri stroked the head of the little elephant again. "And, this one. He seems very special."

Nico's smiled faded and his eyes went cloudy for a moment. He picked up the plush toy, and petted it.

"Yes, Kikos. That's his name. When my parents died—it was unexpected, of course, and there was much chaos in bringing us here. We barely had time to pack our bags after the funeral before we were hurried to the boat. I never knew why there was such a rush. We had to leave so much behind. But I managed to grab Kikos and shove him in my bag." He smiled then, a very tender smile that touched Henri. "He always reminded me of my mother. When I was very small, she would read me a story, or sing me a little song, and then she would tuck me into bed with Kikos. She always told me he would protect me at night, should I have any bad dreams. Whenever I look at him, I can still see her sweet face in my mind. Or, at least, as much of it as I can remember. Time fades memories, even if the feeling abides."

Henri felt tears sting his eyes, but he did not want Nico to think he felt any pity for him, as the young man was clearly so strong to have sustained such a loss and be the better for it.

"I'm sure your mother would be very glad to know that Kikos still watches over you."

"Yes," said Nico, nodding. He studied the little toy. "Maybe she would. Do you know—no, no, never mind." He turned away.

"What is it?" asked Henri. "What were you going to say?"

Nico laughed and dropped back to the bed. "I can't tell you; I feel ashamed."

"You have no reason to feel ashamed, I'm sure," said Henri, now desperate to know. "Tell me."

Nico dipped his head, and twisted the quilt in his fingers.

"Sometimes, even now—sometimes, I bring Kikos to bed with me. If I am feeling unsure or unhappy or worried. To ease my mind and help me sleep. He always helps to put me at ease." Nico shook his head. "It is ridiculous, I know."

Henri sat beside Nico on the bed.

"It is not ridiculous—not ridiculous at all. I find it very touching."

Nico looked at him again, with those eyes the color of chocolate, the lashes around them so dark they seemed as if they might be lined in kohl. He leaned in and kissed him on the lips. Caution told him oughtn't, but he could pay it no heed, not now that both his body and heart had been so touched.

"You know," said Henri as they broke their kiss. "I find myself very jealous of Kikos."

"Jealous?" Nico chuckled. "Of my Kikos?"

"Indeed. I am quite jealous of how easily you take him to your bed. I can imagine he is but one of many who have desired to share it with you."

"One like you?"

"Very much."

Nico kissed him again, repeatedly. "You should know," he said in between kisses, "how very easily I would share my bed with you, Henri. And my body too."

Henri felt entirely ready to investigate this promise when a loud rapping on the door knocked him back into reality.

"Nico!" The steely voice of Nico's sister came through the door. "Dinner is ready. Bring yourself—and your colleague, please."

Nico stole one more quick kiss. "Come, colleague. To dinner we are summoned."

"Are you sure," said Henri, standing and straightening himself, "that it is not actually the gallows?"

⇛⇚

"THE WINE," DECLARED Zetta as they settled around the dining table. "I have forgotten the wine. Nico, go downstairs and see if Κùριoç Persopoulos has any table wine to spare."

"Ah, Zetta, it is no worry," said Aunt Seripha. "We have water to drink."

"This is a meal with a guest," countered Zetta, "and I am sure monsieur is used to having good wine with his meals."

"Water is perfectly fine with me," said Henri.

"Nico," his sister commanded. "Please. The wine. Go."

"But I thought the restaurant was closed today," said Henri. "Which is why we were all able to meet for dinner."

"I do not work at the restaurant," said Zetta staunchly.

"It is no worry," said Seripha. "Persopoulos has given me a key, of course."

"I am going for wine," said Nico.

There was a moment of awkward silence as the three remaining searched for something to say. Seripha smiled warmly as she adjusted her napkin and cutlery; Zetta sat looking at him, her face a stone mask.

"Persopoulos," said Henri finally. "That is the name of the restaurant itself, named after Mister Persopoulos, I assume. And it is also your surname you said, Mademoiselle Persopoulos?"

"Please, call me Seripha." She put her hand to her chest. "Though I do like being called mademoiselle, I must say."

"She is a widow," Zetta said.

"I don't mean to pry, of course," Henri said, his tone polite. "Nico did explain to me that your husband had passed. I was only curious as to the names."

"Nico?" asked Zetta quietly.

"Yes, yes," said Seripha, talking over her niece. "Of course. You see, I married Mister Persopoulos's brother when I came to this country. We were very much in love, you know. When he died, his brother gave me these rooms to live in, and I continued to work at the restaurant. My husband was a chef too, you know. So Nico gets his cookery skills very honestly."

"But he isn't blood-related to Uncle Petros, Aunt. In fact, Uncle had already passed away when we came to England."

Seripha gave a tight smile. "Yes, I know this, of course, Zetta. I only mean to say, he did not inherit his skill in the kitchen from me."

"And he is quite skilled indeed," offered Henri. "Everyone at H&C was impressed by his food."

Seripha beamed.

"Isn't it somewhat inappropriate for an employer to fraternize with an employee?" Zetta asked suddenly.

Henri's brows shot up, but he maintained a causal tone.

"I am hardly Mister Kavafis's employer."

Zetta took the pitcher of water on the table and poured herself a glass.

"His supervisor then."

"Nor that. Mrs. Plaistow runs the Royal Tea Room. I oversee the kitchens attached. Mister Kavafis and I are coworkers."

Zetta cocked her head. "Still it seems incorrect somehow. You share duties in the kitchen now, he tells me."

"Yes, Mister Kavafis has become an important collaborator for an upcoming event. I am quite happy to share my kitchen and any knowledge I may have with Nico. It is unusual to find someone so gifted who has not been trained."

Zetta took a sip of water. "Exploiting a young man's gifts by his superior may be common but that doesn't make it right or good."

"Sister," cried Seripha. "You go too far. Mind your manners, please. Monsieur Henri is a guest in our home. You'll have to forgive her tone, monsieur. She is very protective of her brother."

"My brother can be very impetuous."

"I find his impetuousness to be a very charming quality."

"And also a quality that allows him to be taken advantage of quite easily sometimes."

"Your brother does not strike me as a man who can be convinced to do much of anything against his own choosing," said Henri coolly. "I assure you, Miss Georgia, I, for one, would never countenance the idea. Nikolaos has skills that are hard to find, a new perspective, and the cooking world is always in need of that. The world itself even, for that matter.

"I always knew it," said Seripha. "When he was a boy, I said it. He could make something extraordinary of himself, if only someone would give him the chance."

Zetta seemed unmoved. "Chance always involves danger," she said.

"On that, we are firmly agreed," Henri said.

They exchanged a look then, Henri and Zetta, followed by a tense silence.

Nico returned, all smiles, with a bottle of wine in each hand.

"Have I missed anything?" he asked.

"Only me telling your aunt what a wonderful home she has," said Henri.

"Oh, monsieur, it is too modest for that."

"Not at all, it is a lovely, warm home. It reminds me of the home of my grand-mère in France."

"Imagine that," said Seripha. "Of course, we wish we had more space. Nico's room was an old sitting room, which he and his sister shared when they were young. And now, of course, Sister and I share a room."

Henri noted that Zetta made eye contact with no one at the table. She sipped her water.

"Wine?" asked Nico and began to pour glasses for everyone.

"You say you do not work at the restaurant?" Henri asked of Zetta as they passed around the glasses.

"No," she said. "I trained as a type-writer. I work as a barrister's clerk."

"That seems fascinating work," said Henri, honestly intrigued.

"Possibly for the barrister," said Zetta. She seemed to soften a bit. "Mostly I am responsible for copying documents and transferring script to type and so forth. It does occasionally make for interesting reading. But, more often than not, it is rather rote and boring."

"But it pays well," added Seripha.

"Yes." Zetta nodded. "And it is clean work, not physically demanding. It allows me to set aside a good deal in savings."

"One day, when she finds a husband, she will be able to contribute to a very good home," said Seripha.

Zetta looked at her aunt slightly askance. "Married is not guaranteed."

Seripha opened her mouth to protest and Henri saw to intervene.

"I think it's admirable," he said. "I always appreciate anyone who makes their own way in the world, on their own and of their own devices. I think most especially so with women, as there are so many barriers set up against progression."

Zetta's face revealed very little.

"We all have our barriers in life," she said.

"Quite."

"Speaking of homes," said Nico, taking a gulp of wine. "I believe it may time for me to soon find one of my own."

"What?" His aunt and sister cried in unison.

"What do you mean?" said Seripha. "Haven't I given you a lovely room? I try to make a home for you both to feel safe. I allow you your freedom, both of you."

"Perhaps his point of view has been influenced by his new job," offered Zetta, giving Henri a very pointed look.

Henri allowed himself a small eye roll in reply as he reached for his wine.

"It's not that at all, Aunt. And no one has influenced me one way or another," asserted Nico. "But I am a grown man now. And I am making good money now. I will never not contribute to this household and support Aunt Seripha for as long as I may breathe. But it's time I started making a home of my own now. Creating my own space in the world. I can't always rely on your grace and favor."

"But of course you can, I am your aunt. Do not be silly. You will stay here until you have saved up enough money to begin a good life for yourself."

Henri took up the bottle of wine and refilled Nico's empty glass. Their eyes met briefly and Henri tried to communicate his support. He wasn't sure why Nico had suddenly felt the need to make such an announcement, especially during so precarious a visit to begin with, though his memory did wander back to the pre-dinner "discussion" on the bed, and he understood the need for one's own domain.

"Aunt," Nico said, "I cannot wait for life to pass me by in waiting for the perfect opportunity. I have to try to seize what life I have while it is there to be seized. Before it flees."

"Maybe you needn't seize so quickly," advised Zetta. "Especially before you know all you could know about any opportunity."

Henri dropped his eyes.

"It's time you got a room of your own too, sister. You have sacrificed for me so long."

Zetta stared at him blankly.

"She is a woman," said Seripha. "It is her duty to sacrifice."

"Some may say. But that doesn't make it right or good," said Nico.

Henri met Zetta's gaze then, and, for a moment they both shared a soft, quizzical expression, wondering if they had been overheard, Henri thought.

"I was thinking of a small flat, one room, maybe two, in Bayswater or some such."

"Bayswater?" asked Zetta. "Isn't that rather far?"

"Possibly. But a lot have moved there, and I think I could get a place with less trouble maybe."

"At least you will be near the cathedral," Seripha said.

"And, besides, Zetta deserves some space of her own," Nico continued. "Some privacy as she plans her future. She is smarter than I am, her prospects much wider than my own, she needs something to call her own."

"Nico, you mustn't think that," protested Zetta.

"But it's true, sister. It is not something I am sorrowful about. I have decided my wants in life, and I am set on the path towards them. I have colleagues—friends," he gave Henri a look, "who will help me achieve what I want. I want to do what I can to ease your burden as well."

Zetta still seemed shocked but she nodded slowly.

"You are a good brother, Nico," she said quietly.

"But enough of this," Nico said, suddenly bright. "I didn't mean to change the mood so sharply. I am only thinking, planning. Nothing will happen immediately. I've only just begun at H&C; I might get sacked tomorrow!"

"Then you should have a brother-in-arms," said Henri smiling. "I would quit in solidarity should that ever occur."

"Then who will make the chocolates and petit fours so delicately?" asked Nico.

"We shall construct a cart and sell them on the street. Chocolate hawkers!"

"I will call out to passersby to tempt them," Nico said.

Zetta gave a begrudging half-smile. "You always were prone

to dramatics, brother."

Nico grabbed her hand and gave it a squeeze.

"Chocolates, you say?" said Seripha. "Monsieur, do I understand that you are skilled in the making of chocolates?"

"They're pure perfection," declared Nico.

"He exaggerates."

"I do not require perfection, only samples," said Seripha. "The next time you come to dinner, you must bring me some samples of your work."

"Shall I be invited back then?" asked Henri.

"Of course, monsieur. You must! Nico doesn't normally go through so much trouble for dinner. He wants to impress you and my stomach appreciates it. For all I am concerned, you may come to dinner nightly."

"I am jealous that you have him at your disposal perpetually," said Henri. "Whatever he has gone to so much trouble for tonight smells absolutely divine."

"Yes, let's eat, finally," cried Nico, jumping up from the table to retrieve dinner.

"You won't be disappointed," said Seripha.

"This I already know," agreed Henri.

Zetta lifted the bottle and leaned across the table. "Would you like more wine, Monsieur Henri?"

"Yes, please, Miss Georgia. Much appreciated."

They exchanged a small smile and sat back as Nico brought the dish to the table, his face lit up with a grin.

NICO STOOD, STARING up at the austere Georgian terrace house on Gower Street. It was three stories high, not counting what appeared to be windowed attic rooms, and its brown brick façade was only broken by the white-trimmed windows and the arched doorway. Nico looked to the left and the right and saw all the homes along this stretch appeared virtually identical. He had double checked the house numbers more than once for fear of knocking on the wrong door. He knew that his aunt or Zetta might think this neighborhood forlorn but it struck him as elegant.

He took a deep breath, calming his nerves, and knocked on the door. A gentleman, and around the same age, he wagered, as his Aunt Seripha opened the door. He had a pleasing, angular face and a calming presence.

"Mister Kavafis?" the man asked.

"Yes."

"Very good, sir. Please do come in. Mrs. Newbold is expecting you. Shall I take your coat?"

The older gentleman took Nico's coat and hat, and having stashed them in the nearby closet, led him up the stairwell to the third floor, explaining, along the way, that dinner would not be served for some time and that Mrs. Newbold hoped he didn't think her impolite, but wouldn't he rather visit with his friend, her nephew, Henri, until time.

"Yes, of course," said Nico. "And might I ask, sir, who you are?"

The older man seemed slightly astonished at the question.

"I am Margate, sir."

"Yes, of course," replied Nico, feeling somehow chastened.

"Here we are, sir."

Reaching the third floor hallway, Margate rapped on the nearest door, which like the fronts of the buildings on the street, was just like every other door they had passed on their way up. The bedroom door opened and there was Henri.

Nico's mouth fell open.

"Are you wearing a smoking jacket?" he exclaimed.

Unable to contain his glee at the sight of the silk quilted collar and cuffs, Nico laughed openly. Margate raised a brow but said nothing, only crossing his arms behind his back.

"Yes, thank you, Margate," Henri said quickly, pulling Nico

into the room and closing the door.

"I beg your pardon," said Henri, "but this is a dressing jacket, not a smoking jacket."

"Oh, pardon me, your lordship." Nico affected an accent and gave an exaggerated bow. "I do apologize, sir, for misidentifying your garments, your Highness. Please don't have me flogged, sir."

Henri wrestled Nico into a standing position and pulled him very close.

"I should flog you, indeed. I should put you over my knee and take a ruler to your backside like the insolent schoolboy you are."

Nico gave a little growl and nuzzled his neck.

"Oh, yes, your lordship, more of that." He gave Henri's earlobe a quick nip before pulling back and looking him in the face. "You know, all you need is a Calabash pipe and you would make a perfect Sherlock Holmes."

"Is that so?" Henri lifted his chin and turned his head. "I have always rather thought I would make a good Sherlock."

"Well, a handsome one at least," teased Nico. "And I suppose that would make me your Watson?"

"I do not think Sherlock and Watson shared quite the intimacy we do."

"I wouldn't be so sure. Why do you think Mrs. Hudson is always hiding away downstairs? Methinks the lady doth know verily much about the secret profligacy of the detective and his secretary. And speaking of servants, you have a bloody butler, you posh bastard."

Henri laughed and pushed Nico aside.

"Let me change," he said.

"Shall I ring for the valet?"

"Tu es indecent," said Henri, still laughing.

"I shall learn what that means and be very offended, I'm sure."

"I think you know very well what it means."

Henri removed his lounge jacket and hung it neatly in the nearby armoire, retrieving his dinner jacket.

"Margate isn't a butler, really," he continued. "He's something like a man-of-all-work. He doesn't live in; he just directs things, like a housekeeper might. Only my grandmother prefers a man in the position instead of the usual woman housekeeper."

Nico shrugged. "So you have a butler."

Henri gave him another playful shove.

"If you insist on calling him that, then, fine, yes. But I do not have anything. He belongs to my aunt. I did not have such things in my childhood. In France, we had no servants, only my parents and my relatives around to guide life and all its needs."

"You needn't prove yourself to me, you know. I wouldn't care if you were a costermonger or a duke." He came up to Henri and straightened his jacket. "In fact, I rather like the idea of you as some great man of the manor, ordering people about."

"I wasn't proving myself," he said haughtily.

Nico smiled, always thrilled to have piqued Henri's fiery temper.

"We had servants in Greece, you know. My parents, I mean. They weren't rich by any means, but everyone in Greece was poor—compared to London, I mean—so even those who were less poor could employ others. And my mother did not believe a woman's place was worrying over domestic affairs. Unless she was employed to do so, of course."

"I cannot blame your mother there."

Nico looked around the room. It was far more Spartan than he had expected, but somehow regal in its unadornment. There was a very solid bed in the center, its frame made from what he supposed was mahogany and polished to a gleam. It was perfectly made, the corner tucked neatly and tightly. The matching armoire, also gleaming, hulked across the main wall. A window overlooked the courtyard below, under which sat a small side table with three drawers. Its top held very little besides a comb, a brush, and a photograph of a woman with dark hair standing outside a quaint cottage in what appeared to be countryside. Henri's mother, he assumed. There was an urge to jerk open the drawers of the table and see what treasures were hidden there, what things Henri did not want the world to see about him. On the other side of the room was an armchair, angled next to a small fireplace. The chair was old but solidly built and expensively upholstered with a small table beside it containing a small stack of books. He recognized *The Mystery of the Yellow Room* he had given Henri only last week.

Nico walked over to the armchair and went behind it. He ran his hands along the polished wood of the back rail and the side wings and then let them slide slowly down the soft but tightly woven fabric of the backrest.

"We're two sides of the same coin, really," said Nico thoughtfully. "I left a comfortable middle-class life and came to London to be thrown into the fray of city survival. You left your modest country home to come to your grandmother's comfortable townhouse, complete with man-of-all-work. No matter how you deny it."

"Of course I deny it. I detest the bourgeois."

"Yet you make your living catering to them. And putting on the airs of them."

"I put on no airs of anything but ambition." Henri sniffed. "I'd much rather be back in the cold water flat I had while at the Carlton instead of trapped in this townhouse. I have no desire to be comfortable. I want to be excellent."

Nico smiled. "I do so like to stoke your temper."

"You excel at it."

Nico laughed.

"Your ambitions are successful, monsieur. I think you are already excellent, despite any further aspirations." He saw the beginnings of a scowl on Henri's face melt into a blush. "But, you must admit, it is rather a grand neighborhood."

Henri crossed the room to stand on the other side of the armchair, checking himself in the mirror.

"Is it?" Henri looked genuinely surprised. "I've always found it awfully boring. All that plain brown brick. No character at all."

"Maybe it's just your perspective, having lived here," Nico said. "It doesn't seem lacking in character at all. It's quiet and solid, I think there's beauty in that. I find it very appealing."

Nico approached the armchair and leaned on it, putting a knee in the seat, and grasping the back.

"There are a surplus of boarding houses nearby. You might take up residence there—if you can stand all the medical students and their silly slang. You did say you were looking for a spot of your own?"

"It would certainly be a convenient location. Central to all one's needs."

Henri placed his hands over Nico's on the chair.

"Before we dine, I must apologize in advance for the food. Likely it will be some abomination that my grandmother thinks Continental like mutton with turnip-tops and artichokes fried in tallow. She does not allow me to do any cooking in the home."

"I am not here for the food, Henri." He ran the back his hand along Henri's jawline.

Henri's eyes fluttered shut at his touch.

"But it will be an embarrassment after the delicious meal you shared with me."

"I see your skills daily, Monsieur Chef, you needn't worry about that. I have come to learn other things about you tonight."

"There is not so much to my home."

"On the surface, perhaps not. It is staid, respectable, those things which you wish us to think of you."

"Which I wish?"

"Yes." Nico stepped around the chair and put his hands on Henri's waist. "But I know there is a fire beneath; I have seen it. It shows here too. Corners so neatly tucked, clothes so perfectly folded, objects so perfectly arranged." He pressed close to Henri, their bodies against one another. "But it boils beneath, doesn't it, monsieur?"

Nico let his teeth slide against the skin of Henri's chin and he nipped lightly, following the line of his jaw, until he reached his earlobe which he began to suck. Henri let out a soft moan, like a heavy sigh.

"Do you think of me here?" whispered Nico.

"Every night," Henri whispered.

Nico continued to kiss his neck. "There? In that bed?"

"Oui," the breathy answer came.

"Do you touch yourself? Lying there in that bed. When you think of me?"

"Oui. Every night."

"It's so perfectly made," Nico said. "Tucked in, so smooth, so tight. I would like to rip free the covers and destroy the bed with you."

"You will destroy me."

"I don't think anyone could destroy you, Henri."

"Please try," said Henri.

And Nico kissed him, fiercely, roughly, pulled his mouth to his. His kisses were open, his tongue exploring, each kiss like a gasp of air for them both. He took Henri's bottom lip, chewing on it slightly, sucking. He opened his eyes briefly and saw Henri's smooth, ivory skin flush crimson and it spurred him. He pushed his swollen crotch against Henri's, burying his hands in the soft, luxurious black hair. His passion was such that he had pushed Henri against the wall, pinning him there, as held his head in his hands, kissing and licking his skin. Henri moved his hands around and cupped Nico's arse and Nico growled, his fire burning even hotter. The sound rushed in his ears; he heard a rush of air like the crash of waves at the shore and the distant sounds of cathedral signaling. The sound continued.

He pulled back, panting as he asked, "Do you hear bells?"

Henri, equally breathless, nodded. "It's the dinner bell. We must go down."

"Here we find ourselves again. But how can we go down now, like this?"

"Unless you want an audience of the butler and my grand-mother at my door within moments, we must."

Nico rubbed his face against Henri's, feeling the light stubble electric against his shaven skin.

"Ah, the butler, after all. He was rather distinguished-looking for an older man. Maybe he would not make such a bad specta-tor."

Henri cut his eye at Nico and grabbed him by the arms.

"Shall I call him then?" he snapped.

Nico chuckled. "Oh, I do love it when you act jealous. It makes me feel very wanted, you know."

He leaned in and gave Henri a slow, seductive kiss.

"You know I have eyes for no other man but you, Monsieur Henri Newbold."

"Do I?"

"Of course you do. Do you think I would eat artichokes and mutton for any other reason?"

He pushed himself back from Henri and moved towards the bedroom door. He turned back to look at Henri, still leaning against the wall, undone. "Come now, Henri, straighten yourself up and attend to dinner. You look as if you've been in a brawl. Whatever will your grandmother think?"

Nico winked and dipped out of the door, to wait in the hall-way, but not before he heard Henri mutter loudly, "Bâtard."

And it made him smile grandly to hear it.

DESPITE HIS TEASING exit, Nico waited for Henri at the end of the hallway. Henri exited his room and smiled at Nico as he approached.

"Another dinner jacket?" Nico asked.

"You wrinkled the first," said Henri quietly. "Besides, don't you like it more than the smoking jacket?"

"You are equally handsome in all of them. And I'd prefer to see you wearing none of them at all, if I could have my way."

Henri's eyes widened but he smiled as he grabbed Nico by the arm.

"Quiet with that kind of talk," he practically whispered.

"I doubt old Margate would mind."

"I hope you don't mind, but there will be other guests," Henri said as they made their way down the stairs. "My aunt will be here, as she is weekly, with her husband."

"A weekly family dinner."

"Of a sort, yes."

"Does that mean I am to be considered family?"

"For your sake, you should hope not."

Entering the dining room, Nico felt the instinct to check himself. The dark-paneled walls, the long, formal table, and the stoic-looking woman sitting at its head denoted a sobriety that quickly dispelled his playful mood. He doubted that a royal visit would evoke such severity in mood.

"Grandmother, may I introduce Mister Nikolaos Kavafis. Mister Kavafis, my grandmother, Mrs. Charles Wilson Newbold."

His grandmother gave a nod and said, "Margate almost had to ring the bell a second time."

"Our apologies, Grandmother, I had trouble choosing a jacket."

"At least you bothered," she said. "We always dress for dinner, despite your repeated insistence to disregard. Mister Kavafis, welcome to my home, I am pleased to meet you."

"And you as well, Mrs. Newbold. Monsieur Newbold speaks very highly of you."

The woman seated down the table tittered at that.

"Hello, Mister Kavafis," she said. "I'm Jacqueline Woodstone, Henri's aunt. And this is my husband, Richard Woodstone."

"Mister Kavafis," Richard, across from her, greeted him with a nod.

"Pleased to meet you both," said Nico as he and Henri took

their seats.

"I say," said Richard. "Do you really dress for dinner when it's only the two of you?"

"As she desires," Henri said blandly.

"Why shouldn't we dress for dinner?" demanded Henri's grandmother. "Standards are not determined by the number of people in a room."

"Oh, come now, Mother Newbold," said Richard, chuckling, "no one would know but you and Henry."

"I would know," said Mother Newbold. "And that is sufficient."

"Now, now, Dickie," said Aunt Jacqueline, "do not rile her up. And I have told you before it's *Henri* not Henry."

"When he's in France, maybe. But he's in England now, isn't that right, old chap?"

Henri of France failed to answer.

Margate appeared then, carrying the first course. He appeared to be the only server, but the food was, if not elaborate, certainly done with painstaking detail and Nico surmised there must also be a cook in employ. He told himself that he must remember to tease Henri about this later.

They were making their way through the soup, a rather bland Chantilly Soup, much in need of salt and much in need of saving from the heavy-handed parsley, when they spoke next.

"Is your family local, Mister Kavafis?" asked Mother Newbold.

"In a way," replied Nico. "We come from Greece originally, but my aunt and sister are local, and they are mostly my family as I lost both of my parents when I was young."

Mother Newbold nodded thoughtfully. "Better that way, I should think."

Nico could not respond and he saw that Dickie and Jacqueline blanched.

"Grandmother," Henri said, his tone admonishing, as he smacked his spoon down beside the bowl.

"Do forgive me, Mister Kavafis, but I think I have been misunderstood," said Mother Newbold. "And do not smack your spoon, Henri, like some farmer's child. No, what I mean to say is that to lose both one's parents, especially at a young age, is truly a sad thing. It forms a child, I know. But a parent, most particularly a mother should never outlive her children. It is a thing against God."

"Mother Newbold, if you please," said Dickie.

"Do not silence me, Richard. Not at my own dinner table, I should thank you."

"Do you speak from experience?" asked Nico, hoping to keep the mood from deteriorating further.

"I do," the older lady replied. "Henri's father, Joseph, was the first I lost. To the Russian flu pandemic. They lived in the country, of course, but he traveled into that city—Paris—constantly for business and they believe that it was where he contracted it. He did not survive."

"Grandmother has never approved of my father living in France," added Henri.

"I do not object to France in principle," corrected Mother Newbold. "And your mother, Louise, was very acceptable as a wife."

"I'm sure she will be delighted to know," replied Henri.

"But the reason he left," continued Mother Newbold, ignoring Henri, "was to be an art dealer. What sort of respectable business is that? Everyone knows that artists are little more than degenerates in the best of cases and criminals in the worst."

Jacqueline looked at the large portrait hanging at the end of the dining room, taking Nico's attention there. Though time had been no friend, he could see that it was a portrait of Mother Newbold as a young woman, a stolid, square-shouldered man at her side.

"And which one painted your portrait, Mama? Was he a pervert or a criminal?" asked Jacqueline.

"Jacquie, now, now," cautioned Dickie.

Mother Newbold cut her eye at her daughter but continued her inventory.

"And it was little more than a decade later when I lost another. Our dear Gordon, the youngest child. He died in the Boer War, though why he was there in the first place is beyond anyone's reckoning."

"He wanted to escape," muttered Henri.

"So there was I, steeped in the mire of tragedy. To be a woman and have lost your husband and your children, Mister Kavafis, is a burden unknown."

"Not all your children, Mama," Jacqueline reminded her.

"No, of course not, my dear. But sons, of course, are another thing altogether." Jacqueline exchanged a look with Dickie who gave her a small shake of the head. "Sons are the going on of the family; they are your future, your continuance. You will understand one day when you have sons of your own."

"Yes, Mama," said Jacqueline tartly. "And I shall remind our two daughters how lucky they are not to have the burden of duty upon them."

"How old are your daughters?" Nico asked.

Jacqueline turned to him with a smile.

"They are twelve and thirteen. Rosamunde and Alice, respectively. And they simply adore their Uncle Henri."

Nico turned to his friend. "I am most certain they do. Who could not?"

"No," replied Henri with a bashful shake of the head. "They simply adore the chocolates and sweets I bring them whenever they visit."

"That too," said Jacqueline, smiling.

"They get that appreciation from their mother," said Dickie. "I imagine if I filled her purse with chocolate rather than coin, she would just as happy."

"Perhaps," said Jacqueline, "but my dressmaker might be slightly more disagreeable when payment is due."

"Do you have children, Mister Kavafis?" Mother Newbold's

weighty voice cut through the mirth.

"No ma'am, I do not."

"And do you plan to marry?"

"I have an ambition to settle down with the person I love, yes, ma'am."

"And do you have any prospects?" asked Mother Newbold, leaning in. "I am connected to a great many young ladies of note."

"Here we go," muttered Henri.

"I thank you, ma'am, but I do have a prospect."

"Do you?" Mother Newbold and Henri both asked.

"Yes, ma'am. She is a most wonderful girl. I met her at work, at the department store. She was rather taciturn and stoic when I first met her, but I think I am slowly charming her. Rumor has it that she is a very stubborn person, and she can have a cutting temper sometimes."

"Admirable traits in a wife, no matter what they say," said Mother Newbold, nodding.

"But I do like the challenge of winning her heart," continued Nico. "No matter how much she fights against what she knows her heart wants."

"Possibly your girl is only trying to ascertain what the most sensible decision is," offered Henri. "After all, she is a working woman, as you say, and possibly she has much to lose if she simply turns her heart over to the first charming man with a charming smile who approaches her."

"Nonsense," interjected Mother Newbold. "Mister Kavafis seems a most sensible man, indeed. If he is willing to fight for the one he loves."

"And you must remember," added Jacqueline, "really charming men with charming smiles are few and far between."

Henri raised his brows and looked at Nico.

"It seems, Mister Kavafis, that I am outnumbered."

"It would seem that way, Monsieur Newbold."

Margate, in the corner of the room, cleared his throat.

"Oh, yes, the main dish," said Mother Newbold. "Do serve, thank you."

Margate lifted the tray of sliced mutton, leaving the asparagus on the side table.

"Never have I been more grateful to see mutton," said Henri quietly, and Nico chuckled.

"I must say, it has been good to meet you, Mister Kavafis," said Mother Newbold as Margate made his way around the table with the food. "You are a sensible young man and Henri is lucky to have found you as a friend. Henri is far too devoted to his work. He shall end up in an early grave like his grandfather if he continues at his current pace." She took a sip of wine. "Mister Kavafis seems to have a good head about things. You could be more like this young man, Henri."

"I shall endeavor to in future, Grandmother," replied Henri.

Henri threw Nico a look from across the table, his brows slightly furrowed, a worry line etching itself between them. Nico always thought Henri was particularly appealing when this storm raged across his countenance, and though he couldn't tell if Henri was annoyed by him or amused by him, he was delighted either way.

THE REST OF the meal was enjoyed in relative silence, punctuated only by the occasional chat about current news or local affairs. Henri's grandfather, Nico learned, had been a doctor, a very successful doctor, and had left his wife rather comfortably positioned after his death from a heart attack. From the stories they shared, it seemed the most reliable people in Henri's young life had been the women of his family. Nico wished he could meet Henri's mother, Louise, who Jacqueline spoke so lovingly of. A memory brought up, of a recipe Louise had tried to translate for Jacqueline, but which had resulted in near disaster in the kitchen even made Mother Newbold laugh.

After fruit and cheese, the ladies retired to the drawing room, Jacqueline threatening them with her piano skills, and the men stayed for a drop of port.

"There you are," said Dickie, lighting the cigar he had given Nico. "Take that in and see how you like it."

Nico inhaled deeply, closing his eyes, and felt the icy hotness of the smooth smoke tickle his throat. He exhaled, a cloud of blue wafting around his head, and found Henri watching him.

"Lovely," Henri said, in a near whisper.

Their eyes met and Nico brought the cigar to his lips.

"Can't interest you in one?" asked Dickie. "Fine stuff. Romeo y Julieta—from Cuba or somewhere. They say that chap Churchill who works for Asquith is quite fond of them."

"Non, merci," replied Henri. "I am quite content to watch you smoking them."

Nico leaned back in his seat and inhaled, letting his free hand rest on his stomach. The sweetness of the tobacco gave him a heady feeling. In his mind danced a scenario of himself, laying back in a chair just like this, slowly smoking, as Henri watched, the both of them entirely undressed. The way Henri looked at him now, Nico wondered if he too was imagining a similar scene.

"Have you chaps taken in any of the games?" asked Dickie, unaware of the eye play.

"No, not yet, but we have seen the stadium," Nico said. "On a visit to the Exhibition."

"They say your chaps are doing quite well, in fact," said Dickie. "The Greeks. Scored the bronze in trap shooting, I heard, and expected to take javelin. Looking forward to the Marathon myself. They say it's meant to start at Windsor Palace, don't you know. One wonders if the King and Queen will be waving them on and cheering."

"Nico and I will be attending some games soon," Henri said.

"Will we?" asked Nico, surprised.

"Yes," Henri said, his voice cool. "I had forgotten to tell you, but I secured the rooms."

"The rooms?" asked Dickie.

"You know grandmother does like to retire so early," explained Henri. "So we've decided to make a weekend of it. That way we can enjoy the events and any festivities that might follow."

"Splendid idea," said Dickie. "Two young fellows, nobody waiting at home, why not hang about a bit. You should make a meal of it if you can, I certainly would relish the chance."

"Indeed," said Henri. "To make a meal of it."

He gave Nico a look that made his skin feel as if it were on fire.

Dickie cocked his head; he leaned forward and stubbed out his cigar.

"That'll be the piano, chaps, we ought to head in," he said. "If we don't move quickly Jacquie will be trying to have Mother Newbold singing 'The Boy I Love is Up in the Galley' and then where will we be? Bring your port if you like."

Nico grabbed Henri's arm as they left the room, holding him back a distance.

"Were you serious about the weekend arrangements?" he asked, in a near whisper.

"Yes," said Henri, giving him quite a serious look. "You heard Dickie, I should take the chance to make a meal of you—make a meal of it, I mean. Forgive me, sometimes my English slips."

"Doesn't it, though," said Nico, trying to hide his smile.

"Come, Mister Kavafis, the piano awaits," said Henri as he moved towards the drawing room.

Nico brought the cigar to his lips, watching Henri walk away. The tobacco was sweet and tart, and he turned the cigar, letting his tongue taste of it.

Suddenly, the days ahead of him, until he and Henri would share a weekend, seemed like an eternity.

CHAPTER SEVEN

T HE ROOF GARDEN had been closed off for the special event.
Flowers had been brought in to fill the spaces not being used
by the reserved seating. By the podium, situated at the center of
the space and just at the perimeter of the balcony-like area, were
a pair of two caryatid columns of white marble, in miniature,
meant to resemble the same women of sculpture who resided on
the façade of H&C. Around them had been arranged a grid of
bright blue cornflowers and white lilies, their trumpet-shaped
heads bursting from the narrow patchwork of cornflower leaves.
This was meant to be an homage to Greece, Mister Singh had
explained. Mister Singh was Head of the Exotics and Oriental
Rugs Department, and had been charged with furnishing pieces
to decorate today's event.

In addition to the Greek statuettes, there were ornaments
meant to represent a number of countries. Egyptian-inspired
sculptures with heads like a falcon and a cow, squares of mosaic
tile on tryptic, their teals and purples jumping out against the
cloudy sky, a seeming nod to the beauty of mosques. A black
lacquer Chinoiserie corner cabinet had been set to one side,
topped with printed brochures, which themselves were guarded
by two porcelain enamel Geisha figurines. The back wall of the
garden roof had been hung with Oriental rugs and tapestries from
North Africa.

Nico looked around, partially in awe of the transformation of the usually demure space and partially befuddled by the haphazard mixture of styles and cultures. He wondered if most of the aristocratic patrons filing into the space had any idea that these pieces came from distinct and separate cultures, much less if they could pick their country of origin on any map.

Nico waited by the spiral stairwell entrance with Tommy, Mario, and the other male waiters as the attendees entered. Lily, and the other female staff had been relegated to the dining room during the event. The organizer, Lord Ockley, had demanded this as he felt women did not represent the spirt of adventure he hoped to explore during today's fundraising. He hoped to inspire a passion for world exploration, and women, he felt, too plainly called to mind the domestic, the comforts of the home country. He seemed to have no issue, however, accepting the possible donations of the many women of title who attended today, and Nico wondered what they might think of where they invested their guineas if they knew of Ockley's feelings.

The staff on the roof were not waiting on anyone today, not in the usual sense. Today they were meant to be available for guidance or questions. Once the event began, they would circulate with trays of lemonade, cordials, and barley water, and finish with marrons glacés and granité au citron, which Nico knew Henri and his staff had been preparing all the night before and this morning. The refreshments were a nod to summer but, looking at the gloomy sky, Nico did not know if anyone had bothered to inform Mother Nature.

His ears perked up at a familiar voice.

"You remember my granddaughter?"

"Of course, Lady Clementine, how do you do?"

Clementine waved her small lace fan.

"I do enjoy the occasional beams of sun," she said, "but it is rather close-feeling today, isn't it? As if the air were all weighed down."

"My old bones welcome any heat or closeness," replied Mister Hawthorne. "Not like my youth when I might absorb any chilly breeze without notice.

Hawthorne noticed Nico standing nearby.

"Ah, hello. Mister Kavafis, isn't it?"

"Yes, sir. Good afternoon, Mister Hawthorne, Lady Covington, Miss Clementine."

"Good afternoon," Hawthorne said. "Would you mind showing us which table we ought to take?"

"Of course, sir. Though it is set up to be seated as you feel, not assigned. So you might take any seats you like."

"Can you imagine," said Lady Covington, "if they allowed such behavior at the opera house? Sheer anarchy."

Nico escorted them to a well-placed table.

"I thought I might see your husband today," said Hawthorne as they maneuvered the patio.

"No, he has taken a meeting with his accountant," said Lady Covington. "And then, I imagine, a stroll through Burlington Arcade, as is his wont."

"I hope he refrains from whistling."

"He hasn't a musical bone in his body. No, he has been known to glide into a friendly bonnet shop when boredom strikes."

"And does boredom often strike?"

"Quite often. And like the back of a glove before a duel. But the Mrs. Hawthorne; is she here?"

"No, I'm afraid she's visiting a cousin of some sort. Near Scotland, I believe."

"She has many distant relatives, it seems. Always a sojourn to one house or another."

"Her family goes very far back."

"And very wide as well."

They seated themselves and Clementine looked to Nico.

"Is there anything cooling available to drink?" she asked.

"Yes, miss. I'll bring you some lemonade."

"Perfect."

"And for the Lady and sir?"

"I don't suppose you have any chilled champagne?" asked Lady Covington.

"Not on the roof today, milady."

"Well, I suppose it is charity, after all. Lemonade then." She took out her own hand fan. "One rather feels like one is at a cricket match or something."

Lady Covington had surmised correctly that the event was not, in fact, cricket but more like charity. Lord Ockley was to announce his planned afternoon and dinner event with the visiting Greek diplomat and Olympic team, and then he would pounce on them, employing all his charm for the purposes of convincing them to open their checkbooks to him. At least, that was how it had been announced to the staff, though Nico was extremely doubtful that Ockley possessed enough charm to inspire countenance to his cause.

As Nico brought the party their drinks, Lord Ockley moved to the front of the garden patio to begin his speech. Looking at him, Nico imagined that Ockley might have been an attractive man in his youth, his lack of height notwithstanding. But his naturally pale skin had been defeated by his overlong exposure to too much bright sunshine and desert-like conditions. He was wrinkled beyond his years, every line on his face like an etching in cracked, faded leather and his skin was blotched and discolored, overbaked into an unappealing relief map of brown and red. His once sandy-colored hair had begun to recede, exposing a constellation of freckles and spots, like drops of so much spilled wine, spreading the width of his ever-expanding forehead. His teeth, though straight, were too large for his mouth and when he smiled, as he so often did at his own jokes and supposed witticisms, showed their yellowed fronts, stained from too much tobacco and strong tea.

He was trim to the point of being gaunt, other than the beginnings of a paunch which managed to give his body a rather bowed shape, and when he stood on the dais, decked out in his khakis and boots, the impression Nico had was one of a sickly, old lion. He lifted a paw, as a dictator might summon troops, and held it aloft until the distracted crowd finally took notice of him and began to quieten. He cleared his throat and welcomed them in a loud voice that washed over the roof garden, a voice that, no doubt, had been honed from bellowing orders from a great distance. After thanking his benefactors, the H&C staff, and the assembled onlookers, he began his speech.

"Throughout the last decades, much of British exploration has been sponsored by the Royal Geographic Society. The support of the great Society and others like it has been invaluable, but as we have moved into the new century, perspectives have shifted. The most exciting and illuminating voyages of late have been funded by private investors. We have moved away from mere documentation and discovery. Now we seek to dig further, if you will excuse my obvious metaphor.

"No longer are we content to simply observe the native tribes or suss out the hazy tangle of nations and boundaries. Now we must rescue this history, reclaim it as its proper keepers, before it is lost to the dirt and dust of poverty and the perpetual rot of ignorance. We are the benefactors, and our currency of donation is culture. Before these ancient lands are lost to the ambition and greed which overtakes their countrymen as they attempt to claw their way into modernity. We are the stewards. It is great nations like our own which must be the saviors of history. Like the great Atlases you see on the front of this very building, we must shoulder the weight of our own burden."

A strong, cool wind blew across the rooftop, causing the blue and white flowers to shudder and tremble, and one of the china statuettes to tilt and fall on the tabletop.

"This is where our ambitions have shifted in these years. The Society and organizations like it are content to bring back the pineapple, rotten at its core and inedible, and present it as a picture of knowledge. The knowingness of the exotic. But my cohorts and I want more. We want to go to the pineapple tree and take it fresh, to dig the tree up by its roots if we must, to learn how it grows, how it is fertilized, propagated, and to sequester it here in safety where it can bloom and multiply under the watchful eye of those who have developed systems and procedures to encourage life, not merely leave it to the random and savage chance of nature. Where it can stay that pure beautiful native thing that it is. Ours is not the goal of obliterating history but to coddle it, to swathe it, to protect it—from its own self, if we must. And, I believe, we must. We are the greatest nation on this planet and great nations have a responsibility—like any teacher, any parent—to guide the children from darkness and teach them how to be proper teachers, parents, propagators themselves.

"And that is what these games—these great Olympics—represent as well. We have cradled this ancient idea, this innocent urge to move and express the body and all its physicalities and have brought it into a context in which it can thrive. We offer our hand—to all those nations and peoples still lost in the darkness of history—in order to guide them into the bright light of the future. The proper future we all can understand. We must help them understand it too.

"We entreat you today—if this ennobled idea of guidance appeals to your heart and sentiment – to join us. Anyone who knows the importance of stewardship, knows the importance of benevolent governance, can be a part of our ventures. Take a card, a pamphlet, and immerse yourself in our strategies and plans. We are perched on the edge of creating a new modernity, to illuminate the destiny of sacred enterprise, and we must gather the tools to manifest it."

The clouds, which had grown darker in the sky as he talked, shuddered. A few drops of water fell, dotting his dry skin and making it shine.

"Thank you for your attention and for any aid you might supply today or in future," he concluded.

The heavens, heavy with their burden, opened up above and

rained down heavily and suddenly. There were gasps and curses throughout the assembly, and people jumped up to flee the storm. Parasols opened all around, though they provided little protection from the angry summer rain.

Hawthorne had motioned his party under the awnings at the back, and they had mostly avoided getting wet thus far. Nico eyed the crowd that had begun to form at the entrance to the spiral staircase and turned to Hawthorne and Covington.

"There is a small staff lift just over here behind the prep area," Nico explained to them. "It is only made to hold one person or so and a cart, so it will be a bit of a squeeze. But if you like I can take you down that way."

"You're a savior," cried Clementine. "Come, Grandmama, let's do."

Hawthorne looked skeptical. "Won't that put us rather behind the scenes as it were? What will the others think if they see us emerge from the kitchens?"

"As I will be dry and they will not be, I shan't care," said Lady Covington, holding her hat with one hand and lifting her skirts slightly to hustle in the direction Nico indicated.

The lift arrived, blessedly empty, and Nico assisted the ladies into it.

"What do you think of all that he said?" asked Hawthorne.

"I once had a pineapple, you know, fresh," said Lady Covington, "during one of our tropical tours to somewhere with never-ending sunshine and heat. I found the fruit far too sour and harsh. I much prefer the subtlety of something like a strawberry or an orange at Christmas, if one must have some bite."

Hawthorne seemed confused.

"But will you be donating to his cause?"

"Oh, no, I shouldn't think so. We prefer our charity with more of a flair—being a patron to the arts or educating orphans, something like that."

"The arts? But you've never once donated to my theater."

Lady Covington gave him a look. "Yes. That's true."

The lift came to a stop and Nico opened the doors.

"Here we are."

"Oh goodness," said Clementine. "What a place."

⟫⟪

HENRI HEARD THE service lift open behind the main preparation area. He was bent over the main work table, glazing the fruit tarts with an apricot jam thinned with rose water and orange liqueur. He glanced over his shoulder and sighed.

Lady Covington, her granddaughter, Mister Hawthorne, exited led by Nico of all people.

"Apologies, Chef," said Nico. "There was a sudden summer storm and the exits were getting crowded."

"Yes, I have heard the commotion in the dining room," said Henri as he turned back to his work.

Clementine meandered about the space, her mouth agape, eyes wide.

"Your kitchen is rather marvelous, monsieur. Everything is so shiny and neat and calm. It reminds me of a great Transatlantic liner."

"Yes, I have been told this before."

"Do you know my mother had a French chef when I was a girl but his kitchen wasn't at all like this," continued Clementine. "It was cluttered and chaotic and he seemed always to be bellowing at one person or another. But I did enjoy his soups."

"Your mother only said he was French, dear, but he was not," corrected Lady Covington.

"Wasn't he?"

"No. He may have trained somewhere or another, and learned to make a sauce or two, but he was decidedly Russian. Which I think went some way to explaining his temperament."

Henri sighed, placing his pastry brush down delicately on the table.

"Ladies, sir, while I do most appreciate your unexpected visit and your compliments on my kitchen, I must ask you not to linger. We will begin afternoon tea service momentarily and with the new influx from upstairs, I'm afraid we all must be at the ready."

Lady Covington nodded and gathered herself.

"Of course, monsieur. If there's anything I appreciate, it is a well-run house. We shan't tarry. Come, Clementine." She paused, looking at Nico. "Afternoon tea, you say. Would you have a table for us, perchance?"

"For you, Lady Covington, we will always make accommodations," said Nico.

"Yes." She gave him a quick study. "You're the Architect are you not?"

Nico grinned. "Yes ma'am. Well remembered."

"Yes. Yes, I think I am starting to like you, in fact."

"Milady." Nico gave her a small bow.

"Oh, I say," interjected Clementine as they moved towards the door. "Architects disguised as waiters, Russians posing as Frenchmen, this is all starting to sound like one of those marvelous books by Marie Corelli."

"Clementine, dear, do share your opinion less often," advised Lady Covington. "You're so much more attractive that way."

As Nico held the door for their exit, he threw a look to Henri, a cheeky grin with raised brows. Henri smiled back.

"Bonne chance," he called.

Henri slid one tray of tarts to the side and stirred his pot of glaze. He had just dipped in the pastry brush when he heard the great door to the staff stairwell behind open and close.

"Zut," he muttered. "Are we running a kitchen or a museum tour?"

Heavy footsteps stopped just behind him.

"Do excuse us, Monsieur Newbold," he heard Lord Hartridge say, "but we were only escaping the deluge."

Henri wiped his hands on his apron and turned to find his

employer standing with Lord Ockley. They had been followed by Ockley's secretary or servant of some sort, Henri had not yet been able to ascertain the man's role. The fellow was named Grey, an apt name as he seemed to represent the color himself. He held himself with a meek air and was ashen in complexion, fair-haired and pale-eyed. He seemed at all times on the verge of fading away.

"Not at all, monsieur, it seems to have provided the most expedient exit," replied Henri.

"Deuced weather. It's been so very unpredictable all summer," said Lord Hartridge.

Lord Ockley took in the room and gave an oily smile.

"Ahoy there, Frenchie. Back in the kitchens again, what." He turned to Hartridge. "Illuminating, isn't it? To see how those laborers behind the scenes pull it all together. Rather like one of those exhibitions down at Shepherd's Bush."

Henri bristled. "Perhaps we ought to charge admission in that case," he said.

"Judging by the cost of the menu," Lord Ockley said, chuckling, "I expect you already do. To which end, how is the menu coming for our luncheon with the Olympic team?"

"It is coming along well. We expect it to be a success."

"Glad to hear that," said Lord Hartridge.

"Yes, yes," said Ockley. "Splendid. And is the boy helpful— the Greek? What was his name again?"

"Mister Kavafis," Henri answered tightly. "He has been instrumental in making it the success it is."

"Quite sure, quite sure. Seems like he knows how to make things flavorful." Ockley smoothed out his waxed moustache. "I expect I ought to get to tea then. Come now, Grey. Still so much to be discussed with the attendees. You don't want them to get their bellies full before they've opened their checkbooks, eh?"

"Au contraire, that is how we prefer it," said Henri.

"Yes, well, just goes to show the difference between service and real work, I suppose. Will you be joining us, Hartridge?"

"In just a moment, if you don't mind," Lord Hartridge said blandly. "I would like to speak to Monsieur Newbold for a moment."

"Fine, fine." He placed his hand on the door. "Make sure the scones are nice and warm, Frenchie. Can't stand a scone that's not fresh."

Henri simply looked at him, without reply, until he had pushed open the door and gone, Grey slipping in behind.

"Monsieur Henri," said Hartridge, coming closer. "Is everything indeed a success?"

Henri sniffed. "My work is always impeccable, monsieur."

"Of course it is, dear man. I apologize. That wasn't my question at all. I rather meant to ask, how are things coming working with Old Boney?"

"Old… Boney?"

"Yes, sorry, Ockley. I am not unaware that he can be a difficult personality. In fact, I don't care much for himself, if I'm honest."

"No, monsieur? But we are working so closely with him. I assumed by choice?"

"Yes, I know. Whatever his motivations are for this event, I applaud how it looks. I think it is much-needed that we open our arms to the communities who have been visiting London for the games. I know Ockley has set his aims on other results in the end, but I like that the store can be associated with such things. And, too, it's bound to be good word-of-mouth."

"I agree, monsieur. I think it seems a worthy gesture. Though, what do you think Ockley aims by it?"

"Oh, who knows, really. He has always fancied himself the Great Explorer, the Great Liberator of History and all that nonsense. I think he wants to ingratiate himself with the Greek government so that he can more easily divest them of their antiquities. He was a good friend of my uncle, you know, and Uncle rather fancied himself a world adventurer. Of course, he was just a schoolboy playing at it, but Ockley knew the ins-and-outs and how to make things work so Uncle admired him greatly. He's the one who gave him the nickname Boney because of his skills as an archaeologist. But even he knew what a dreadful pill he could be."

Hartridge seemed to realize something.

"Apologies, Monsieur Henri. I'm sure you aren't the least concerned about the silly trappings of my family history. I only mean to make sure you are not having too much trouble."

"No, monsieur. I appreciate your concern, but I think I can manage Lord Ockley. He is a type I have known many times over in my years. Other than an occasional popping in to make sure things are moving forward, he has been fairly distant. He expects Mister Kavafis and myself to do the work, and we have enjoyed it greatly. Nic—pardon, Mister Kavafis has taught me very much about Greek food and I am excited to incorporate what I have learned into our dishes in future."

"Splendid. That's when Bones is at his best—distant. But you will let me know if any issues arise?"

"Of course, monsieur."

With a nod, Lord Hartridge took his leave.

"You know," said David, approaching the work table, "I must say I don't care much for that look of that Ockley fellow. Something about him reminds of the baker what used to be on the end of our street. Cut his bread dough with all sorts—ash, plaster, anything—to where he made half the neighborhood sick from it and they ran him out. Not a care for his neighbor. All for the love of making a ha'penny into a guinea, weren't it? Ockley seems that sort."

"Do you know, David, for once I actually agree with you."

David looked shocked. "Thank you, Chef."

"Have you done the sandwiches yet?"

"Yes, Chef. Cucumber and cress, and tongue as well. All done delicate cut and that."

"Very good, monsieur. We'll make a real cook of you yet."

"Begging your pardon, m'sier, but I am a real cook."

"A kitten may call himself a cat, but first he must grow the whiskers, non?"

David eyed him suspiciously.

"I'm not much for those foreign sayings, Chef, so I shan't try to decipher your meaning. Besides," he said, tucking his towel into his waist, "I always preferred dogs anyway, didn't I."

CHAPTER EIGHT

WEATHER-WISE, IT WAS a gloomy day and the sky constantly threatened rain, but Nico couldn't have noticed. So buoyed by his happiness was he that the grey sky seemed as sunny as the best day, and getting soaked by a sudden shower might have inspired a smile. He looked around him and the awe he felt at examining the White City Stadium radiated within him and matched the awe he felt at what seemed finally a day or two of freedom. He and Henri sat, watching the race, along with thousands of other people. He had overheard someone say it was twenty- or thirty-thousand estimated. Never had he been in such a swell of humanity, surrounded on all sides by people cheering and clapping and waving pennants and flags of all sorts, the rush of their noise like the crashing waves of a storm-filled ocean. In the covered stands, there were large swaths of color where fellow countrymen had grouped together to support their national teams. They raised them en masse when achievement was gained and seemed to wave them even harder when failure might be imminent.

There was a great wallop of cheers suddenly as the men running the third heat of the 800 meters semi-finals came round the final turn. John Halstead, an American runner, had taken the lead and was determined for the win. His legs pumped, and he threw back his head, beating the British athlete just behind, a Mister

John Lee, by only two yards and winning a place just like his countryman Mel Sheppard—all jawline and ears by Nico's estimation—had done earlier in the day. An explosion of gleeful yelling broke out from the American contingent in the crowd, many of whom jumped to their feet waving their flags. *"When you hear them a bells go ding ling ling,"* a group of them began to sing, *"All join 'round and sweetly you must sing,"* belting out a popular American tune. Not to be outdone in enthusiasm, another man leapt from his seat when his countryman finally crossed the finish line, jumping onto the runner's back and kissing him soundly on each cheek. Nico couldn't help but laugh, pointing it out to Henri, who joined in.

"Such enthusiasm," said Henri, seemingly in awe.

Nico watched the Americans return to their fellow team-mates, and Nico had to admit they were a handsome bunch. Earlier, when boredom had sunken firmly in and he left ostensibly for refreshments, he had passed two of the runners, John Carpenter and John Taylor, and had noted how striking the two fellows were. It certainly gave a little more interest to the actual games which Nico truthfully found a little soporific. He hadn't the heart to say so to Henri, who had arranged such a lovely set of days for them both, but he did suspect Henri was just as eager to abandon the stadium and explore their own feats of athleticism in the hotel room he had arranged. Nico looked forward to missing tomorrow's games if he were to have his way.

"I fear the rain will strike soon," said Henri suddenly, staring up at the sky.

Nico could see no change from the rest of the day but he nodded.

"Do you mind if we cut short our time at the stadium?"

"I couldn't mind anything less."

"Shall we return to the hotel then?" asked Henri. "And then dinner?"

"Yes, let's," said Nico, standing. "Though I haven't any appetite for food."

He winked at Henri and stepped by him to leave their row, intentionally pressing against him.

"It's a pity," said Henri as they reached the ground level and headed towards the exit, "that you don't have an appetite. I found a restaurant that I wanted to show you that produces a dinner as fine as I might myself."

"I thought sweets were your specialty," said Nico, cheekily. "Desserts and all the decadent things."

"I think you'll find I'm rather talented in many areas, monsieur."

"Of that I am truly hopeful." Nico gave a small bounce on the balls of his feet. "You know, I'm inspired. Shall we race back to the hotel?"

Henri laughed. "You are so impatient. Besides, I am sure you could take me easily."

"Promises, promises, monsieur."

Henri guffawed and reached out to swat at him playfully, but Nico jogged just out of his reach. Henri was forced to jog a little to keep up with him and when he finally overtook him, he threw an arm around his shoulder and pulled him close.

"I have caught you, you devil," Henri said, sticking him in the sides to make him laugh.

It worked and ticklish Nico squirmed out of his grasp, his hat falling to the ground. They paused for a moment, both laughing, as Nico retrieved it.

"Monsieur Henri? Is that you?"

Nico snatched his cap from the ground slapping the dust off it, as he watched Henri go stony, alerted by the now familiar voice.

"Lord Ockley," Henri replied, his voice grave.

Nico came to stand beside Henri, still and statue-like as he suddenly was.

"Now, I do say," said Ockley, his eyes narrowing, "who would have guessed I'd find the two of you today. Enjoying time together outside of work, are we?"

Henri was silent but Nico gave a stiff nod. "Lord Ockley," he said.

Ockley handed his walking stick to his man, Grey, who as usual was hovering just behind him like the ghost of an unsettled relative. Nico saw that Ockley was speaking to Henri but his eyes were fixed on Nico. Grey, too, seemed to be sizing him up. He felt as if he were caught between a tailor and a boa constrictor.

"I was only just remarking to Grey that I haven't seen a crush of people like this since the coronation. So imagine that I would come upon both of you at once."

"Imagine," said Henri.

"I knew you two were inseparable at H&C but I had no idea the bond extended past the front doors. Though I can't say it surprises me; there is a shared spirit that you both seem to have."

Henri pointedly ignored this.

"We came to see the games," he said flatly.

"Yes, I had heard that the Association had been persuaded to reduce the price of tickets to the game so that all classes could afford to watch."

Nico glared at him as he smoothed over his moustache.

"It sounded like the Americans had taken another heat just now," Ockley continued. "Boisterous bunch they are; I can imagine they were heard from miles around belching out their college songs. It's a shame they couldn't ship them all out to Brighton with their representatives. Complaining about the lodgings? It beggars belief. They're lucky we put them up at all. In all my travels, I have always found Americans to be the most insufferable of foreigners. They never seem to know their place or how to behave. They even have that Taylor running for them tomorrow."

"I hear he is an extraordinary talent," said Nico.

"'Extraordinary' is apt. It is beyond the pale. My man Grey brought me an article that very much made the point." Grey, behind him, landed his anemic gaze on Nico and nodded. "Even if it was from the *Irish News* of all places. The chap said that when the games were held in Athens in 1906, the Greeks made every effort of comfort and welcome. Despite the little country being pitiably poor, they made the visiting Brits feel honored. And here the Americans are, in Great Britain of all places, acting as if they've been treated without consideration. Possibly they would prefer to go back to their pickled olives and straw mats of Athens."

Nico could not imagine how to respond to this with anything resembling social nicety, so he gritted his teeth and remained silent.

"This is probably why your king didn't bother to show up for the parade, I imagine," concluded Ockley.

Nico cocked his head and answered in a measured tone. "King Edward was absent at the parade?"

"No, no, of course not. I meant King George. Your king. Of Greece."

Nico straightened his cap on his head and inhaled deeply, averting his gaze to the sky.

"There is so much going on in the world," interjected Henri. "What with the Young Turks and the Ottoman troubles. Perhaps, King George had other concerns other than athletic showmanship."

Ockley shook his head. "Pity I wasn't able to meet King George really. I wanted to know if perhaps he was as fond of that Maud Allan woman as his brother-in-law is. I thought I might have her come swing her skirts round during our event, if she can be located."

"More schemes to prompt donations?" asked Henri.

Ockley pointedly ignored this.

"Surely you must have seen her do her Salome dance?" Ockley asked Nico directly.

Nico cocked his head.

"Me? No. I have not seen her. Only postcards. Why should I have seen her?"

Ockley twisted his moustache and a little smile danced on his lips.

"I rather thought the works of Oscar Wilde would be of interest to you."

Nico pointedly ignored this.

"Judging from the photographs, Lord Ockley," he replied. "I doubt very much that the Greek team attending the event would recognize Miss Allan and her dance as having very much at all to do with their home."

"Yes, well, what do athletes know of art?"

"Or politicians for that matter," added Nico. Henri seemed to be frozen, staring at Ockley. "Lord Ockley, we must take our leave, as we have dinner reservations. Good day, sir."

"Dinner? The two of you?" asked Ockley, a sly look on his face.

"Maybe some hungry Americans will join us should we happen upon them," Nico said as he began to walk off, lightly touching Henri's arms and prompting him into animation.

Ockley turned to Grey to retrieve his walking stick. He cleared his throat.

"I shall see you tomorrow then, monsieur?" he called.

Henri stopped, turning back. "Pardon?"

"Tomorrow. Our meeting with Lord Hartridge to discuss the progress of the event?"

Henri did not reply.

"Monsieur is not working tomorrow," Nico offered.

"No? What a pity. Well, I will certainly send your regards. I am sure he will be delighted to learn his employees have developed such… camaraderie. I'll be sure to let him know. Come, Grey."

Grey stood watching them a moment, his fish-like eyes revealing nothing, before following his employer. Henri's face was all sharp lines, his nostrils flared, as Ockley made his way in the direction of the stadium. A trickle of worry swirled around Nico's chest. That wall had gone up again, and today, of all days, when he thought the bricks had finally crumbled in the promise of shared joy.

"Come, Henri," Nico said softly. "The hotel."

Henri gazed at him, and blinked as if emerging from sleep.

"Oui."

Henri strode with determination and Nico had to move fast to keep up with him. Nico forced a light tone.

"That man, Grey, he gives me the morbs and makes my skin crawl all at once. He's like something out of Edgar Allen Poe."

Henri continued silently.

"Henri?"

"Comment? Oh, yes. Grey. A serpent to be sure," he said distractedly.

"Then he's in good company with Ockley."

Henri made a noise of disgust. "Indeed."

"Henri—"

"Perhaps we should skip dinner, non?"

Nico felt a little flutter. Perhaps, when they were alone together, he could soothe Henri, calm his nerves that had clearly been so ravaged by the encounter with Ockley.

"I would like that. Some time to ourselves."

Henri nodded, barreling ahead towards the junction of Norland and Uxbridge Roads.

BACK IN THEIR shared room at the Royal Hotel, Nico washed his face in the basin, after taking off his jacket and cap and undoing the top buttons of his shirt. He was getting comfortable but Henri only sat, stiff-backed by the window, looking out on the street below. He could not get the image of Ockley, walking stick in hand, slithery smile on his face, calling out that he would inform Lord Hartridge of their time together. He knew exactly what Ockley had implied; he knew exactly what power he wielded; he knew exactly what the wrong words could do to his position.

Lord Ockley was detestable, a slippery and slimy serpent no one would want to handle. But that did not change his position in society. If anything, his position gave his manipulations all the more weight. With just one twirl of his waxy moustache, he could turn the trajectory of someone like Henri's life in an unyielding direction.

He tried to push the thoughts from his mind but he could not. His whole body was tense with the worry of it.

Nico came up behind and placed his hands on Henri's shoulders, massaging them. Henri wanted the touch so badly, yet the anger and dread swirled in his gut. He pulled the curtains on the window shut quickly and closed his eyes.

"Come from the window, Henri," Nico said soothingly. "There's so much more to see inside."

Henri let Nico take his hand and guide him to the bed where he sat. He let Nico take off his jacket, his tie. Nico leaned in for a kiss but Henri inexplicably turned his head. He did not even know why he did it and he was angry with himself. And Ockley. And Nico. All at once.

Nico sighed, and took Henri's hand in his own. He pressed his thumb into Henri's palm and his fingers over the back of his hand and began to massage it.

"Is that better?" Nico asked.

Henri could see the want in his eyes, the need for approval, for a kind word. He wanted to say something, something to meet the expectation he could feel pulsing off of Nico, but he could not. And he was ashamed of his lack. He could only nod.

Nico was silent for a moment, his eyes shielded. Then he smiled, and Henri could see him forcing brightness into his countenance.

"That man, Grey. Do you think he is simply Ockley's secretary, or is there something more afoot? I think we both know that Ockley has certain interests."

Something scratched at the back of Henri's mind and his expression went sour.

"Oh, Nico. Not this. Not always this."

"What is wrong?"

"Why does it always have to be about this?" Henri asked sharply.

Nico dropped his hand. "About what?"

"All of this. What we are doing."

"We've hardly done anything, Henri. So I'm not sure what you mean about all of this."

"Is that the only concern in the world? The only thing of importance?"

Nico looked dumbfounded and stood from the bed. He stared down at Henri.

"You must be joking."

"I am not."

Nico began to pace. Henri could feel the anger churning as his legs moved; he realized he had never seen Nico angry before.

"Good God," said Nico. "The only thing in the world? We've done little else but everything else in the world. I would say all of this, as you say, is bloody important to the souls of people." He sighed and took a step towards Henri. "Henri, you do not have to be afraid."

Henri sucked his teeth and turned his head away. "Stop always telling me that I am afraid. Who said I am afraid of anything? I merely do not understand why you must always make such jokes."

"Such jokes?"

"These quips about Ockley and Grey, about others. About Plaistow and Crombie—Hartridge and Casas, even. Not everybody can be an invert, Nico."

"'An invert'?"

"A deviate, whatever the term is."

"It is disgusting. Both these terms. I am neither of those things."

"I was not talking about you."

"Weren't you? And you know the same things. You yourself

told me you knew of Hartridge and Casas when you worked at the Carlton and they were guests."

Henri shook his head. "I knew rumors. Nothing more."

"Oh, come now, Henri," Nico cried out in exasperation. "'Rumors'? Hartridge has left his grand pile to the management of his mother and spinster sister who are in residence and fully run the estate. He only goes home for the holidays and village events. Tommy once told me that Casas even came for Christmases. The poor family-less foreign friend, to hear them tell it. Casas has more friends in London than most people have hairs on their heads. He could go anywhere, but he chose his place." Nico practically laughed in disbelief. "Their townhouses are next door to one another in the city. They might as well be married, for God's sake!"

"None of that means anything. They have never once proclaimed themselves."

Henri knew it was a paltry argument but something compelled him to disagree. He felt like a small child who had been caught doing something he oughtn't and he wanted to defend himself.

"How could they proclaim themselves Henri? That is not the world we live in." Nico sat on the bed beside him. "You said there was something in seeing them together that drew you to them. Something unsaid, something unacknowledged—that made you feel safer, more secure—that allowed you to trust them."

Henri didn't want to admit it but it was true. Part of the reason he could pull himself away from the comfort of the Carlton was because of Hartridge and Casas themselves. With them he did, in fact, feel more secure, less on edge. Outside of that boiling pot of hypermasculine egos that was the Carlton and Escoffier's stable of chefs, he felt like he could breathe that little more easily. Not having to watch every single word uttered for fear of challenge or having to prove himself in any way other than culinary.

"But all of us?" he asked. "In one store?"

"We are talking of six people, Henri. Six out of the over a thousand H&C employs. Do you really think we're the only six at that? You know the world. We may be invisible to the average eye, but that doesn't mean we are ether, intangible. We are there. You are neither blind nor a fool."

Nico's words stung and Henri turned away.

"I apologize," said Nico softly. "I know you are not a fool."

"There is no need to apologize."

"Isn't there? We hurl insults at one another instead of affection."

"I did not mean to implicate you. I was not speaking of you when I said those words."

"You were speaking of me, Henri. You were speaking of me, and you were speaking of yourself. Invert. Deviant. Whatever terrible word you use, you are speaking of what the world declares as shameful. But I will *not* be ashamed. And you should not be either."

Henri shut his eyes, wishing away the torrent of emotions he felt.

"I am not blinded by my own urges, Henri. I know what a difficulty this can be. We do not have the privileges of Hartridge and Casas."

A force, like a running train, moved through Henri's head. He tossed Nico's hand aside.

"Non," he said and rose quickly from the bed. He returned to his spot by the window, tearing open the curtains. "You do not know what a difficulty this can be. I know exactly what I am. I am not afraid of it."

"Aren't you?"

"No!" roared Henri, spinning around. "I am afraid of losing everything because of what I am!"

"And what is the difference?"

"The difference is that I cannot control how the world responds to me; how they see me. But I can control myself. I can control how far I let myself go."

"At what cost?"

"It is not a cost. It is a saving. It is preserving who I am in this world."

Nico stood from the bed, his shoulders sagging.

"Who I am in this world wants you, Henri. I am not content with kisses in the larder or stolen glances or coded words exchanged in public. These are the things reality demands, but they are not all. Not for me. They are not enough."

"Then perhaps I am not enough for you."

Nico was wounded, Henri could tell. He grasped the frame of the bed to steady himself. He closed his eyes, dropping his head. The sight tore at Henri's heart.

"I cannot—I will not carry plates the rest of my life, Nico. I must be more than that."

Nico shook his head, laughing bitterly. Henri felt confusion tear at his soul.

"You've got it backwards, monsieur."

"What?"

Nico looked at him and the look sent shivers down Henri's spine.

"Remember what you told me when we first met. I am the waiter, and you are the chef. You cook. I am the one who folds napkins and carries the plates."

Henri opened his mouth to respond but could not. His petty, miserable words came back to haunt him. He had forgotten his anxiety inspired temper, but Nico clearly had not. And, yet, he had endured. What a fool Henri knew he had been all this time. What a fool he still was.

Nico suddenly grabbed his jacket and cap from the hook where they hung. He snatched his bag, still unpacked, by the bed. A wash of panic overcame Henri as he watched him prepare to leave.

"Nico?"

Nico was silent. Henri took a jerky step forward.

"Nico. Nico, where are you going?"

Nico paused at the half open door.

He did not turn around as he said, "Good-bye, Monsieur Newbold. I suppose we'll see each other next at work."

He hesitated a moment longer before closing the door behind him.

"Nico, wait," Henri whispered. But he was already gone.

Henri's eyes burned, his throat felt raw. He had an urge to tear at his hair; to scratch his own face. Instead, he turned back to the window and looked down. Down below on the street. Horses and carriages moved past, small children ran, tossing balls and rolling hoops, hawkers pushed their carts of ware, men and women, couples walked arm-in-arm, smiling and talking to one another, nodding at other couples who passed, content in their place, their shared happiness.

Henri grabbed the curtain and snatched it shut so fiercely it was almost torn from the rod.

He closed his eyes and fell against the wall. No sound came from him, no sobs, no moans. He only slid down until he was sitting on the floor where he leaned forward, arms on his knees, and covered his face with his hands. There he sat, as the sun began to set, slowly plunging the room into darkness.

NICO SAT AT the desk in his room. He pulled another wax pastel from the vase on his desk and tried to draw. Drawing usually relaxed him, freed his mind from any anxiety or worry. He had no illusions about his talent; he was not an artist. It was merely a way to concentrate his feelings, to let his mind glide. But, now, he could not create anything. The paper contained nothing but dashes of color, lines and amorphous shapes that signified little but the chaos he felt inside.

Aunt Seripha and his sister had been quite surprised when he'd burst in earlier. Both of them were curious about the games at the stadium and why he had returned so early. Zetta studied him though, and he knew her questions probed at the more serious undercurrents of the truth. He knew she did not entirely trust Henri and worried over his involvement, even if she had said little since the night they first met. So Nico had ignored their questions and gone straight to his room, shutting the door firmly.

Now, of course, Nico was embarrassed and annoyed. Could it have been that she'd been right all along? He should have trusted her intuition possibly. All this time he had devoted to convincing that smug bastard he was worthy of love. And, on the first chance afforded them to secure their connection, he had given in to fear and apprehension. What a fool Nico had been. What a fool this whole time.

And, even now, after what had happened, he could not escape those eyes. That set of jaw that always elicited a shaking within him. How close he had been to Henri in that hotel room, how close he had been to exploring his body, to tasting his kiss, to giving himself over to the man. How close, and yet it was dashed. He could not reconcile himself to that; it was like an acute pain, a palpable hurt wracking his body.

He tossed the pastels across his desk and snatched the paper up, crushing it into a ball and tossing it to the floor. He slumped over his desk and stared at the wall. There was a noise at the front door, probably Zetta returning from her errand.

A knock on his door was followed by his aunt's voice.

"Nico, you have a visitor," said Seripha.

A visitor?

"Are you sure?"

"Of course, Nico. Come. Someone important, I'm sure."

He opened the door to find Henri standing beside his aunt. He recoiled as if he had been slapped across the face. His instinct was to push the door shut and retreat, but Seripha had held out her hand preventing this.

"I was only just heading out," she said.

"At this hour?"

His aunt fluttered her hands, a sign that she was extemporizing.

"Mrs. Persopoulos wanted my help with something she was making—a blanket, I believe. I will just head out. Please, allow Monsieur Henri to visit with you in your room so he does not think me rude."

Nico looked at Henri whose gaze fell to the floor.

Good, Nico thought, he should feel badly.

"Monsieur," Nico said, waving his hand as invitation.

"I will take my key," said Seripha. "If I am back late, I will simply go into my bedroom. Don't mind me."

"You needn't leave, Aunt. Monsieur Newbold is not staying."

"Stay, don't stay, I am sure monsieur can decide his own mind," his aunt replied. "I will be going."

Henri entered the room and Nico turned away from him, going to the desk.

Neither of them spoke until they heard the sound of the front door being closed.

"May I sit?" asked Henri, indicating the small sofa.

"Does it matter?"

Nico tried to ignore the pained expression on that handsome face.

"Nico, please. If we could only talk for a moment."

"I'm sure we said all that needed to be said earlier today," Nico snapped.

"I don't think we said anything at all, really. Those were words of anger."

Nico scoffed. "And in anger, monsieur, there is usually much truth revealed. It is reassuring to know where I stand with you. No, reassuring is not the right word. It is insulting, monsieur, but, still, at least I know."

He began to turn away.

"You have to know—" Henri blurted out. Nico looked at him, waiting. "You have to know how much I care for you."

"I'm not sure that I do. You said that you were not enough

for me, which can only mean that you really think that I am not enough for you. And I should never want to be less than enough for a person. Goodnight, Monsieur Newbold."

"Bloody hell," exclaimed Henri. "Enough with the fucking 'monsieur'. I am Henri and you are Nico."

Nico felt the anger surge through him.

"And what the bloody hell does that mean?"

He watched Henri run his hands over his face, burying his fingers in his hair.

"What does it mean that I am Nico and you are Henri?" Nico pressed. "Those are but names and what do names matter? This is not the House of the Lords, let's not pretend that what we call each other changes anything fundamental about us. You insist on my calling you Henri. Why? Henry, Mister Newbold. Henri Dufresne Newbold, Le roi du cuisine, all just words. All empty. What does it matter if I call you something different from everyone else?"

Henri threw back his head and let out a roar of impatience. His arms fell to his side and he clenched his eyes shut. When he brought his head down to look at Nico, his eyes were stormy, a mix of fire and sorrow.

"Because you are different."

"How?" Nico challenged. "Why?"

Henri took a step forward, as if he were about to charge.

"Because I love you, you bloody fucking fool."

Nico fell silent. He did not know how to respond and then suddenly anger overcame him again. He scoffed and shook his head.

Henri rushed forward, grabbing him by the arms. "Did you hear what I said?"

Nico tried to twist free, but Henri held him tighter.

"Can you ignore me so easily?" demanded Henri.

Nico wrenched one arm free and snatched the other as he tried to turn away. The action caused him to lose his balance and he stumbled.

"Nico!" Henri caught him by the waist. Henri pulled him upright, clutching him.

"I meant what I said," Henri declared hotly.

Nico looked at Henri. He saw his clenched jaw, the flashing eyes, the furrowed brow and his full mouth, tightly pursed, like a pouting schoolboy. Nico had the urge to slap him squarely across the cheek and kiss him at the same time. He settled for grabbing him roughly by the shoulders.

"How do you know how you feel about me? We've never even spent the night together."

"And that is my fault? I tried today, with the hotel."

"And you exploded that." He shoved Henri. "Why must you always be so bloody bull-headed?"

"And why must you always question everything? I do not say those words easily, Nico."

"And what of your words today?"

"I am a fool, I know it. I am a silly, frightened fool." Henri's confession came out in a tumble. "I am not like you, Nico; I don't have your confidence, your assuredness. You see what you want, what you need, and you stride to it without doubt. I don't—I cannot. Everything I want, behind it I see the shadow of doubt. The specter of calamity, disaster, of being found out and being denied everything. And when the specter threatens too largely, I cower. I push it back so that I am safe. I do not know how to embrace my desire."

Nico placed his hands on Henri's biceps. He was sure he could feel the blood racing through the veins. "But don't you see that's not true?" Nico said. "Look at how you have pursued your dreams. You left Escoffier to come to H&C, not because it was a sure thing, not because it was a guarantee of good reputation or respect, but because it offered you a chance to achieve what you wanted." He ran his hands up and down Henri's wiry muscled arms. "And you pursued me, when possibly I should have been left well enough at arm's length."

Nico felt his resistance melting away as he touched Henri.

Henri smirked. "I believe, sir, it was you who pursued me."

Nico punched him in the shoulder. "Only because you were such a frigid French bastard. I might have needed an ice pick to get through that exterior."

Henri laughed. "Not you," he said. "You could melt it with a look."

And then suddenly he was serious. He grabbed Nico by both his wrists and pulled him very close, so that their faces were almost touching.

"Nico, I meant what I said. For whatever bastard I may be, it's you that I want. I don't care that we haven't spent a night together; I don't care that it may be against the rules—all of them." He placed Nico's hands on either side of his face, so that they rested on his cheeks. "Do you feel at all the same way about me?"

"Oh, you bloody fucking fool," said Nico, half-smiling, "don't you know that of course I do. I was damned as soon as I knew you."

"Let's be damned together," said Henri softly.

Nico let go of Henri and went to the bedroom door to lock it. He took Henri's hand and began to lead him to the bed.

"Come," he urged.

"But your aunt," protested Henri.

"She won't be back for hours yet. She knows we are meant to have a fight."

Nico pressed against him and began to unbutton his jacket.

"Are you sure?" asked Henri.

Nico let his tongue glide over his lips.

"I am quite sure. This is well overdue, Henri."

Nico pulled Henri to him. He kissed him then, passionately, deeply, slowly sucking on his bottom lip before releasing and letting his tongue trace its shape.

They started to undress. Nico, already half undone, shucked his untucked shirt over his head and tore it off. Henri unbuttoned his waistcoat, undid his cuffs, and began to unbutton his shirt.

"You're always so bloody pulled together," growled Nico. "Always so perfect."

He placed both hands on Henri's chest, curling the fabric in his hands, and tore it asunder. There was a ripping sound as buttons flew and Nico pushed the material aside. Henri gasped.

"I was impatient," Nico said with a shrug.

"That was a very expensive shirt," he said.

"Now it is a very expensive dust cloth," replied Nico, wrapping his arms around Henri.

"What do you expect me to wear home?"

Nico kissed him, pushing his tongue in.

"You may never return home," he said between kisses, "if I've anything to do with it."

He lifted Henri's coat-cut undershirt and slid it off him, kissing his chest, his neck, his shoulders as he did so. He took Henri's nipple between his lips and sucked it, grazing his teeth over the sensitive skin. Henri gasped and let out a small moan.

"Yes," Nico encouraged him.

He grabbed Henri by the hips and walked him backwards. He shoved Henri onto the bed and Henri fell back, laughing and sighing, his arms thrown above his head. Nico was overcome with the temptation and buried his face in one of the exposed underarms. The wiry hair pressed against his face and he inhaled deeply of the manly scent, the smell sending a jolt through him that awakened a circuit of nerves all over his body.

Nico moved his head and let his tongue explore, tasting Henri's skin. Henri ran his hands through Nico's hair, moaning softly. Nico moved his mouth down, letting his kisses linger on the stomach, lined with muscle and dusted with soft downy hair. He followed the dark line of hair southward, kissing all the while. He made short work of removing Henri's footwear, socks, and garters, tossing them aside, and then began to unfasten his trousers, which he pulled down, along with his knee length drawers, and removed. Henri lay there, naked, peering up at him.

Nico loomed over him, rubbing his swollen crotch.

"How long I've waited to see you like this," he said, his voice rough and heavy.

He quickly began to remove his own trousers and Henri sat up on his elbows.

"Slowly," he said. "I want to enjoy watching you."

Nico slowly unbuttoned his trousers, letting them fall naturally to the floor. He began to unbutton his union suit sliding it over the sinewy muscles of his well-rounded shoulders. He shrugged out of the sleeves and pushed the knitted body garment down to his waist. He grabbed his swollen cock, now pressing against the material below, and began to run his half closed fist along its length.

"Slow enough for you?" he asked, his eyes locked on Henri.

"Oui," Henri whispered, captivated.

Nico began to push the fabric, sliding it over his swollen member, which bounced up, freed. He slid the union suit off his legs and tossed it to the floor. He stood there, letting Henri take in his form.

Henri sat up and ran his hands all over Nico's body. He traced the lean, defined abs, he ran his hands over the muscles of his chest, little more than a handful, but perfectly, formed. He began to kiss and suck his nipples and one hand moved down, caressing first Nico's balls and then his shaft. Nico began to moan, throwing his head back, his eyes fluttering shut.

"Tu es divine," said Henri.

Henri looked up, his eyes glistening, and met Nico's gaze when he dropped his head.

Nico grabbed first one wrist and then another and pushed Henri back onto the bed. He climbed over him, straddling Henri's hip, and pinned his arms to the mattress. He leaned close, kissing Henri deeply. He lifted up, releasing Henri's arms.

"Tonight, Henri Newbold, you will have me," Nico commanded. "And I will have you. Many times over."

He leaned in again, pressing his hard cock against Henri's. He ran his hands through Henri's hair and studied his face.

"Yes?" asked Nico.

"Yes," said Henri.

"And why is that?"

"What do you mean?"

"You know very well. Why is that you will have me?"

"Because…"

"Why?"

"Because I love you."

"Say it again. Please."

"Because I love you."

Nico sat astride him, grinding his hips, their hard cocks rubbing against one another.

"Say it again," said Nico, breathless.

"Because I love you. I love you, Nico."

Nico threw his head back and began to grind against Henri with more force. Henri was hardly able to catch his breath, overcome with the power of his desire. He sat up quickly, and wrestled Nico onto the bed. Nico, surprised, gasped as Henri ran his hands all over him and flipped him onto his stomach.

Henri wrapped his arms around Nico and pulled him roughly against him, pressing Nico's arse against his crotch. Henri reached down and stroked Nico's throbbing cock. Nico craned his head back so Henri could have his mouth.

"You have completely undone me," growled Henri.

"It's about time," Nico said in a throaty whisper.

Henri pressed him down to the mattress and pulled Nico's hips back to his own. He wet his cock and rubbed it between Nico's buttocks. He slowly began to enter and when he was fully inside, he moved his hips, falling against Nico's back. He wrapped one arm around Nico's shoulders and pulled him into his rhythm.

He pressed his face against Nico's as he built speed and they both moaned, their voices blending and falling like a band playing music on a perfect summer afternoon in the park, the notes shimmering through the crisp, bright air.

THE MORNING LIGHT broke through the window and fell across the bed.

Henri opened his eyes and saw the room illuminated. Glancing to his side, he saw Nico sleeping on his side and realized, with no shortage of surprise, that he had spent the night in the man's bed. He reveled in the golden tone of his bare skin, made even warmer by the early morning light. He ran his hand over it, tracing the lines of his body, dotting his back with small kisses.

Nico, awakened, turned over to face him.

Henri caressed his face, tracing his brows, his lips, his jaw.

"You astonish me. How are you real?"

Nico looked up at him, his head on the pillow and his eyes bleary with sleep.

"I am just ordinary, Henri."

"You are far from that; quite far." He kissed Nico's shoulder. "And you astonish me in how bold you are. It heightens your beauty beyond measure."

"I have never been able to be anything other than who I am. I am not built to withstand it otherwise."

"Where do you get such assuredness? Is it your background?"

Nico gave him a quizzical look. He rested his head against his arm.

"Being Greek?" he asked. "Is that what you mean?"

"I suppose," said Henri. "I have never known a man like you in France or in England."

"Maybe you have not known enough men."

Henri raised a brow, causing Nico to chuckle.

"Not that I want you to have known so many men," he said.

"Men like us," Henri said, thoughtful. "It goes very far back in Greece, no? Almost every aristocrat I've known—of the persuasion—had spent a year in Greece once they leave school. They seem to find much validation in the ideals of antiquity."

Nico laughed. "The educated Englishmen are obsessed with our ancient ways. But it is no easier today in my country than anywhere else. Those days and beliefs are ancient history to us as well, as much mythology as they are to the Europeans who visit to gawk at the Parthenon. Had I stayed in Greece, it would be no less a challenge there; perhaps, even more difficult in certain ways." Nico nudged Henri. "But it is true, I think, that the average Etonian imagines us all running around in togas and laurel wreaths, spouting poetry and sucking one another's cocks."

Henri nuzzled his neck.

"I don't see this as a particularly objectionable way to live," he teased.

Henri ran his fingers through the hair on Nico's chest. He traced a line down his muscled stomach.

"If it is all mythology, then you must have been a god." He wrapped his arm around Nico's torso and pulled him close. "Mon petit Jupiter. King of the Gods."

"Ah, but Jupiter is a Roman god. I would be Zeus." He ran his fingers through Henri's hair. "But I am no god; only a man."

"I disagree. You are much more than simply a man." He let his hand slide down, caressing Nico. "If you are Zeus, does this make me Ganymede?"

"Only in that you are the loveliest born of mortals, true. But not in personality. Besides, you are older than me."

Henri guffawed. "A compliment or an insult?"

"Only compliments, to be sure." Nico smiled cheekily. "I never liked that story regardless."

Nico took Henri by the chin and turned his head from side to side, examining. Henri reveled in the attention, lifting his chin.

"I think you must be Ares," declared Nico.

"Ares?"

"Yes. Ares. The God of War. Always in battle."

"Am I so combative?"

Nico eyed him. "A question for your kitchen staff, I think."

"Why you!" Henri laughed. "I am not so sure of your

knowledge of mythology anymore. Perhaps you should revisit your books."

Nico poked him. "You see, even now, the fire is in your eyes. Even now you are ready to grab me by the wrists and grapple me until I admit defeat."

Henri furrowed his brow and gave him a smoldering look.

"Perhaps I am," he said.

He lifted himself over Nico, and pressed their bodies together.

"What do you say of my fire now?" growled Henri.

"I say I like it very much."

Nico stretched his neck forward to kiss Henri but Henri playfully ducked out of the way. He straightened his body, his weight supported on his elbows, so that he covered him entirely. Henri pressed his crotch hard against Nico's and began to kiss his neck until Nico began to moan softly.

"I do not think Zeus and Ares ever exchanged such passion," said Henri.

"Perhaps they should have," said Nico. "If I had written the myths, they would have."

"You would rewrite history?"

"Only those parts ignored." He wrapped his legs around Nico. "Only the parts that need rewriting."

"Then we must fetch the God a pen," said Henri as he covered Nico's mouth with his own. "You know; I still have the hotel in Shepherd's Bush for one more night. Shall we return there?"

"Maybe, but I don't want to leave this bed just yet. We can stay here all day."

"But your aunt, your sister? Aren't you worried if they know I am here. A day locked in a room together is not the same as a friend stopping after a late evening."

"My sister already knows about me, Henri. I think she knew even before I did. She worries about me; she is frightened that I may be compromised or worse. But she does not ask me to be anything but myself. And my aunt," Nico gave a small chuckle.

"My aunt found me with one of the boys in the restaurant when I was younger. She was slightly scandalized but I don't think she worried overmuch. Until she found me a second time with another boy."

Henri's mouth fell open.

"Twice? In the restaurant too?"

"Yes." Nico shrugged. "Restaurants can get very monotonous sometimes. I think she hopes I will change one day, grow out of it. She sent me to the cathedral twice a week for years. But I think she loves me more than she wishes to force me into anything. She is good that way."

"Still, for me to be here."

"Do let me worry about my own home," said Nico pulling him close. "I think they both prefer I am safe in my own bed than out in the streets or at the mercy of some stranger."

"They prefer you to be at the mercy of a sour-faced chef?"

"I certainly hope they do." He kissed Henri. "Now, do stop talking so much. I did not bring you here for a history lesson."

"You did not bring me here at all," Henri reminded him. "I brought myself."

Nico slipped his leg between Henri's and grabbed his arse, pulling him down beside him on the bed.

"If you say so. I shall fight you no more."

Henri smiled then, overcome with giddiness. He looked into those dark brown eyes and was overcome.

"I certainly hope that isn't true. I like it when you challenge me."

"Not today, Ares. I have other plans."

Nico kissed down the length of his body until he nestled below Henri's waist. He took Henri in his mouth. Henri threw his head back, lost in the bliss of the feeling, his skin flushed brighter than the new morning light flooding in.

CHAPTER NINE

APPROACHING MRS. PLAISTOW'S office, Nico couldn't stop smiling. He had been distracted all morning, ever since Henri had left his home, distracted by thoughts of the man. Nico fell against the hallway wall, closing his eyes and remembering the last night. Henri had left before dawn today, wanting to get back to his own home and change for his day of work ahead. Nico had escorted him out, his sister and Aunt both still asleep, and then gone back to his bed. He couldn't sleep for all the emotions swirling inside, imagining scenarios and possibilities, the future open and bright and filled with Henri.

He had taken breakfast with his sister and aunt and everything appeared normal. As he ate his toast with butter and honey, he watched them. Aunt Seripha jabbered on in her usual manner, laughing and commenting on the tasks of the day, while Zetta ate her simple meal of kasseri cheese, cherry spoon sweets, and coffee. Once, as she lifted her coffee to sip, he managed to catch her gaze and they studied one another. Her expression was guarded, almost curious, but he knew his sister well enough to know there was no censure in her look. Worry, perhaps, but no censure. They both left for work and he returned to his bedroom. He had meant to draw or write but, sitting on his bed for a moment, he awoke hours later, almost late for work. He had rushed out in a flurry of buttons and untucked shirts, all the while still smiling.

"Good morning, Mister Kavafis."

Fanny Clay, one of the telephonists from the switchboard office, passed him in the hallway. She smiled at him.

"I do hope there's no trouble that brings you to this part of the store today," she said.

"None at all, Miss Clay, thank you."

"That's good then." She paused as she passed him. "Do tell Monsieur Henri I say hello, won't you? It's been quite some time since he and I chatted."

"Of course," agreed Nico with a nod.

Once she had gone, Nico headed for Mrs. Plaistow's office. He was slightly hesitant but knocked and heard her clear voice tell him to enter. Inside, he found her seated at a small table to one side of the office with Mrs. Crombie where they appeared to be taking tea.

"On, I'm sorry," said Nico. "I didn't mean to disturb."

"Not at all," said Mrs. Plaistow. "Only a spot of tea."

"I always take my elevenses with Mrs. Plaistow," explained Mrs. Crombie. "It's so much quieter up here than in the canteen, as I'm sure you know. I'm just on my way, at any rate."

She rose and gathered her apron and sleeve protectors, which she had hung over a nearby chair.

"What can I help you with Mr. Kavafis?" asked Mrs. Plaistow.

"It's only my collar, ma'am. I seem to have lost it somehow and my others are still with the laundry. Is there somehow a spare I can borrow?"

Mrs. Plaistow touched the corners of her mouth with a napkin primly and stood.

"That's very irresponsible of you, I do say." Plaistow moved to a small case nearby, opening a drawer. "One should always have at least two collars available at all times, Mr. Kavafis."

"Of course, ma'am."

From the drawer she withdrew a fresh white collar and handed it to him.

"It's wingtip," she said. "Usually reserved for the senior staff, but I don't suppose anyone will object in the Tea Room. Trust you don't lose this one."

"I shall return it in perfect condition," Nico promised.

"Keep it." Mrs. Plaistow gave him a very direct look which made him fidget. "I expect you may need it again."

Mrs. Crombie, from near the door, gave a little laugh.

"Don't worry, Mister Kavafis. Her tone may be sharp but I've heard nowt but good things about you from Mrs. Plaistow."

Mrs. Plaistow narrowed her eyes, which sparkled a bit.

"Yes, thank you, Mrs. Crumble," said Mrs. Plaistow flatly. "I am sure you're missed in the kitchens."

"That's me told then." Mrs. Crombie laughed and gave Nico a wink as she stole out of the door.

Nico studied Mrs. Plaistow. There was something in the twinkle of her eyes just then that made her seem new. For the first time he noticed that, despite her stern appearance, she was a very handsome woman, much younger-looking than her style of presentation would lead one to think. That twinkle suggested mischief, which was not at all in keeping with her persona within the store. And how easily she had called Mrs. Crombie by the mocking nickname Nico assumed only traded amongst the staff. It seemed a joke between the two ladies rather than a putdown of any sort.

"Is there anything else Mister Kavafis?" she asked as she turned away from him.

"No, thank you, ma'am. Shall I clear your tray?"

"Thank you but I can manage." She began to gather the saucers and cups to the tray.

Nico knew he should leave but something made him linger. Before he could stop himself, he asked the question at the front most in his mind.

"Is it true that you and Mrs. Crombie share a house?"

Mrs. Plaistow froze in mid-action, her hands hovering above the tea things. She looked at him sharply.

"That's rather an impertinent question, Mister Kavafis."

Nico felt his throat constrict. He had perhaps gone far too far.

"Of course, ma'am. Many apologies; I forget myself."

She went back to the business of the tray and he decided he ought to leave quickly, to run off before her wrath grew.

"But, since you ask, the answer is yes," she said before he had time to move. "It is certainly not a secret of any sort, and clearly widely known within the store if your question is to be any judge. Mrs. Crombie moved to London, you see, when Lord Hartridge offered her a position here—she was formerly at his estate, of course. So I offered her a room at the home my husband and I had previously established here."

"And Mr. Plaistow did not mind?"

"You really do excel at impertinent questions, Mister Kavafis." But despite her chastising tone, her face softened as the corners of her mouth turned up in a faint smile. "As Mr. Plaistow has been dead some twenty years, I shouldn't think his opinion much mattered."

"Oh, ma'am. I am sorry for intruding."

She turned to hand him the tray.

"Here," she said. Nico took the tray and she looked at him for a moment. "My husband had the good sense to die very early in our marriage. He left the townhouse to me and since it was not in a very fashionable part of London—not then, at least—and as his cousins got the vast bulk of the money, they did not object. I was determined to hold onto what I had come to know as my home. Thus began my life as a woman of employment."

Nico felt her scrutiny but was also surprised at her openness.

"And you have become very successful, ma'am."

"So might you if you learn to be more circumspect. Now, I assume you have no more intrusions into my private life that you would like to venture?"

"No, ma'am. Thank you, ma'am."

"Good, now take that tray to the Tea Room, won't you?" She gave a crooked little half-smile and Nico saw the mischievous light in her eyes again. "After all, I am sure Monsieur Henri will be looking for you expectantly by now. He always is, isn't he."

Nico eyes widened. "Ma'am?"

Her eyes danced as she turned from him.

"Put on your collar, Mister Kavafis," she said, "And attend to your work."

HENRI CROUCHED IN front of the prep table. He examined the creamy custard pie in front of him, glistening in the half-light of the darkened kitchen. He took a fork and tapped the crusty top, burnished to a golden brown under the heat of the oven and glistening from the sugar syrup poured over to finish.

"And what do you call this again?"

"Galaktoboureko," Nico replied.

Nico was at the window of the kitchen, opening it. It was late in the evening and the rest of the Tea Room staff had left for the day. Behind Nico the night sky, cut by the buildings of London, their lights sparkling, framed him. He turned back towards Henri but leaned against the windowsill. He had discarded most of the layers of his uniform and had removed his collar, opening the top buttons of his shirt. He fanned himself with the towel he held and closed his eyes. Henri delighted in how the falling light caught his dark hair, highlighting its sheen, and his skin, dewed with perspiration glowed golden.

"What do you think?" asked Nico, his eyes still closed.

"It looks delicious," said Henri, not looking at the dessert.

Nico opened his eyes and walked towards Henri, dabbing the towel against neck and clavicle.

"It's terrible warm tonight," said Nico.

"You're going to have to get used to it if you intend to work in the kitchens."

"Maybe I will be the maître d'hôtel. The secret recipe developer behind the Great Chef."

"I don't think Mrs. Plaistow would appreciate you taking her job," answered Henri as he lifted the plate and sunk his fork into the galaktoboureko.

"Has she been giving you recipes too?" Nico swatted him with the towel. "Both I and Mrs. Crombie will become very jealous."

Henri grinned widely and dodged the towel, as he tasted a mouthful of the dessert. He hummed in appreciation.

"But this is delicious," he exclaimed. "Silky-smooth and per-fect."

"You don't think it's too sweet?"

"No. I think it is just the right amount. Why do you want to change it? We should serve it as is."

Nico nodded. "We could, but I wanted to do something to make it our own."

Henri beamed inwardly at "our own."

"Like?" he asked.

Nico leaned against the prep table.

"I thought of maybe infusing the custard with tea, to keep it on theme for the afternoons, of course. And then possibly, with the sugar syrup, adding lemon or bergamot. With the custard already so rich, I thought it might lend itself to it."

"An entire cream tea in one bite?"

"Something like that. And possibly if we cut it into smaller squares and grill all sides of it, it would be a lovely addition to the tea tiers. What do you think?"

Henri placed the dish and fork gently on the table. He studied it a moment more, his brows furrowing. He knew he looked quite serious when he did this and he wanted to throw Nico for a moment. He saw the questioning in his eyes; he knew he had succeeded.

Henri shook his head.

"I am afraid I must say," he began as he walked towards Nico, "that unfortunately, you are as talented as you are beautiful."

Nico's mouth fell open in surprise. Henri grabbed him by the waist and pulled him close.

"You intentionally made me worry," Nico chastised him.

"Only because I love to see you surprised."

Henri dipped his head and kissed Nico slowly, sweetly, letting his fingertips graze the soft, golden skin of neck.

Nico traced Henri's lips when they broke apart.

"I can't believe you actually convinced David to spend all afternoon making phyllo," Nico said with a smile.

Henri gave an exhale of breath coupled with a very serious look.

"Convinced? I did not convince him; I simply assigned him the task. I am the chef, mon chéri."

"I do like it when you are forthright," Nico said, kissing him again.

He pushed slightly away from Henri and headed back to the window.

"Although I'm quite sure you mean you told Michel to tell David to make the phyllo. You are not such a tyrant as you sometimes like people to think you are."

Henri pursed his lips. "Pure slander."

"I like that you are soft on the inside, it makes cracking the shell so much fun," said Nico.

He leaned against the window sill, searching for a breeze. He opened his eyes wide.

"Listen, do you hear it?"

Henri stood still and listened. Sure enough, under the murmur of voices and carriage wheels which floated up from the street, he heard the sound of distant music outside. They both stood silently for a moment and the music was easy to make out, its tune a joyful but slow waltz.

Nico moved towards him, extending a hand.

"Come, come, Henri, dance with me."

"Comment?"

"Don't be coy. That day, at the Exhibition, you said that you would not dance with me in the open, with all those people around, in the broad daylight. So, come then. It is dark; we are alone, there is no one else here. Don't you hear the music?"

The idea sent a shudder of sweetness through Henri. He was being pulled towards Nico but his self-consciousness made him hesitant.

"I told you I don't dance anymore."

Nico grabbed his hands and gave him a pull.

"And I told you that I don't believe you."

He dragged Henri to the wide open space of the kitchen; Henri worried he might trip over his own feet. But Nico steadied, held him. Nico took Henri's right hand and placed it behind him so that it rested on his back. He lifted Henri's left hand, and pressed the palm of his right hand against it. No matter how many times they touched, Henri always felt a jolt of electricity. Though they had explored every inch of one another's body, there was something more charged about these small, subtle touches. Energy radiated from their palms, like a small flare of electricity coursing between them.

"You should lead," Nico said. "I can follow."

Henri nodded, unable to speak. He was glad for the task of leading as it distracted him from the overpowering urge to bury his face in Nico's neck and taste his skin.

They began to glide in small circles, dancing a slow waltz, Nico pressing his hips against Henri's. Henri forgot about anything else, only the force of their bodies together. After a few minutes of moving, Nico laid his head softly against Henri's shoulder and Henri could feel the warmth of his breath against his neck. Despite the heat of the evening, it gave him chills to feel it. His eyelids grew heavy, feeling lost somewhere between a dream and the waking world, and all of his concentration focused on keeping the two of them connected, on supporting the weight of the beautiful man in his arms.

The music faded to a close. Nico lifted his head and looked at Henri through his lashes.

"You should dance more, Henri. You're really quite good at it."

Henri smiled down on that handsome face and leaned in for a kiss, soft, deep, their tongues playing languidly against one another. Nico placed his hands on Henri's shoulders and though he seemed to be the one clutching on, Henri felt as if his legs might give out at any moment and he might be the one to swoon. The room was a blur around them; he could only see Nico.

Slow, pointed claps broke into their cocoon and the light of the room came back into view, shattering Henri's haze of emotion.

He turned towards the source of the noise. There, leaning against the doorway of the kitchen, was Ockley. He continued to clap. Henri felt sick.

"How long have you been there?" he snapped.

"Long enough to see that the two of you move marvelously together," Ockley said, his tone unctuous and sly.

Henri and Nico broke apart, but not suddenly, and not far apart. They both stood facing him.

"You really should charge admission, monsieur," added Ockley, "if you intend to be putting on shows of this nature."

Henri felt a coldness swell in his chest; his limbs turned to stone.

"This is not a show. Not any of your concern. Why are you here anyway?"

Ockley advanced towards them. "Don't trouble yourself, lad. You can't think I am at all surprised to see this. I've pegged you two from the moment we first met. In fact, I think you'll find we are birds of a feather, you boys and I."

"I very much doubt that," said Nico.

"Now don't be testy because you feel caught out. You needn't feel too worried. I understand such urges." He cast his eye over the prep table. "Only I have better sense than to leave myself open to their inspection."

He glanced at the milk pies they had just been working on.

"Sweets," he said. "I do have rather a sweet tooth. That's one thing I missed in all my travels. Other cultures don't have quite the appreciation of sugar that we Brits do. That is, of course, until we show them the proper way of taking it. And then they cannot get enough. Ravenous as little children for it. Simply feral for a taste." He looked at Nico. "You must like sugar, no?"

"I appreciate the finer applications," said Nico. "If it isn't handled correctly, it can be too much. In fact, it makes me sick."

"Ah, an aesthete." Ockley chuckled. "Who would have known? These weeks at H&C have finely tuned your senses so quickly. But, then again, you clearly have had a masterful guiding hand. Once you've had haute cuisine, it dulls your taste buds to all else. So I'm told, at least. I'm afraid I've never developed the taste for it myself. My urges have all run for the simpler, the plainer."

"Maybe you should learn to cook your own food then," Henri answered roughly.

Ockley laughed. "Don't be silly, old boy. I'm not some scullery maid. That's exactly why one has staff, people like you, to cater to one's appetites."

Henri ran his tongue against the back of his teeth, trying to keep his words measured.

"We have much work to do, Ockley—"

"That's *Lord* Ockley, monsieur."

"As I have said, we have much work to do. Do you want anything in particular?"

"Is that any way to speak to a collaborator, monsieur?" He walked closer to the pair. "We are meant to be working together, after all. Perhaps, all three of us could work together more closely. Get a proper feel of things."

He ran his finger down Nico's sleeve.

"I've never seen you out of your livery. You look even more than the part in this. More like you ought."

Henri felt his blood boil.

"The menus have been decided," he spat. "We need not collaborate further."

"Is that so?"

"Yes. We will do our job as instructed, and we trust you can find someone else to help you with whatever other needs you may be in want of."

"If they were so lacking in pride," snapped Nico. Henri could tell he was losing his fight against his anger, and understood completely.

Ockley's face changed, the slimy grin, the purring voice, gone. There was flint in his eyes and he stood straighter, his lip twitching, the mustache dancing on it like a dead caterpillar.

"You want to watch your tone, boy. Just because your little French friend has you stirring his sauces, doesn't mean you have the right to speak to me however you like." His head snapped towards Henri. "Nor, I very much doubt, would you want Lord Hartridge to know what has been going on in his kitchens after hours. Sights sickening enough to curdle the milk, most would think. Shocking. Certainly not the type of behavior expected from an uppity chef who claims to have been trained by the supposed best."

Henri was at the end of his tether and could barely control the urge to strike the man. He would not fall prey to these petty threats again, not after they dimmed the light he had with Nico so recently. He would not stand for it tonight.

"My kitchens are closed," said Henri, his voice like ice. "I shall have to ask you to leave."

"Your kitchens?" Ockley barked in mockery. "Nothing around here is yours. You couldn't afford a table or a soup spoon in this kitchen. You are just a cook. Don't get above yourself."

Out of the corner of his eye, Henri saw Nico look at him. He knew he wondered if he would erupt.

"Be that as it may," Henri continued, moving steadily towards Ockley, "the kitchen is closed."

Now he was inches from Ockley, and he curled and uncurled

his fist. He was so close, he could smell the sickly scent of the wax Ockley used on his moustache, the scent of his cologne, rank and suffocating.

"You can still exit by way of the lift, Lord Ockley. Or I can show you the faster way down the staff stairwell. I repeat, my kitchen is closed."

Ockley's eyes narrowed, his stare like a viper's as it waited to strike. "You wouldn't dare expel me."

"As you have said, I am shocking." Henri raised a brow. "Do you wish to test exactly how shocking I may be?"

They stared at each other for a long moment and Henri felt sick, but he fought the feeling and willed himself to be like stone. He knew he treaded dangerous waters, but he would not allow himself—and most especially Nico—to be threatened so openly. He must make it known.

Finally, Ockley dropped his gaze and examined his nails.

"It really is a pity, monsieur," Ockley said, his earlier tone returned, "that you choose to act like a brute. Not surprising, I suppose, but still a pity."

He turned on his heel and headed for the kitchen door.

"It really could have been a revelatory collaboration, our trio. But it's evident you choose to work alone." He stopped at the door and gazed back at them. "Which will suit you well, I imagine, should you ever lose your place at H&C and have to face the cruel sting of the pavement. A cook without a kitchen is sad; a chef without one is all the more pathetic. Let's hope you have enough sense to know your place."

He pushed through the doors and was gone.

Henri turned to Nico. Nico had a hesitant expression in his eyes, and he held his face a mask. But something in him was beaming, Henri could feel it. It felt something like pride, and affection too.

"Are you all right?" asked Nico.

"I am fine," Henri reassured him. "And you?"

Nico nodded and his mask turned to a warm smile.

"That was awfully risky, you know. Talking to him like that."

Henri nodded, trying not to think on it too much.

"But, my God, were you marvelous," said Nico, beaming. "Marvelous indeed."

A snap of relief fell over Henri, like the rush of a cold breeze on a sweltering day. "We should go," he suggested.

Nico nodded and turned to gather his things.

"Maybe," said Henri, his body relaxing. "Maybe we can find the source of that music. Or some other place where one might go to dance?"

Nico looked surprised.

"You want to dance tonight?" he asked.

Henri shrugged and raised a brow. "I have been told I am rather good at it."

He delighted at the bark of laughter Nico gave in reply. Nico grabbed his hand and began to pull him out of the kitchen, eager, even more now, to leave.

"Perhaps we ought to take the staff stairwell," suggested Henri. "Just in case."

Nico glanced back at the door through which Ockley had just left.

"Yes. Quite. Good idea."

CHAPTER TEN

IT WAS LIKE a collage of beauty. Spread out before Nico on the table were watercolor sketches, dried flowers, swatches of silk and other fabrics, photographs and charcoal drawings of scenes both epic and intimate. Mister Singh, head of the Exotics and Oriental Rugs Department, was showing Nico and Michel his final ideas and sketches for how the Royal Tea Room would be decorated for Ockley's Olympic luncheon event. He informed Nico and Michel that Señor Casas and Lord Hartridge had asked him to make it as opulent as possible—to transform the space into something worthy of the grand games being played at the stadium. Something redolent of history and culture and deep pockets. They wanted to impress the crowd. Nico knew that Hartridge and Casas had arranged for photographers to be present, reporters, all members of the media of words, newsworthy and gossip-worthy. They wanted to create a scene; they wanted the name of H&C to be on everyone's tongues.

And Mister Singh had taken to his task with notable aplomb. It was obvious from the schematics he laid before them that this task was not only one up to his talents but inspiring for him. Still, even with this landscape of color and allure before him, Nico was distracted. He welcomed Michel at any time, of course, but Henri was noticeably absent. In fact, he had not seen much of his beloved chef since the night they'd gone dancing. Knowing

Henri's tendency to retreat after being courageous in love, he worried that he had fled again, back into his emotional hideaway. Of course, Henri had been busier than ever these last few days, and their occasional interactions had been glowing and warm, so Nico knew he likely ought not to fret. Even so, occasionally was not enough when it came to Henri. Ever since they had broken down those barriers, it seemed he needed Henri even more than before. Every moment away from him felt empty, every minute they were apart, he found himself thinking of him, wondering of him, waiting for the next time they would see each other. Henri was a hunger and he was insatiable it seemed.

"Mister Kavafis?" asked Mister Singh.

"Oh, I'm sorry, what was that?" said Nico.

"I asked if you had any final adjustments you might suggest?"

"No, not at all. In fact, I was distracted by the beauty of it all, Mister Singh. I think you have outdone yourself. It feels alive and I cannot wait to see it on the day. And, frankly," he added with a smile, "I'm glad there are no statuettes this time," offered Nico. "To be honest, it felt rather like a museum tour previously."

"Yes," agreed Mister Singh. "All the bibelots and such the day of the charity speech were a bit much, I do agree. But that was at the request of Lord Ockley. He seems to have a very specific idea of what makes something appealingly exotic."

Nico grunted softly and rolled his eyes.

"If you don't mind my asking, how did you end up at H&C?" asked Michel. "Your knowledge seems so extensive. I have heard you attended Oxford?"

Mister Singh nodded as he closed his portfolio.

"Cambridge, actually. I read history at Cambridge," he said and gave a little shrug. "I had entrée through familial connections. But you might be surprised how little need there is for brown historians in London, or, indeed, England as a whole. Here, at least, I can use my knowledge to inform choices made in the department, and possibly, though much more rarely, to inform customers of a place or culture they might know nothing about." He took a sip of his coffee. "And, of course, the pay is good. I hope to one day marry, and H&C, for now, is something stable that I can build on. Even if it isn't where I saw myself being."

Michel nodded.

"This I understand. When I was a young man in Paris, I never imagined I would be making a life for myself in the city of London, spending my days at a bejeweled shop."

"I have a cousin," said Mister Singh, "who recently spent some time in France—quite a bit actually. He told me so many stories. He is the son of my uncle who has given me a home here in London. My father was the personal secretary to a maharaja, which sounds illustrious but doesn't fill the coffers."

"Did your cousin like France?"

"Oh, yes, I think it somehow changed him forever." Mister Singh chuckled to himself. "It's funny, you know, my cousin could so better pass as an Englishman than I and yet I think I am far more the proper son Uncle wanted."

Nico was suddenly struck with a memory of Mother Newbold's words about sons. "How do you mean?" he asked.

"In as much as Monty is fair-skinned and there is so much of his English mother about him, in the looks, I mean, as well as disposition. He was educated at all the proper schools, he met all the proper society, and has existed in those proper circles all his life. Yet I will be the one to have a wife, and make a family, and establish myself in a respectable line of work. These are my ambitions."

"And they're not those of your cousin?" asked Nico.

"No, it is not in his nature. That is not a criticism—not coming from me, at least. It is simply how the man is made. His father shall never see it though, I am afraid. Uncle so desperately wants his son to be the proper thing so that he might avoid the struggles Uncle faced coming to this country. He wants it so desperately that I fear he often looks past his son's contentment.

"And my cousin has become so worried about doing things

the improper way, the improprietous way, even, that he has hemmed himself in so much he hardly allows himself to enjoy life properly. But a man can only push down his natural inclinations for so long until they express themselves as something entirely haphazard or without reason." He looked at his pocket watch. "I ought to get to work. I didn't mean to burden you gentlemen with such talk of my family and their troubles. It's not at all relevant."

"Not at all," said Nico. "I appreciate your words, Mister Singh. You seem very wise."

"Wise? No, not very. I am only a very good salesman. And that comes with the gift of being able to see things about people they don't even see in themselves."

"Like how many rugs they might need for their townhouse?" asked Michel, smiling.

"Precisely," said Mister Singh with a laugh. "And if they do not see within themselves the need for six vases, all imported and steeply priced, well, I must convince them, mustn't I?"

Mister Singh stood and gave a small bow.

"Gentlemen, I wish you good day. I expect the event to be a smashing success and I have enjoyed our talk."

For a moment, Nico and Michel sat at the table, both taking in the view. It was a nice day, perfect for the meeting here, with the sun bright, but not too hot, and the clouds rolling softly against the grey-blue sky.

Something had been troubling Nico all morning, and he was glad that he might discuss it with Michel. Still, he was awash with mild trepidation, the source of which he did not entirely understand.

"I had thought Monsieur Henri would be here this morning," Nico said finally. "Since we were finalizing the event."

"Yes, he did mention that he might not be able to attend. Some meeting he had this morning; I think it may have been related to his family or some such."

"So nothing is wrong then?"

"No, no, I do not believe so. Something routine."

Nico nodded and stared at his demitasse cup for a moment.

"Monsieur Michel," Nico began.

"Yes, Mister Kavafis?"

"Nico, please."

"Nico, then. And you must call me Michel. We are practically family at this point, at any rate."

"Are we?"

"If not now, then soon, I feel. After all, you have become Henri's closest friend of late. And Henri is like my brother, so I think that connects us some way."

This prompted a question in Nico's mind that he had not been bold enough to ask before. Now seemed the time.

"And has he always been only a brother?"

Michel chuckled and straightened his demitasse on its saucer.

"You needn't worry, Nico," he said. "We have only ever been friends. There is no threat from me."

Nico dipped his head. "I didn't mean to insinuate any threat, of course. I was only curious. I am surprised, to be honest, given how close the two of you are."

Michel nodded.

"You must never tell him that I told you, but, at one time, Henri was interested in more. We formed a bond very quickly when we first met, which I think was unusual for him. Of course, that did not mean he courted me." Michel laughed. "No, I suffered many months of his jutting jaw and snappish quips, before he made a veiled confession. But I let him know, in the kindest way, that we did not share that particular interest."

Nico was surprised.

"Was it that easy? Most men would have broken his nose for such a confession."

Michel gave him a wry smile.

"Knowing Henri, he might have preferred that I had broken his nose. You know how he can be. I know now, as I knew then, that he cherishes me as a friend." Michel leaned forward a bit and looked thoughtful. "The truth is, if I were capable of loving men in that way, I would have loved Henri. Probably very much; but that is not my way. Besides, it is much better this way—look at the partners we have become. Even if I had preferred men, and I had chosen Henri, he would have driven me absolutely mad. How many times I have thought to smack him about the head with a spoon, and that is only the passion of friendship. You are brave to wade into those waters—mind you don't lose your toes."

Nico laughed. "How are you so easy with this? Most men I've known would rather strangle you than utter any words about 'unnatural acts.'"

Michel sat back, waving his hand.

"Unnatural? Bah. What is unnatural? Possibly I am unnatural in the brain myself if I have never understood such attitudes but I shall never concede to them. If my own son were so inclined when he reached maturity, people would expect me to shun him, despise him? My own beautiful, wonderful son. I could never. Jamais. Non. That. That is unnatural."

Nico had always been quite fond of Michel, but now he could see why Henri had clung so closely to this friend, this true friend. "I think you are wonderful," he said.

"Don't let Henri hear you say that. He is very jealous of those he cares about. You may have noticed."

"Oh, yes, I have noticed indeed. But I find his jealousy slightly charming."

"You will feast for years, then."

"Was he ever jealous of Edith?"

"Oh, yes, bien sûr. Quite. At first. But, as is his way, he was silent about it. So silent, in fact, that I worried he might poison her sherry. Once he trusted her, however, it was pure devotion. He is like that."

Nico hesitated. "You know... he has said he loves me."

"Mon dieu! Then you are as special, as I suspected. More so even."

"Am I? I often feel so unsure."

"You mustn't. That is just Henri's way. I have never heard him once confess that sentiment for anyone in all the years I have known him. It is not given easily, his devotion or love. If he has managed to pry those words from his stubborn lips, then they are true. Despite his irascible qualities when he is devoted, little can break his devotion."

Nico nodded thoughtfully.

"Do you mind my asking," Michel began, "But is this feeling one you share?"

"Yes," Nico said without hesitation. "Perhaps I am a fool to know so definitely, but it is. I think maybe I have loved him since the moment I saw him."

"Yes. He is an extremely loveable man. And yet it is entirely a mystery to as to why, *n'est-ce pas?*"

They laughed.

"Come," said Michel. "We will be needed in the Royal Tea Room soon and we don't want Le Roi himself to come looking for us."

IT HAD BEEN quite some time since Henri had been in a gentlemen's club. While working at the Carlton, he had been invited to one or two of them a handful of times by various patrons, sometimes working for an event, but he had never enjoyed the atmosphere. The paneling and trim work all around felt oppressive despite its opulent aim. There was always the smell of age and cigar smoke and one too many spilled whiskies. No amount of Nixey's Blue, or Black Lead, or Watson's Matchless cleanser could defeat the cloistered decades of a place like this. He judged that it gave many comfort in its solid, indestructible sameness, but it put him on edge.

The library of The Travellers Club was admittedly one of the brighter spaces he had attended while at a club, with its bookcases going round the room and the homely chandeliers hanging above the leather chairs. Even so, as soon as he entered, he felt the urge to flee. He was led by the steward to a wingback chair near the fire where he found Lord Ockley, reading the morning's paper and smoking a pipe. Ockley greeted him gruffly and suggested they find a more private table to have their meeting. Only a room away, it was a small table for two against a large window.

Ockley nodded at the steward once they were seated.

"A drink, shall we? I'll have a brandy. What about you?"

"Wine, please," Henri said.

"Ah, of course. I'm told we have a Greek variety, which might be to your taste."

Henri gave him a weary look.

"Burgundy is fine, thank you."

As they waited for their drinks, Ockley examined him.

"Are you actually French?" he finally asked.

Henri was caught off-guard. What a ridiculous question.

"I beg your pardon?"

Ockley leaned forward on an elbow, puffing his pipe.

"Or is it just an affectation? Everyone is always so impressed by French chefs. I wonder if you aren't from Cheshire or some such and have everybody fooled."

Henri steepled his fingers in front of him.

"My father was the son of an English physician who married my French mother and I grew up in the Loire Valley. Which is in France, monsieur."

"And did your mother own a vineyard?"

"My mother was the daughter of a vigneron; they did not own the vineyard."

Ockley chuckled. "Don't tell me your grandfather was stomping grapes barefooted and all that."

"No. He was more of a land manager. And well-respected."

Ockley nodded and knocked his pipe out in the small dish on the table.

"Still," he said, "quite a step down for an English family, even if they were middle class. Can't imagine your father's parents were too happy about all that."

Henri was unable to check his impatience. "Why are we meeting today? I'm sure it can't be to discuss my family history."

Ockley shrugged. "Just trying to get a feel of things."

"What sort of things?"

"Well, mainly what type of resources you might have. As I suspected, I'm likely your only option."

Their drinks arrived. Henri took a sip of wine to steel himself. "My 'only option', you said? I'm afraid I do not follow your meaning."

"My man at the bank told me you were there." He swirled his brandy in the snifter. "Looking for a loan, he said—for your restaurant."

"What? How do you know of this?"

"Oh, don't be troubled, old chap. I've many friends there, of course, and when my chap heard you were the chef from H&C he was quite curious, of course. I often reward him for being quite curious, you see. Since he knew that I was working with Hartridge and the Spaniard, he paid attention."

Henri stared at him in disbelief.

"Quite a shame they weren't able to grant you the loan," Ockley continued. "Quite a shame. Of course, you can't play them. You might have saved up a guinea or two, but they can't put much reliance on a cook in a department store who doesn't have any family backing, can they?"

Henri sipped his wine and tried to keep his tone as even as possible. "Did you have anything to do with my being denied?"

"I can't see how. What have you got for a loan, really, my boy? No real capital or collateral. Businesses are not built on good ideas alone."

"Unless the ideas come from someone of a particular class."

"That's neither here nor there," Ockley harrumphed. "The point is I am prepared to help you. I can stand for the loan."

"Why would I want you to fund me?" Henri snapped.

Ockley smiled and smoothed his moustache. He leaned forward onto the table. "You know, we're not so different you and I, really. We both know exactly what we want. When I was young, I knew the expectations of me. I left, sought out new countries, new adventures, to fend off the inevitable reach of duty. I thought once I had gotten out into the world a bit, sown my wild oats, as they say, I could come back and take my place. But I came back from my explorations knowing two things for certain: that I was no longer a Christian and that I desired only men.

"But I wasn't enough of a fool to not know what that meant. And I know you are not as well. At school, there were touches, gestures, friendships, that had awakened both my body and my heart, but they could not exist in my life. I could not touch an English man, could not tarnish that part of myself, make myself known in that way. But those lands so far away—there I could indulge in anything I wanted. With those naive boys, in Italy, Greece, North Africa—the boys who were almost savage in their ignorance of propriety and shame—with them I did not have to worry. I could fulfill my desire with no consequence."

Henri could hardly contain his disdain. His hand itched to throw his wine in this man's face and be done with it, but he resisted. "The only thing savage in all these musings seems to be you, sir."

Ockley laughed. "I know you know the allure, monsieur, do not play the saint with me. Look at your boy, the Greek. Your Nico."

"He has nothing to do with this. Don't you speak his name."

Ockley gave him a look and leaned back in his chair, taking a long sip of brandy. "Do you know; he reminds me of a boy I met once. Years ago, on the docks in Sicily. A beautiful black-haired creature. Made a living carrying sacks of lily flour. He was more ardent and more pliable than a bitch in heat. You could have him for a pack of cigarettes and a litre of wine. They're like that, you know, those Mediterranean types. The North Africans too. I think it's the heat of the climes; makes then languorous, both in mind and morality." He sneered at Henri. "Not at all like you French, with your withering looks and philosophies of contempt."

Henri narrowed his eyes and leaned in. "I cannot speak to the true nature of your lily-flour friend. But I shouldn't think you ought to judge an entire race by one or two encounters. Any more than I would assume all English are lacking and lecherous, having been acquainted with you these past weeks."

Ockley smacked his glass on the table.

"I will have the boy," he stated.

"He is not a boy; he is a man. He is not an object, and he is not mine to give. You will have nothing that is not freely given you."

Ockley shook his head, running his tongue over his lip. "Nevertheless, I will have him. What choice does he have? He's a black-haired little servant boy with barely enough coin to pay for his own livery. What exactly do you think you can give him, monsieur? Nothing except more drudgery, scraping to earn every penny. For all your airs, you're still just a bloody cook, man. And you want to open a restaurant—you hope he runs it with you? Then you will still be just two cooks. Still sweating in a kitchen, bowing and scraping to your social betters all for want of a bank bill. I, on the other hand, can keep him how he deserves to be kept. I can give him anything imaginable, so long as he gives me what I need. What can you give him but a bent back and chilblains? I would be his escape from all that."

"You would be anyone's prison."

Ockley examined him. "You would do well to think it over, young man. These kind of opportunities don't come along often."

"Your terms are impossible. Any other man might wring your neck for suggesting them."

"Any other man would have better sense. Don't let your cock get in your way. It's all right for you. You have training, connections, and a history of a notable beginning. If you fail spectacularly now, you will go on. You will be given a character reference, you will have somewhere, whatever place, to go. You may be starting at zero again, but you will go on. What about your boy? He has no such pedigree. If he fails, he has nothing, nowhere to go."

Henri could feel his skin burn with fire, his jaw felt like it might crack loose from his face. He gulped the last of his wine. "He will have me."

"That? That is very little in the scheme of things."

"And what makes you think I shall fail spectacularly?"

"I shall make sure of it, monsieur. I shall make damned sure of it. Relinquish your hold on him or I will ruin you both. Spectacularly."

"What is your obsession?"

"I have no obsession. I have everything I want. I get everything I want. And I will get this too. Think it over." Ockley sat back again, raising his hand. "The steward will show you out. Good day, monsieur."

✦ ━━━ • ━━━ ✦

CHAPTER ELEVEN

HENRI SAT AT the small desk in the kitchen cubicle. It was little more than a large closet of a room that he, Michel, and Plaistow used for the administrative things of the kitchen. There were ledgers to check balances, supplies, and inventory, as well as a telephone which connected to the switchboard for placing orders or contacting the staff offices. Henri sat, staring out of the small window to one side, the façade of the building across the street a blur in his vision, lost in thought and feeling wretched.

After doling out instructions for the day, he had made himself scarce. As long as he kept himself sequestered, he thought, he would be hemmed in. Unable to make any more terrible decisions. If only he had listened to himself all those weeks ago. If only he had ignored his feelings and ignored that man, that beautiful man who had haunted his waking life ever since.

"Why are you hiding out back here?"

Michel stood in the doorway and peered in. Henri blinked and shook the thoughts from his mind.

"Michel. How are the preparations coming?"

"Everything that can be done has been done. All the supplies are ordered and stocked. Now it is just to have it done in the morning. Mrs. Plaistow is closing the Tea Room before the dinner shift tonight, so that all the canteen staff who shall attend tomorrow can have the night off to rest up. She tells me a toast is planned this evening to thank them all for their help. Mister Singh and his crew of helpers from the soft furnishings department will be here in the morning to prepare the space. The floral department may need to use the larder to keep the arrangements until just before the event."

"Fine. Good." Henri's voice was flat, listless.

Michel approached the desk, looking worried.

"But, Henri, what is wrong? You look as if you haven't slept in years. Can you be so worried about tomorrow? You will be a triumph as always."

Henri covered his face with his hands and sighed.

"I fear not."

"I've never seen you so stressed. Tell me, mon frère, what is troubling you so."

Henri turned to his friend, and from the expression in Michel's eyes, he could tell he wore every inch of his emotions on his face.

"Oh, Michel. How can I begin to—" Henri halted. "What are you doing here? What do you want?"

He was staring at the doorway and Michel turned his head to follow his gaze. Mister Grey was standing there, as somber as a corpse, seemingly appeared from the ether.

"Lord Ockley has sent me," said Mister Grey.

"Obviously," answered Henri. "I do not expect you have enough will of your own to propel you down a sidewalk."

There was a slight shifting of facial expression, that on anyone other than Mister Grey might have been a smile.

"His lordship sends me to make an inquiry. He wonders if you have further considered his proposal that you discussed at his club? He needs an answer today."

"At his club?" Michel interjected. "Henri?"

Henri shook his head at Michel. He glared at Mister Grey. "There was no need to consider further. Tell your master that I reject his offer, wholly and completely."

Mister Grey looked at him, his reptilian gaze unreadable. He glanced at Michel and then back at Henri. "Excuse me, Monsieur Newbold, it is not my place to offer my opinion on his lordship's personal affairs—"

"No. It is not," snapped Henri.

Grey continued unfazed, his voice soft but steady. "But I really think you ought to contemplate the ramifications of your decision. Lord Ockley takes no matter lightly when it comes to an ambition or want. He will achieve his goal. Or erase the barrier completely."

Mister Grey folded his arms behind his back and stared at Henri, waiting for a reply.

"Then let him do his best," Henri said. "My answer remains unchanged."

Grey waited a moment longer, his expression bland. Finally, he made a noise that sounded something like a sigh but with less animation.

"Very well. If that is all—"

"It is. That is all there is to say."

Mister Grey gave a small bow. "Best of luck, Monsieur New-bold."

Michel watched him leave and turned to Henri. "What the hell is going on, Henri? That was the most unveiled veiled exchange of threats I have yet to see. Something feels quite sinister."

Henri collapsed in the chair.

"Ockley has threatened to make known what he knows of us. Nico and I."

"Why that bastard. But—But I assumed that—I got the impression that Ockley was…"

"Yes, yes. He is like us. That is why."

"I don't understand."

"He wants Nico. He thinks that I am standing in the way of his—his conquest, I suppose."

"But that is ridiculous."

"Of course it is. But he believes it. And he is determined to ruin me, to ruin us both, if he cannot get what he wants."

Henri felt the desperation screaming behind his temples.

"What am I to do, Michel? Before Nico, I only had one goal; now I am torn. I tucked the rest of that away. I ignored that part of myself, the deep want, the need—so that I could be the chef I wanted to be. A chef is not a piano player or a painter. Without a place, without someone to present his work to, he is nothing. Nothing but a silly man in an apron standing over a saucepan. They do not let me be both a man and a chef. I cannot be whole."

Michel put his hand on Henri's shoulder.

"If you really, truly love him, then none of the rest of this matters, Henri."

"Would you give up everything else for Edith, Michael?"

"Of course, without question. Wouldn't you do the same?"

"Yes, I would. That's what frightens me. I do not think I can let him go."

"But then that's it, why should you?"

"But Michel, how can I destroy him too? I am willing to destroy this, destroy myself to be with Nico. But I cannot ask him to throw his chances away for me."

Michel shook his head.

"That is his decision to make. He loves you; he will not want to lose you."

"How can you be so sure?"

"Because he has told me."

Henri looked at him in surprise. "Has he?"

"Yes. In no uncertain terms."

"But I cannot bear to see him suffer, not because of me. All of this is my fault."

"If he has you, he will not suffer, Henri."

But Henri was not so sure of this. He was not certain that he was enough; that his love for Nico could sustain a life of ruin at his hands. He hopped up from the chair and went to the window, leaning against the frame. He wondered if he ought not to call the whole thing off. Tell H&C that it could not happen. Maybe he could escape. Abandon this city, this country. Maybe Nico would be willing to flee with him. They could go somewhere; they could go to the countryside in France, visit his mother, stay there, buy a cottage and live off the land, secluded, disconnected, safe.

"I think maybe you have made too much of this. Do you really think Ockley would do something to jeopardize his own event? Out of spite?"

"I think he is capable of it, Michel. He is a man who is used to getting what he wants in life, and he will not be dissuaded. A ruined event will be little more than an anecdote to tell his friends over a weekend retreat."

But it would follow him. And Nico. No matter where they ran. To the countryside of France, to the other side of England, across the oceans. It would follow them. Ockley would see to that. He had the connections, the reach, the power. They would forever be marked, be stained, not only in the eyes of London society but all society.

"He is trying to bully you into giving him what he wants," Michel said. "Like a spoiled child. Sometimes you must hold out against their tantrums to teach them a lesson."

Henri only shrugged. Michel took Henri's face in his hands and stared into his eyes. "You will know what to do when the moment is here, Henri. You will know."

"Will I?"

"Yes."

But Henri feared he already knew what he must do.

"Is everything all right?"

They both turned to see Nico.

"They told me I could find you here," he said. "Is there any-thing the matter?"

Henri shook his head and turned back to the window.

"No, no," said Michel. "Only a bit of nerves that needed calm-ing. I think you have arrived just in time. I will be in the dining room, if anyone needs me."

Michel left, closing the door behind him. Nico came across and stood near Henri, but Henri could not turn to face him. He picked at the paint on the window ledge, his head down.

"Henri? Is there anything I can do?"

Henri closed his eyes tightly and breathed in deeply. He willed himself to keep his voice steady. He stepped into his chef persona; slipping it on like he did his toque. He must be convincing, he told himself.

"I think it is better if you are not here, Nico."

He did not look at him, but Henri could sense the surprise in Nico.

"Right now, you mean? Are your nerves so bad as that?"

"No, not right now. But – yes, right now. But also… Tomorrow too."

"What?" Nico was shocked.

Henri straightened his back, felt himself adopt the persona. He turned to Nico. "I think it is best if you do not attend the luncheon," he said in his most reproving tone.

Nico took a step back as if pushed. "Henri? What are you saying Henri?"

"Of course, I will give you all the credit deserved for any success."

Nico's face was a mix of emotions, none of them good. "I do not understand. You're kicking me off the event?"

"I think it is best if it is only me here tomorrow."

Nico lifted his hands. He shook his head. Henri tried to steel himself.

"I do not understand. Are you so desperate for the recognition as that? If it means that much to you Henri, you can have all the credit. My ambition is not why I am here."

Henri flailed inside; he felt as if he were hurling himself down a flight of stairs. He must make Nico hear him. He chose the easiest avenue, the nearest narrative to the truth.

"But—But, my ambition is why I am here. I have appreciated your assistance—"

"My assistance? We have worked together as a team. We have collaborated in this creation. I have not been merely a sous chef, Henri. I—we have been more than that. And you know it. But, as I said, if you need it to be such—"

"I am the chef. I should be here. I should take responsibility," Henri proclaimed. "This—all of this—it is mine to claim."

He meant to be stern, but the nerves made him practically shout. He sounded on the brink of rage.

"Henri, I do not understand…" Nico's eyes were so full of pain.

Henri felt a stabbing pain in his chest, like a knife brought to heat over a flame, cutting through him. His nerves seemed to light on fire, burn into ash, crumble beneath his skin. He stomped his foot to bring himself into focus. "As I said, I am the chef. This is my responsibility."

Nico's shoulders fell. He seemed to collapse from the inside.

"And I am a just the lowly waiter. Is that it? Only meant to carry plates and fold the napkins?"

"That is not what I—"

"Enough, Henri. I cannot believe we are back in this place again. I know what your career means to you, but I cannot believe you would cast me aside so easily as this. For this. Not after all we have shared."

Henri railed against himself. He wanted to fall to his knees and beg for Nico's forgiveness; tell him everything. But all he could see in his mind's eye was that vicious bulldog face of Ockley, and the threat of ruin. How could he throw Nico on the open flames like that, destroy what he managed to start for himself here at H&C? He had everything in front of him; he could not let himself be the thing that halted Nico when he was making his first steps towards a new life. How could he let Ockley manipulate him like that? Perhaps, if Nico only disappeared, if he separated himself from this debacle, he would not be stained by whatever the outcome may be. Maybe Ockley would relent and see sense, and they could get on. Separate but safe. Apart but whole.

But would they be whole apart?

"This world does not give us pathways to happiness so easily," he blurted out, his voice hard. "We cannot have everything we want, Nico. Not those like you and I. Sometimes we cannot have anything we want, or need. Sometimes we must choose in order to survive."

Nico lifted his chin. He stared at Henri, his expression defiant. "But that is the difference then. I would choose you over all of this."

Henri tried not to show how those words were like a blow to the gut. "You cannot. You do not really mean that."

"I do. I mean it with every inch of my soul."

They looked at each other for a long moment. Henri could not withstand those eyes, that face. Finally, he turned away. He clutched onto the desk chair behind him, his eyes burned, his throat felt like sand. "And that is why you must go."

"Henri—"

"Go, Nico. Go."

Nico let out a noise, a sound like being struck. Something between a sigh and a cry. Henri heard a cacophony of thuds and wallops as Nico angrily shoved a pile of ledgers onto the floor.

"I do not understand you, Henri Newbold. I do not understand you one bit."

"I know," Henri said, though he could not be sure if he spoke above a whisper.

"I hope you get what you want, Henri. I hope you get what you deserve for this."

Henri nodded, closing his eyes against the tears burning there. "I am sure I shall."

Henri could not turn to watch him go. But he must, he told himself. What if this is the last time they see each other? He could not bear not to see his beautiful face once more.

He turned and saw Nico's ragged posture as he slunk towards the door.

"Nico," he said, his voice a fierce whisper. He forced the words out. "Nico. You must know that I really do—"

"Don't!" Nico stopped. "Don't you dare say you love me, Henri."

Nico's words were raw and heavy. He turned to Henri, his eyes red-rimmed, his expression pure pain. "How dare you use that word against me? How dare you kick me into the gutter and then throw me cakes to eat?"

"Nico…"

Nico hesitated at the door, turning his head before exiting.

"Adieu, monsieur," he said. His voice was soft, low, but the words sounded like a snarl.

Henri fell back against the desk, resting on its edge. His head spun, his heart beating in his chest as if he had run a mile. He pressed the palms of his hands against his closed eyes and tried to steady his breathing. It took all the strength he had left in his body to keep the sobs at bay, the sobs he felt clawing at his chest, trying to rip their way out of his body.

His mind was like a rush of white noise as one phrase repeated over and over again silently: What have I done?

NICO STORMED DOWN the back hallway, towards the staff stairwell, every inch of his skin on fire. He did not understand, he could not understand, how Henri could speak to him in such a fashion. Did these last few weeks mean nothing to him? The hesitancy, the fear, even, Nico could deal with. He understood the time and place they found themselves in and the maze they had to maneuver to express their affection. Mazes he could handle, strategy he could manage, but running repeatedly into brick walls, he could not. If only Henri were not so reactive—so bull-headed and temperamental. All Nico asked for was a bit of space, just a small shaft of light shining through in which to wedge his foot. He didn't expect all the doors and windows to be thrown open to the world; all he wanted was a space, a place near Henri. He could accept arm's length but not a closed fist.

The thoughts made him itch with frustration and anger. He wanted to lash out, to strike something down. He had half a mind to march back into the kitchens and clip Henri in the jaw. But he knew that would solve absolutely nothing. It would only make things worse. He must get out of this damned store immediately.

He stopped suddenly, surprised to see two figures crouched in the back hall. Looking closely, he saw it was Lord Ockley and Mister Grey. Ockley's posture suggested he was on guard, and his face fell into a mocking gaze when he saw Nico.

"Why if it isn't the handsome Greek," Ockley said. He stashed the small bottle he was holding in his jacket pocket. "Has Henri convinced you to change your mind after all?"

"What are you talking about? Out of my way."

Nico tried to push past them both, but Ockley grabbed him by the arm.

"Where are you going, dear boy? You can't leave yet."

Nico shot daggers with his eyes.

"I can. And I am."

"But we're only just about to celebrate, to toast the entire staff." Ockley waved his hand at Grey and Nico saw the opened bottles of champagne he held in his hands. Two more sat at his feet. "But maybe we can toast just the two of us?"

"I am in no mood to celebrate, sir. Most especially not with you."

Nico began to move again and Ockley's grip tightened.

"Now, now, dear boy, I insist. If you won't stay with me, then you must be feted for all you've done. You and your chef."

Nico jerked his arm out of the man's grasp.

"I wouldn't want to be feted by anyone such as yourself."

"Don't be insulting, boy. After all, I still have some sway over your beloved store owners. You wouldn't want to risk your job, would you?"

He placed his hand on Nico's shoulder and began to massage it. Nico shrugged him off fiercely.

"Keep your hands off me," he spat.

"Now, see here, you swarthy brute," Ockley's voice was loud and hard; he stepped forward. "You will not speak to me like that. Do you know the power I hold?"

"I could not care less about anything you hold."

"I do not care if your simple little feelings have been hurt. Or if you have had words with that dirty French friend of yours. This is *my* event, and your presence in it has only been allowed by my grace. So when I tell you to attend the toast, you shall attend. Now get in that room and take a drink like everyone else."

The fire that had danced on Nico's skin only moments before swirled through his body, lighting up every limb and curling into a rage in the center of his stomach. He took a step forward, his fists clenched.

Ockley saw his fists and laughed. "There it is, that equatorial temper. Men like you are even more beautiful when your anger flares; you only need someone knowledgeable to properly stoke the embers."

And in that moment, the fire raging within Nico was extinguished with a blink. A heady calm, like the moment after one splashes icy water on one's face, came over him. The bonfire in his gut disappeared and was replaced with an oily, sick feeling.

He looked at Ockley then and every bit of anger and repulsion he had ever felt for the man coalesced into pity and disgust. He spat at Ockley's feet.

"And men like you disgust me," Nico said, his voice cold and steely. "You think you hold power over others when the truth is you do not even hold power over yourself. You are but a meager-minded child, ruled over by your lack of character and unable to overcome the depths of insecurity you lack knowing how pitiable and tragic you really are. You are totally devoid of empathy and soul." Mister Grey gasped loudly. "I won't take a drink from you. Nor anything else your hands might have touched. I wouldn't care to be stained by the soil of their association with a creature like you."

"Why you," Ockley roared. He stepped forward, raising his arm as if to strike Nico.

"If you dare, you had better make sure it is a blow that fells me completely," said Nico. "Else you will deeply regret what comes next."

Ockley froze, his arm still raised. Nico could see the beads of perspiration on his forehead; his upper lip, beneath the appalling waxed moustache, trembled. His eyes seemed to glisten as if tears threatened, but he did not move.

"Sir." Mister Grey stepped forward, still holding the bottles of champagne. "Lord Ockley. Sir. We really ought to be going. The champagne, sir, will go flat."

Fire flashed in Ockley's eyes. He shoved Grey hard. "I know that, you bloody fool."

He spun round and snatched the other two bottles from the floor. "Get moving, you idiot," he commanded Grey.

He did not look at Nico as he turned and headed down the hallway but he did call out.

"Don't think this is over, boy," he announced, his tone once again supercilious. "It is you who shall deeply regret what comes next."

Nico felt aswim, rocked by a storm of conflicting emotions crashing within him. He did not have the energy or sense of mind to respond to Ockley, he only turned and jogged down the corridor. He reached the back stairwell and as his legs pumped, skipping two, three steps at a time, he propelled himself toward the exit, desperate to fill his lungs with the stifling, heavy air of London's summer evening.

"Henri, are you coming out?" asked Michel.

Henri, still sitting at the desk, frozen in expression like one of the caryatids on the store front, turned his head.

"What?"

"They've closed for the evening, and they're about to toast the staff before dismissing them." Michel hesitated. "Lord Ockley has brought the champagne."

Henri spun in his seat. "Ockley? That brute is here? Now?"

Michel nodded.

"Give my apologies, Michel. Say I am not feeling well. Say I am busy. Say I have thrown myself through the kitchen window and onto the street. But I will not come drink champagne with that man."

"I will give the staff your apologies." Michel turned to go. "Henri. Where is Nico? I have not seen him since I left this room."

Henri could not answer his friend. He turned in his seat and the tears threatened to cascade again.

"Henri, what has happened?"

"Non, non, non," he said, his voice a rapid gasp. "Je ne veux pas en parler. Pas maintenant."

"Henri?"

Michel came towards him.

"Non!" Henri held up his hand, his voice a plea. "Non, Michel. S'il te plaît. Non."

"Oh, Henri."

He could tell his friend wanted to do more, but Henri knew Michel knew him too well. He quietly left the room, leaving him to his thoughts.

A few minutes later, there was the sound of someone entering the room.

"Michel." Henri sighed. "J'insiste."

"Afraid I don't speak French, what."

Henri turned to see Lord Ockley come into the kitchen cubicle carrying a flute of champagne. He could hardly contain the urge to leap at the man, to throttle him where he stood.

"It isn't particularly good form, old man, if the general is hiding in the larder while the troops celebrate," said Ockley.

"I'm sure the staff will be able to celebrate just as well whether I am present or not."

"I only mean to celebrate your achievement tonight and you turn away my hospitality. My dear sir, you wound me."

Henri snarled at him. "I shouldn't think your feelings are so easily hurt, Lord Ockley."

"It is true I might not be as temperamental as some," said Ockley, his voice slick with derision. "But even a proper Englishman still has emotions, monsieur."

"I don't doubt that to be true," said Henri. "Perhaps we can find one to test the idea."

"It's a shame your Greek isn't here, you know. I get the impression that the two of you have had a falling out of some sort."

Henri glared at him. "If your plan is to ruin me, I suggest you get it over with. I do not have the further patience for your games."

Ockley looked at him smugly. "I think you thought somehow you were saving him, did you not? Whether he is here to witness your failure or not doesn't matter, monsieur. Scandal has never needed a willing participant. People will believe what it not true without question, but half-truths, suspicions, are even more powerful. They become like gospel. And what is thought gospel determines what leads to damnation."

Ockley came to the desk and put down the glass of champagne. "You ought to enjoy one last glass."

Henri held Ockley's gaze. "Before the day ends, of course," added Ockley.

"This is still my kitchen," Henri said as coldly as he could. "And I insist you leave it immediately."

"Quite obliged to. Wouldn't want to get dirty back here, around all this muck."

STILL, HENRI DID not move. He sat there, immobile, at the desk, replaying the afternoon, the last weeks, all of his mistakes, in his mind. He tried to quell the urge that struck him every few minutes to race from the building and get to Finsbury Circle as quickly as possible, to rap loudly on the door until it opened and he could see Nico's face again. To throw himself at his feet and beg for his forgiveness; to plead for him to forget any of the foolish and harsh things Henri had ever said.

But there were so many things, where would he begin? Henri knew he had made a complete shambles of everything.

"Henri."

Michel had returned. Henri sighed in exhaustion. This was too much; maybe he should leave, wander the streets, contemplate the Thames.

"Henri!"

"Michel," Henri snapped. "I have told you I will not be in the company of that man!"

"It isn't that. Ockley is long gone. It's far more grave."

Michel was not prone to dramatics and, as he turned to him, Henri saw his friend's face looked stricken.

"Tell me, Michel."

"Come." Michel waved and Henri followed. "It's the staff, Henri."

"What about them?"

Just then the main doors of the kitchen burst open and in ran in two cooks. They pushed past Michel and Henri and were headed towards the water closet. The one in the back must have gauged his state and stopped midway, grabbing a nearby pail for used for mopping. Suddenly he wretched, violently, and continued to do so, clearly overcome with sickness. From the Tea Room came the unpleasant groans and noises of others retching as well.

"They were suddenly struck, a number of them," Michel explained. "Great pains in the stomach. They've gone a sickly pallor, groaning, and—"

"Michel?"

Michel doubled over. He groaned and pushed Henri aside to run to the nearest water closet. Henri's hands balled into fists and the image struck him, the champagne flute, still filled with wine, which sat on his desk.

CHAPTER TWELVE

THE STORE WAS quiet at this time of the morning. Most of the shoppers had not arrived, and the murmur of voices that always filled the air was lower, quieter. It reminded Nico of attending mass as a child. The voices in the air, like the chants, the ding of the lifts, like the bells, the waft of perfume all around, like the incense burning. He felt, as he approached the Books and Library Department, that he ought to cross himself and go prostrate before the counter.

Likely he was a fool to even think of coming here this morning, but he had not been able to think of where else to go. He had talked so much about the luncheon event to Seripha and Zetta that he knew he could not stay home this morning and face their barrage of questions. He had avoided them when he returned home the evening before, begging off dinner to rest in his room, a sign they interpreted as nerves, and then leaving quickly in the early morning under the guise of rushing off to work. But today he had no work to rush off to.

Part of him felt a grand temptation to show up in the Royal Tea Room. To be there, against Henri's wishes and harsh words, just to see the look on his smug face. That is, if he were ever allowed again in the Tea Room. After the words he'd exchanged with Ockley as he stormed out, there was no telling what the aftermath may be. The oily devil may have reported him to

Hartridge and Casas, or to Mrs. Plaistow, or any number of people, and his job might be at stake. Still, he regretted nothing he had said to that tragic specimen. Henri, on the other hand. He was full of regrets there. He could have reacted in no other way than how he did to those words. And the wounds were still fresh, still hurt as if they were physical and not just emotional. Still.

Still.

Still, it was Henri. That scared, anxious man he had so come to love. Maybe he should have fought harder. It couldn't be true that Henri really pushed him out for glory and recognition, could it? He'd turned the afternoon over and over all night as he lay in his bed, and he could not make sense of it. Of any of it. It felt unreal, like some sort of cheap theatrical. Composed and executed without rehearsal. How could he have lost both his job and the man he loved so deeply all in a matter of less than an hour? Could it be possible?

He was sure Zetta would tell him it was. She would remind him of her warnings, her cautions, her knowing how dangerous a love like Henri could be. She had told him not to trust the man, and perhaps he should have listened to her. Even now he did not trust his own thoughts, and if he could not trust them, how could he have judged anyone else properly? It was all a shambles in his mind.

So he had come here. The one place he knew gave him solace and sanctuary. He switched the book he was carrying from one hand to the other. If he could escape nowhere else, he knew he could escape into the pages of a book. Distract his mind from the worry of reality. Find hope and the belief in love again. Behind the counter he saw a familiar face.

"Good morning, Hosea."

Hosea looked up, surprised, and slapped shut the book he was perusing.

"Blessed be," he said. He shoved the book to one side. "Crombie was right! You know, I've always suspected her of witchcraft. Not in the true sense, I mean, please don't spread that around. But I certainly would not be the least surprised if she carried a deck of tarot or had some polished gemstone with mystical emanations squirreled away in her underskirts."

"I don't follow. What do you mean about Crombie?"

"She said you might turn up today. Of course, I thought you'd be here anyway, what with you assisting Monsieur with this whole Mediterranean luncheon affair. I'm not much of one for diplomats, strictly speaking, but the athletic angle is always intriguing. I attended some of the swimming events earlier this month. Did you see it? Not open water at all—a giant pool, it must have been a hundred meters long. And the men did move quite lithely." He caught himself. "I'm sorry, I do go on so. At any rate—you must go."

Nico's confusion only deepened.

"Go? But I've just come. I'm here to change my book."

"Oh, I have something you'll love! Leave it with me. I'll change it for you, and you can pick it up anon. But, now, you must go to her. Now! She insisted."

"To whom?"

Hosea sighed. "Crombie, of course. Our resident cooking clairvoyant. She was quite adamant about it. So, go. Before you distract me again with talks of mysticism and mermen."

"But, I am not working today, Hosea. I am only here for my book."

"Entirely not the point," said Hosea, taking the book from his hands. "Now, off with you."

"I beg your pardon?"

Hosea had become thoroughly exasperated, apparently not aware of the irony of such emotion. "Do, listen. Clairvoyant Crumble said that if I were to see you today—and she supposed I likely would—that I was to send you to the kitchens posthaste. Your assistance would be needed desperately, she intimated. But, tread carefully, for there is chaos afoot, as the pinky toe said to the ankle."

"Chaos?"

"In the kitchens, I believe, and the Tea Room as well. It's all rather gone to seed, I take it. Though I can't imagine the cause." He turned to place Nico's book on the shelf behind the counter. "This morning I wasn't even afforded a bun. I mean, can you imagine? I was forced to drink a solitary cup of tea, without so much of a crumb to sustain myself and when I asked whatever the matter was, why the pickings so slim to empty, that's when Crombie said…."

Nico turned and trotted towards the employee lift, waving his hand at his friend, who he could hear go on even as he moved across the floor.

"Well," Hosea called out, rather crestfallen. "I daresay that was a bit rude!" Nico heard him harrumph, and a lady in walking dress approached the counter. "Without so much as a by your leave. I expect it's all those detective stories. All that dashing about, you know. All very well when one is chasing a spring-heeled jack but it doesn't serve you well in polite society, now does it."

"I am sorry," said the lady. "I'm not sure I follow what you're speaking about."

"Not at all, milady. How might I assist you?"

"I was hoping to find a book on French cookery."

Hosea frowned and gave her a knowing look.

"I shouldn't recommend it, milady. Seems to lead to trouble of all sorts, French cookery. Stick with Beeton, I always say. Boiled sweets and beef tea, you'll never be steered wrong there."

DOWNSTAIRS, IN THE employee canteen, everything was go, go, go. They were noticeably short-staffed and people hustled past him. He followed the sound of orders being bellowed and found Mrs. Crombie. When she saw him she broke into a smile.

Mrs. Crombie might otherwise have seemed shattered, if the

state of her uniform was any indication, but instead she glowed with purpose. Her frock was stained, her cap was askew, and she was constantly pushing errant curls of hair from her face, but she held herself like a general who lived for battle.

"Thank goodness you didn't tarry," she said. "I thought it might be later when you finally showed up. There's still time now."

"Why did you think I would come?"

"Listen," she said, getting to her point. "They're all sick. You've got to get up there and help in any way you can, Mister Kavafis."

"Mrs. Crombie, what on earth is going on? And get up where?"

"The Tea Room, of course. Don't be simple, my boy. I'm surprised you didn't go there first.

"What do you mean sick? Who?"

"All the Tea Room staff, of course. All the cooks, all the waiters, every one of them. Vomiting their eyes out like poisoned street cats, they are. I've never seen such a sight."

Poisoned. Nico remembered. Ockley and Grey in the hallway, stashing a bottle in a pocket, open bottles of champagne.

"But why?" he asked out loud.

"Who can say? I've not seen such a time," Mrs. Crombie said, "since the Prince—pardon me, His Majesty, the King—came for a shoot at the Hartridge estate and one of his lady friends choked on the claret. I've sent all the staff I can spare up there. It's not much, really, a few trainees, but until someone else shows up, there's nothing to be done. You must go help Monsieur Henri."

"I don't think Monsieur Henri wants my help, Mrs. Crombie."

"Don't be daft. Of course he does."

"No, you do not know the things he said to me yesterday. Even if he is in need now, I am not sure I ought to."

Mrs. Crombie gave him a quizzical look. She untied her apron and tossed it onto a nearby table.

"Elsie," she said to a woman nearby, "you mind the front. Mister Kavafis needs to borrow some linens for upstairs. Back in two shakes."

Nico did not have time to object as she grabbed his hand and pulled him down the side corridor and into the linen room.

"You can't really think that Monsieur would turn you away, can you?" she said when the door was closed.

"He said as much yesterday. He made it clear that he did not want me here today."

Mrs. Crombie paused for a moment, seeming to gather herself.

"When I worked for Lord Hartridge's family," she began, "I had just been promoted from tweenie to a proper kitchen maid. I had a friend; a great, dear friend. She was the closest friend I ever had and the first person I felt I could truly be myself with. I feared I couldn't live without her. And she felt the same way. We walked to and from church together, behind the cart, just the two of us every Sunday. We took our afternoons off together—even went into the village together. But, then, one day, out of nowhere, she cut me dead. I couldn't understand and I tried for weeks to get her alone again so I could ask her why. But she wouldn't speak to me. Never did again—only once, just to say she had changed her mind on our being friends.

"Not too long after, she left the estate and left service altogether. Last I heard of her she had gotten a job in a shop in the village and ended up marrying the shopkeeper's son. They had a child, maybe more, I never knew. I couldn't bear to know, if I'm honest. The worst part was not so much that she had changed her mind about our friendship. That part I could understand; in some way, I reckon I expected. No, the worst part was never getting to say good-bye to her, never getting to acknowledge how much she meant to me, how much we meant to each other, when it was we meant something."

She was quiet for a moment.

"Do you know why she ended our friendship, Mister Kavafis?"

"No," Nico answered quietly.

"Because she was afraid. Afraid of what she felt. Of what I felt. Of what it could mean if she pursued it."

"I don't see what this has to do with—"

"Of course you do," countered Mrs. Crombie before he could finish his denial. "You're a bright lad, you've got the right side up of most things. And you know very well what I mean."

Nico looked at her, he chewed on his bottom lip, unable to respond.

"You're younger than me. And you're stronger than me too. Stronger than my friend. You've seen a different world."

"Are you unhappy?" Nico blurted out.

"Not anymore, I'm not. Not anymore. But, listen when I tell you, it took a long time. I wasted many a year. I was lucky to find happiness again. There's many that's not so lucky as that."

Nico's thoughts drifted back to Tommy's words, the picture in his mind of Mister Johnston, alone in his room in the dormitories, playing his violin, his paper and his sherry his only friends. The visceral reaction that imagining caused surprised him. He felt a swelling in his chest. He knew he must act.

"Thank you, Mrs. Crombie."

She nodded, grabbing his hand and giving it a squeeze. "Now, get out of my closet," she said. She shoved a stack of folded napkins into his hands. "And here take these with you."

He moved swiftly towards the front of the canteen, breaking into a jog, hugging the napkins to his chest. Suddenly, he was determined.

WHEN HE GOT off the lift in the kitchen, Nico was shocked at the quiet. To one end of the kitchen he heard a clatter and saw Michel leaning against a prep table.

"Michel?"

When Michel turned, Nico saw that he was sickly, yellowed like jaundice, and his shoulders were slumped. He was trying to prep a dish but seemed too weak to continue. Despite the relative cool of the room, he wiped sweat from his brow.

"Oh, Nico," he said, his voice filled with relief. "You've come."

Nico rushed over to him and offered him an arm. He led Michel to a chair, where he collapsed. Nico fetched him a glass of water.

"They're all sick," he said between gulps.

"I heard," said Nico. "Listen, I think it may have been Ockley."

"Yes, the champagne."

"You knew?"

"Henri suspected when everyone got sick, because of..." Michel looked up at him. "Nico. Henri. You must know. Henri, he suspected something like this. He feared that Ockley—he thought—well, he only wanted to save you the destruction."

Nico put his hand on Michel's shoulder.

"I think I understand, Michel. Do not trouble yourself."

Michel nodded and his eyes fluttered shut; he fell back weakly into the chair.

"Where is Henri?"

"He's in the back. He didn't drink anything, so he's unaffected. But it's a failure, Nico. At least it will be. I think he'd rather have been poisoned than deal with that."

Just then David emerged from the back of the kitchen.

"Blimey," he exclaimed. "At least you're here. Good lad. But I don't know how much help you can be now. M'sieur won't leave the larder. I think he's gone balmy."

Nico started towards the larder—he stopped.

"But you're not sick?" he asked.

David shook his head and stuck out his chest.

"My father was a blooming drunk. Never touch the stuff, do

I. Not a bleeding drop. Must have been the wine that did the rest in so poorly."

"See what you can do for Monsieur Michel. He's in a bad state."

Inside, he found Henri. He was squatted by the long table, the one he used for chocolates, with his arms crossed on the table and his forehead resting against his arms.

"Henri," Nico said.

Henri sprung up and spun around. He gasped and staggered back a bit; Nico wondered if he might lose his footing.

"But you have come back," he said, his voice rough. "Pardonne-moi, oh, mon amour."

Nico thought he might burst into weeping. It was not a sight he thought he would ever see from the collected and tightly-knit Henri. It struck him profoundly.

"Forgive me, please," Henri continued. "These last days I have been a wretch. What a fool I have been—for so long. Can you ever forgive me?"

"Henri," Nico began.

Henri rushed forward and, catching himself, stopped. "It was Ockley," he declared. "Only he had tried to demand that I give you up, that I let you be his."

"I would never be anything to that man."

"Of course, I know. But he threatened to destroy us, to destroy us both, if I did not heed his demands. I thought, maybe if you were not here, he could not blame you. That he might somehow take his wrath out on me and me alone. But I have been a fool."

"Bugger his wrath. I do not care what he does or says, whether he ruins me or not. There are some things worth being ruined for."

"Yes. I agree."

Nico was piqued. "Are you sure?"

"What?"

"I mean, are you sure, Henri? This job, this career, this place and making a name for yourself. This is your dream. How can you be ruined and not resent me?"

"Resent you?" Henri seemed genuinely shocked. "It is true. This is my dream—no, it was my dream. My dreams were all I ever had before, Nico. But my dreams have changed. I realize that nothing, no dream, is worth having without you. My dreams are now. They have been since the day I first met you."

Nico had to be sure.

"The day you ignored me and belittled me?"

Henri sagged, his face went slack. He did not speak for a moment.

"I was afraid. Afraid of you, Nico. Afraid of how you made me feel. I was afraid that if I allowed myself to believe in those feelings, to believe in the possibility of having you in my life, of having you close to me, calling you mine, that I might be destroyed. It did not seem possible to have all of that—all of you—and not pay some price somehow. I was not afraid of the destruction loving you would bring to my life, but the destruction I would bring to myself if I had you for a moment and then had to live without you."

Nico felt a force within him, pulling him towards Henri. It was like that invisible rope that had encircled them both on that first day, threatening to crash them into one another. His anger was gone, only the imprint of the hurt was left, like a scar on the skin that fades with time.

"Don't you see this how I felt about you as well? This is why I fought so hard for us. This is why I ignored your moods, your cutting words. Because I knew that somehow we were meant to be together. And I want nothing more. But, Henri, you must not think I am in need of protecting from the world. My hopefulness does not come from not knowing how cruel the world can be, but knowing the cruelty, the lost, the hurt all too well. I chose to defy it, not be cowed by it. I am not some damsel in distress, Henri. Trapped in the tower waiting to unravel my hair so that you may climb up and free me."

Henri walked towards him. "I know you are not. Of course not. If anything, you have freed me, Nico."

He stopped just in front of Nico and they looked at one another. Nico knew in that moment that he could never be truly free of his feelings for this man. No matter how much he chastised himself, no matter how hard he tried. And now, just now, he did not want to try—he had no desire to be free of these feelings. He took Henri's face in his hands.

"Then you must be free of the fear, Henri. I cannot take these swings. One minute fire, the next complete ice. You wound me every time; I want to be whole. For you. I shall need you to be honest with me in future. No more subterfuge."

Henri nodded, tears in his eyes, though he smiled through them. "In future," he said, his smile widening.

"Yes. In our future. I cannot sustain such confusion. You will need to be—"

But Henri grabbed him and kissed him deeply. Nico felt himself give in, letting his body melt against Henri's. How he had wanted this feeling; how he had ached for it this last day, thinking he might somehow be without it. It was a feeling like finding home again, the feeling of their mouths together. The anxiety and fear fled his body, he felt strengthened, sustained.

"Henri..." Nico said when they broke their kiss.

"I completely understand, my love. I must be always truthful, apparent in what I feel. So let me start by telling you that I love you. There is no indecision, no wavering. Even if you were never to speak to me after this moment I would understand why but I must make it plain now. If I am thrown out on the street today, a total failure, none of it would matter. Not without your love. If you no longer love me I cannot blame you. I have been wretched. And I will try to find a way to cope, but even if I do not, you must know the truth. This is the truth, Nico. There is no other truth; there is no other thing which I hold important right now. My love for you is the truth, the only truth."

"All I want is truth," said Nico. "And your love."

They kissed again, but Nico began to push Henri away.

"I must go," he said.

"Where are you going? Are you leaving? I don't blame you but—"

"Do not worry, Henri. No matter what you say, your career is important to you as well. It is in fact, part of why I love you so—your ambition, your fire, your passion. Today you will not fail." Nico pulled him close and kissed him quickly.

"It's all right," he said. "I will fix this."

"But how?" exclaimed Henri. "It does not matter now, Nico."

"I should go."

"But will you come back, Nico? Please say you will not leave me."

"I am here now. Am I not?"

"Oui. You came back to me. Like something magical. How is it possible?"

"The truth, monsieur. It can be magical if you let it be. I will be back, Henri. I will not leave you."

Nico turned and dashed through the kitchen. "David!" he called as he moved through. "You've got the menus? Start the prep. Anything that can hold for a bit."

"Are you sure?" David asked.

Nico stopped at the kitchen door. "Give me an hour," he said. "This luncheon will succeed."

JUST OVER AN hour later, Henri was at the prep table working frantically. He doled out sliced vegetables, dolloped stewed meat, grabbed a bowl of grated cheese. He glanced around, searching for something. As he sprinkled the grated cheese, he faintly registered the kitchen door opening, and he silently cursed David for not staying at hand.

"Merde, I need the sauce," he muttered. He called out, as he concentrated on the task before. "David! Where is the damn béchamel? David, the béchamel!"

"I don't know who David is," he heard a voice say. "But I do hope you won't be speaking to me in that tone of voice."

He looked up.

"Zetta?" he cried in shock.

Nico's sister put her hand on her hip. "Are we using Christian names now?"

"My apologies. Miss Kavafis. I did not expect to see you."

Zetta grabbed a towel and tucked it into the hem of her skirt. "I shall need an apron," she declared.

He heard a ruckus in the dining room. "What is going on out there?"

He paused his work and headed out to take a look. But the door swung open before he reached it and he was caught in a flood of moving bodies. All around voices called to each other, in a tongue he did not know, throwing what he could tell were instructions.

"Que diable! How many people are here?"

"We are all here," exclaimed a short, older man. "Monsieur Henri? I am Persopoulos, maybe you have heard of me?"

"Monsieur Persopoulos. But of course, you run the restaurant. I have heard much about you."

"If you have heard it from Seripha, you must regard it all as lies," said Persopoulos in a jolly tone.

"But what are you doing here?"

"We have come to help, monsieur. Nico told us of your emergency and we are glad to help."

"What?" Henri was overwhelmed. All these people here to help him? And because of Nico? "But your own restaurant, monsieur?"

"We have closed for the afternoon," said Mister Persopoulos. He waved his hand. "It is a slow day. No matter."

"But I don't want you to lose coin for helping me."

"You needn't worry about that," said a deep voice behind

him. Henri turned to find Señor Casas. "H&C will be paying Mister Persopoulos and his staff for their help here today. Plus more to cover expenses and lost business of the afternoon."

"But…." Henri stammered.

"Mister Kavafis sent word of his plan to save the event by way of Mister Hosea. It was rather an unbelievable shock to hear of the unfortunate accident to which the staff succumbed However, once I got Mister Hosea to actually get to the point of the story, it was easily decided that we should help."

"But señor, what can I say?"

"Say nothing now," said Casas. "You have far too much to do in too short a time. So you must work. We have every faith in you and Mister Kavafis and his wonderful crew. I shall leave you to it, then."

As Casas opened the door, Henri followed him into the dining room. There was a large group of wait staff being instructed by Nico. To the side Mrs. Plaistow, Lily, and Seripha seemed to be discussing plans. And, he blinked to see it, Mrs. Plaistow was laughing at something being said. Henri looked back at the wait staff just as Nico turned in his direction. They locked eyes. Henri wanted to shout, to jump in the air and proclaim his thankfulness, to cry out how touched he was. His hands shook from the rush pulsing through him. Instead, he just mouthed "thank you" to Nico.

Nico smiled and nodded before turning back to his staff.

"I can't believe what I have seen," he said as he returned to the prep table.

"The staff will do well, no matter if they aren't as polished as yours," said Zetta.

"No, I don't mean that. I am positive they will be wonderful. I mean, I don't believe I have ever seen Mrs. Plaistow laugh like that before."

"She is the schoolmistress? With the grim expression?" Asked Zetta. Henri nodded. "My aunt must have gotten hold of her. She is a miracle worker, our aunt."

She studied the dishes in front of her at the table. "Is this the dish Nico designed?"

"Yes," Henri said proudly. "I thought it would make a fine centerpiece for today's affair."

Zetta turned a dish one way and then the other. She conceded a nod. "It will do," she said.

"M'sieur," David called out, as he approached. "Monsieur Michel and I come from the larder and found this group of fellows all around. Gabbling like turkeys, they are."

"Not Turkey, no. Wrong country," said Zetta. She looked at Henri. "This must be David then?"

Henri barked a laugh. "David, these gentlemen have come to assist today. You see that gentleman there?" Henri pointed at Persopoulos. "You are to report to him today. Whatever he says, consider it said by me."

"But m'sieur—"

"You needn't worry," interjected Zetta. "He also does not speak Turkish."

David gave her a confused glance before moving off. Michel came up, seemingly stronger than before, if still a bit peaky.

"Henri?" he exclaimed in awe.

"A miracle, Michel."

"By way of Nico no doubt?"

"Biên sur."

Michel shook his head, smiling. "You do not deserve him, Henri. I will be working in the cool room by the chocolates. There I think I may survive."

Henri took his place and began working beside Zetta.

"Your friend is wrong, you know," she said.

"Oh?"

"You are deserving of Nico."

Henri was shocked into stillness. "I never thought to hear you, of all people, say that."

"I have never seen Nico as happy as he has been in these last few weeks," she said as she continued to work. "Nor as motivated. Nor as devoted. For the first time, since he was a boy, I feel like he has found his place."

Henri was overcome. "Even after how I have behaved you still say this to me?"

"Nico explained to me the situation, broadly. You only wanted to protect my brother; I understand that urge. I, too, share it."

"Yes, but he does not need our protection."

"No, in fact, he does not."

Henri could do nothing but stare at her, Nico's sister. His chest felt like it might crack in half from the force of his feelings.

Finally, she looked up. "We do not have time to stand idle, Monsieur Henri," she said. She handed him a dish. "This must get in the oven now."

He took the dish and for a moment they both held it. He caught her gaze.

"Thank you," he said quietly, sincerely.

"Do not thank me yet, monsieur, the afternoon is not over."

He turned to take the dish to the oven, and for a moment he could have sworn he floated instead of walked across the kitchen.

THE AFTERNOON WAS more of a success than Henri could have wished for. The room appeared like something from an art museum, or a fairy story, once Mister Singh and his staff had finished with it. It was regal and tasteful and yet wholly fantastical and breathtaking. The Tea Room was transformed into something resembling a palace. Even Mrs. Plaistow seemed overcome at the transformation. She and Aunt Seripha served as hosts, guiding the arriving Olympic athletes to their tables and making sure they were taken care of in every possible way. Mrs. Plaistow herself escorted Dr. Diakos, along with Ockley, who had the good sense to keep his gaze away from the kitchen at all times, to their special table at the front.

The mixture of Henri's special dishes along with the new recipes by Nico were a tremendous success; Persopoulos himself even crying out at one point that he must have the recipe for Nico's "cream tea" galaktoboureko. The luncheon wound down and the athletes snacked on a selection of fruits, along with coffee, tea, and other beverages as the speeches began. Various members of the Olympic committee, along with notable people of the city, the local Greek community, and friends of Lord Hartridge and Señor Casas all offered words of congratulations and praise to the team. Henri and the rest of the kitchen crew stood in the back of the dining room to listen. Henri stood between Zetta and Seripha.

"And you said you would never work in a kitchen again," Henri said, during a lull, teasing Zetta. "But you were magnificent today."

"Of course I was," answered Zetta. "I never said I was not good at it, only that I did not want to do it."

Henri guffawed.

Zetta studied her hands.

"I have never seen him so devoted, monsieur," she said. "He was always impetuous but this is different somehow. You are different somehow."

"Is that difference good?"

"I haven't decided," she replied, giving him a sharp look. She smiled. "But I am willing to find out."

"I hope Nico is as well. I am afraid I have been a task for him."

"What man is not a task?" asked Seripha. "Even the best ones are exhausting. But you must not fret, Henri. Nico is the most forgiving person I know. He does not make an effort unless he cares for a person. And today he has made a great effort. Whatever harsh words you have shared, I am sure they can be healed."

"I am not sure I am deserving of forgiveness."

"Everyone is deserving of forgiveness, monsieur." She looked up as Ockley passed a few feet in front of them. She glared at him. "Well, maybe not everyone."

"You know, you talk like a poet, just like your nephew," Henri said.

"Of course," exclaimed Seripha. "Where do you think he gets all of his talents?"

THE KITCHEN PRACTICALLY empty, Nico took a moment to enjoy it. Service had been challenging, coordinating Persopoulos' staff who were unfamiliar with the space and how to serve some of the dishes, but it was gratifying. And everything had gone exceedingly well. He was proud, prouder than he could say, of what he and Henri had achieved, and it had thrilled him and warmed his heart beyond measure when he saw his aunt, sister, and Henri all chatting away. So much so that he had not wanted to disturb them and slipped into the kitchen through the lift entrance hall.

He glanced around the space, now still a mess, but a beautiful mess, and beamed. The last day had been one of the saddest days in quite some time, but, in the end, it had been one of the most joyful as well. He could not imagine feeling better than he did in this moment.

"I suppose you think you have succeeded."

Nico jerked around, a bark at the back of his throat. "What do you want, Ockley? Leave me be."

"We could still right this situation, you know," Ockley said. "I am a forgiving man. If you have the good sense to change your mind and consider what I have offered you, it could all go your way."

"This situation has been righted. I have no need of anything from you. Nor would I want it."

"You think this is done? Simply because you served up some

of your slop and made those imbecilic athletes grin. So you pulled off a luncheon, and I had the common decency to not spoil it in front of the guests. This changes nothing. I have not yet got my satisfaction. But I will, one way or another."

"Do your worst, you cretin," snapped Nico, rushing forward. "If we are to be thrown into the streets, at least I will be comforted in never seeing your face ever again."

"Of course you would be comforted in the streets. That is where you and your dirty Frenchman belong!"

"I have had enough of you." Nico grabbed him by the collar and drew back his fist.

"No, Nico, don't!"

Henri was in the room. He held his hands up as he moved towards them. "Don't let him make you do anything you would regret, Nico."

"I do not think I would regret it."

Henri placed his hand on Nico's arm and calmed him; he let go of Ockley, who fell back sputtering.

"Savages," he cried. "The pair of you!" He smoothed the front of his suit, tugging at its hem to straighten it. "Rushing in here to play the hero for this boy," Ockley said. "What a fool you are."

Nico saw Henri's nostrils flare and he stepped close to Ockley. "He is not a boy."

"That's right!" Ockley roared, shoving Henri. "He is not a boy. He is nothing. He is not worthy of pouring my drink. He is just island trash, like his family, and my scullery maid wouldn't deem herself low enough to spit at him in the street."

Nico gasped as Henri reared back and socked Ockley on the jaw. There was a loud smacking sound as his fist connected with the craggy terrain of Ockley's face. Nico rushed forward and threw his arms around Henri to keep him from striking again.

"He is a man," boomed Henri. "The man I love. And you will respect him."

Ockley looked at them both with wide eyes. He wiped the

blood from his lip and let out a bitter laugh.

"'Love'? My god, man, you can't be serious. What a preposterous notion. Yes, I hope you are quite happy with your ridiculous fantasy of love. Because you have cost yourself a career. How dare you put your hands on me? If I don't have you shipped back to whatever peasant village you crawled out from, you'll be lucky to get work peeling potatoes."

"Do your worst," spat Henri. "I am not afraid of you."

"You French really are madder than I had imagined," Ockley said. He headed towards the door, stumbling a bit but then righting himself. "You will remember this moment, Frenchie. And you will regret it."

Nico placed himself in front of Henri, his hands on Henri's biceps, stroking them up and down in a comforting motion. He stared into Henri's eyes and willed him into calm. Slowly, Henri's breathing returned to normal, the red flush of his skin settled back to its usual complexion. Nico studied that handsome face, which seemed more alive than ever before, and smiled.

"So much for not being my rescuer, eh?"

Henri's eyes went soft. "I am sorry, Nico. I could not help myself."

"No, no, do not worry yourself," Nico said with a small chuckle. "I am only teasing you a little. He deserved every bit of that."

"He is a bloody bastard."

"What do you think he will do?"

Henri grabbed him and kissed him roughly at first, and then softly. He pulled Nico close, wrapping him in his arms. Nico felt his hot kisses on his face, his cheeks, his eyes. He leaned his head on Henri's chest.

"I do not care," Henri said, his voice rumbling through his chest. "I do not care what Ockley does. Or Hartridge, or Casas, or any of them. Let this damn store fall down brick by brick, let the whole of London society starve, I do not care. Not without you."

Nico smiled, burying his face against Henri's neck. He was

not sure the man he loved would feel so confident in his proclamation after whatever outcome awaited them, but he looked forward to taking it on by his side.

"Come," he said, "shall we see what damage has been wrought?"

"MISTER KAVAFIS, MONSIEUR Henri, I was just looking for you."

Señor Casas was heading towards them as they excited the kitchen. He was followed by the diplomat who had been speaking, and just behind them Nico saw his aunt and sister following, curious expressions on their faces. A cold shot of worry zipped through Nico.

"I have someone who wants to see you both," said Casas. "Gentlemen, may I introduce Dr. Diakos, our esteemed guest."

Dr. Diakos stepped forward and Nico extended his hand. The diplomat did not immediately take it and Nico was left confused. Diakos stared at him, seemingly in disbelief.

"My God," he exclaimed. "But you are the spitting image of him."

"I'm sorry?" asked Nico.

"Georgios, your father."

"M-my father?"

Diakos shook his head and grabbed Nico's hand. "You must forgive me. When Mister Casas was telling me about the team of people who had produced today's wonderful food, your surname sounded so familiar, so I had to meet you. I wasn't sure it could be true, but I see now that it is.

"You see, I knew your father, when we were very young. I held him in quite high esteem. I was away for many years pursuing my career and he and I fell out of steady contact, and then I heard about the accident. My dearest apologies, dear boy. By the time I was next in Greece, you were gone and I never knew what came of you and your sister."

Nico felt breathless. Other than his aunt and his distant relatives in Greece, none of whom he'd seen in years, he had never met anyone who knew his parents. Hearing these words was like having some piece of his parents with him suddenly, and he felt his throat close up, as if he might sob.

Henri must have sensed this, because he leaned against Nico briefly, their shoulders touching, reassuring.

"This is my sister here," he managed to say.

Dr. Diakos turned towards his sister and aunt. While everyone looked in their direction, Henri slid his fingers over Nico's and squeezed his hand.

"Are you all right?" he whispered.

Nico smiled; he could feel his eyes shining, the tears only held at bay. He nodded.

"Thank you."

"And you too," cried Dr. Diakos. "Just as lovely as your mother, Charicleia."

Zetta's eyes shimmered and she gave a bashful dip of her head.

"Thank you, sir."

"Seripha? Is that you?" asked Diakos.

"Ioannis? I did not recognize you earlier." Seripha came to him and embraced him like an old friend. "You looked so distinguished up there! And so old! I did not know Diakos was your family name."

"Well, it is not, not really," said Diakos. "I took it when my mother passed away. It is her surname. I liked the sound of it, and I like paying tribute to her. And it gave me a new identity outside of home, to use in my work as a diplomat."

"I, too, have a new name," said Seripha.

"Your husband's?"

"My late husband, yes."

They smiled warmly at one another. Nico raised his brows and looked at Henri.

"He died some years ago," said Seripha.

"I am so sorry to hear that," Diakos said as he took both of her hands in his.

"No need to be sorry. God sent me these two beautiful children to fill the space in my heart."

They were joined by two more as Lord Hartridge came up suddenly, Lord Ockley at his side. Dr. Diakos threw a glance at Ockley, his smile drooping.

"Lord Hartridge," said Diakos. "Thank you again for such a splendid event today. It will be much talked of for a long time to come."

"Of course," said Hartridge with a nod.

"Now, I am afraid there is more to the day ahead," said Diakos, turning back to Nico and the others. "But I am in London for many days yet. I hope you all, Nikolaos, Georgie, Seripha, will join me for dinner some night—or nights—there is so much to talk about. So much time to fill in."

They all agreed. Diakos took Nico and Zetta by the hand.

"Children—well, you are no longer children, of course—but I want you to know how proud I am of you. I have always wondered what became of you, and wondered how you had fared in the world. Your parents, both such great people, wanted so much for you. And I am happy to see that they would have been so proud to know how well you have turned out."

Nico saw a tear roll down his sister's face and he averted his eyes to keep his own at bay. Diakos and the rest made their good-byes, and the diplomat went off to attend to his duties, leaving his card with each of them to connect later.

"Now that the family reunion has concluded," prompted Ockley. "Lord Hartridge, I believe you have something to say."

Nico glanced at Henri and nodded. He braced himself for what was to come, but having Henri, and his family, at his side, he knew he could face it.

"Good lord, man," said Casas. "What happened to your lip?"

Ockley's hand shot to his mouth and he fidgeted nervously. "I ran into something."

"Yes, I imagine you did," said Casas. "Mouths too often open tend to encounter such accidents. At least you had your moustache to soften the blow."

Ockley went wide-eyed.

"Now, see here," he began, but Lord Hartridge interrupted him.

"Lord Ockley is quite right," he said, turning to Nico and Henri. "I do have something to say. I have come to say we are quite pleased and proud of the job you have done with this event. And we appreciate how Mister Kavafis was able to rally the troops after the bizarre accidental poisoning of the entire staff. To which end, having discussed it with Mrs. Plaistow, of course, we would like to propose a promotion for Mister Kavafis to Assistant Manager of the Royal Tea Room."

Nico was thunderstruck; he looked at Henri, blinking in disbelief.

"A promotion, sirs? So soon?"

Hartridge nodded. "Talent, my good man, is talent. And when it is evident, it should be rewarded and applauded. You and Monsieur Henri have proven yourselves a most capable team, and you are a worthy addition to the management. I think you shall work closely with Monsieur Michel in coordinating between kitchen and dining room. If that sounds like something of interest?"

Nico nodded furiously. He peered at his sister and aunt, who beamed at him.

"Of course, sir. Thank you very much, Lord Hartridge, Señor Casas."

"Thank you, indeed," added Casas.

Henri threw his arm over Nico's shoulder and congratulated him.

"Well done, Mister Kavafis."

"Thank you, Monsieur Newbold."

"There, you see," snapped Ockley. "Exactly what I was just

talking with you about, Hartridge. This blatant display."

"Of one colleague congratulating another?" asked Casas.

"Don't be absurd," sneered Ockley. "This is not what was meant to occur. I told you what I saw Hartridge. Those shadowy, scandalous things I have borne witness to you. And this is what you do? They should be sacked, not rewarded."

"It is a funny thing," said Casas, "about those things seen in shadows. For example, our staff claim to have seen you and your man, Grey, hidden in the back hallway prior to the toast pouring something into what looked to be champagne bottles. An emetic of some sort I would imagine, no? At least, I hope that is the worst. The symptoms the kitchen staff described did remind me of when our beloved pet ate some of the laundry bluing and was sick for two days. But no one would dare be that vicious, I hope."

"Who says they saw me in any hallway? Absurd lies," said Ockley.

Casas shrugged. "Two cooks visiting from the canteen."

"Preposterous!" cried Ockley. "The only one we saw in that hallway is there before you! The one you should be attacking instead of me."

"So you were in the hallway with the bottles of champagne then?" asked Casas.

Ockley shook his head. "What? That proves nothing. We were preparing for the toast."

"After which the entire staff took ill?" said Casas calmly. "Except those who had not drunk anything."

"Slander," cried Ockley. "We shall see what aspersions you cast when the papers get a whiff of the tales of this place. The sick, degenerate acts going on behind the scenes at this faux palace. Do you know who I am? The connections I have? How dare you?"

Lord Hartridge stepped closer to Ockley. "No, how dare you, sir."

"I beg your pardon?"

"Neither I nor my partner will not be threatened. Especially in our own store. You can try your hand at a war of the words if you so desire, but let me remind you that I can buy far more newspaper journalists than you can. My family is older and richer than yours, and the press have been known to adjust their opinions quite easily for the right number of banknotes. How many do you possess at the moment? Have you counted up your collection buckets yet?"

"You bastard," hissed Ockley.

"You forget that I know you, Boney," continued Hartridge. "All too well. And you forget how well my uncle knew you. All the secrets of yours he knew, which he shared in confidence. You forget, also, that he kept thorough and explicit diaries of your travels together. Diaries full of stories that would shock even the most heathen of London society if they found their way into being published."

"You would never," growled Ockley.

"Would you like to try me?" asked Hartridge, a cool menace to his voice.

"I have had enough of this farce," Ockley bellowed, his voice cracking. "I wash my hands of all of you. You will never see me again in your store."

"Ah," said Casas brightly. "There, you see, more welcome news of the day."

"Grey!" Ockley shouted. "We are leaving! Now!"

He stormed off as Mister Grey, carrying his hat and walking stick, moved swiftly to catch up with him.

Lord Hartridge turned to them. "I do sincerely apologize that you had to witness that scene."

Nico and Henri both shook their heads, speechless.

"But we meant everything we said with regard to the event. Splendid. And we look forward to seeing you in your new position, Mister Kavafis."

"Thank you, sir."

"Those diaries must be something powerful," said Seripha. "They seemed to have that little man shaking in his scruffy boots."

"I suppose they would be powerful," conceded Lord Hartridge. "If they existed."

Nico's mouth fell agape.

"Do you mean," Henri sputtered. "That your uncle—the stories? You lied?"

Lord Hartridge held his chin up and smiled.

"Monsieur, I am a businessman, thank you very much," he said grandly. "I never lie. I only make speculation work to my advantage."

He and Casas made their goodbyes and left the Tea Room.

The kitchen door opened and Michel came out, blinking, and still a little green around the gills.

"Mon dieu, have you been sleeping in the larder this whole time?" asked Henri, on the verge of laughter.

"Only since the speeches began," admitted Michel. "I still do not feel so well. What have I missed?"

Nico let out a laugh. "Hardly anything at all, Monsieur Michel. That cannot wait until tomorrow to share."

Michel nodded; he clapped Nico on the shoulder. "Nikolaos, you have proven yourself beyond measure today. Monsieur Escoffier himself would hire you in a minute without thought if he saw the work you have done."

"Thank you, Monsieur Michel. But Escoffier can keep his grand establishments." Nico looked at Henri. "I have my place."

"I am happy to hear it, mon frère. Now you must excuse me. I know Mister Singh has one or two comfortable sofas in his department and I shall hastily retreat there to expire. If my body is still in situ when they close the doors tonight, please send word to my wife that I have loved her dearly and truly."

"Edith will raise you from the dead if you do not return home," said Henri. "Of that, I am not worried."

"Come," said Aunt Seripha, "let us go home and have a proper dinner."

"Yes, monsieur," said Zetta. "We would welcome you."

Nico saw a crooked smile on Henri's face as he tried to cipher his emotions.

"You are too kind," Henri said, "but I do not think I can look at food again today."

"That's fine then," said Nico. "We can simply share a bottle of wine and enjoy one another's company."

"Yes," said Seripha. "We must. You are family now, Henri. There is no need to worry about anything formal."

Henri seemed overwhelmed and Nico was bold enough to reach out and grab his hand.

"Thank you, mon amour, for coming back for me today."

"I always will, monsieur."

EPILOGUE

Eighteen months later

DEVOID OF FURNITURE, the space felt cavernous. It was towards the back of the building on this floor, a large area that had been used previously as a storage room. But H&C was expanding, if that was conceivably possible, and new uses were being found for all available space. Lord Hartridge and Señor Casas, never ones to sit idle, wanted to expand the reach of what they offered. The food halls and the Tea Room were nice, but why not fine dining too? H&C should have it all, they decided.

Nico examined one corner of the space, where the single row of windows resided, overlooking the streets of London. Aside from the front of the space, which opened onto the central area of the store, this was the only source of natural light.

"It will be darker than the Tea Room," he said.

"Yes," agreed Henri. "But I think it will work for the atmosphere."

He jogged to the other side of the space. "Over here, you see, I want to put an American-style bar. And just at the end here, where no patron would want to sit, I was thinking that we could make this the musicians' corner."

"But I thought you objected to music in restaurants?"

Henri shrugged. "My time at the Royal Tea Room has

opened my mind."

"Is that so?"

"Oui. And you have also opened my palate with those American cocktails you make at home."

"I seem to remember you declaring my drinks cart very gauche when I purchased it."

"Can a man not change his mind?"

Nico chuckled. "Some, it seems, can do so three or four times a day."

"So here we will have the musicians, here the American bar. This will give us options if the restaurant stays open into the night. We shall create a mood. Also, I was thinking we might have a female bartender like Miss Ada at the Savoy Hotel."

"How modern you have become, Henri."

"You act as if I was some stuffy old curmudgeon when you met me, mon amour."

"On the contrary, mon chéri, I never once said you were old."

"Bâtard."

Nico smiled at his favorite appellation.

"What will you call it? This delicious modern restaurant of yours."

Henri paused and looked at him. He let his eyes wander up and down Nico's body. Here, in this half dark space, they had no need to worry of passersby.

"I shall call it *Le petit Jupiter.*"

Nico felt himself blush and he tried to contain his smile. "You mean…"

"I am naming it after you? Bien sûr. What else?"

Henri approached him, lifting his chin. He smoothed an errant curl in his hair. "You know, your eyes shine so brightly, even here."

Nico lifted his chin higher, letting Henri trace his lips with his fingertips. Henri leaned in for a kiss.

"But I told you before," Nico said, before he could be kissed.

"It's Zeus in Greek mythology."

Henri pressed his forehead against Nico's and gave a little growl. "Yes, yes, yes, my little scholar. But Jupiter sounds better in French."

"Does it?"

"Évidemment. Besides, it will be our little secret."

Nico ran his tongue along his bottom lip.

"I have told you," he teased, "that I do not like secrets, monsieur."

Henri pulled him close. "You must not be so rigid, Nico. You must learn to be more flexible, more accepting." He raised his brows. "This is what I have constantly heard from a friend of mine."

"Your friend sounds very wise." Nico laughed. "But, yes, Chef. I surrender."

"You had better."

He kissed Nico, a warm, affectionate kiss, his fingertips dancing across Nico's skin, his tongue lovingly caressing Nico's.

They walked towards the front of the restaurant space, the light from outside getting brighter as they did. As if they were emerging from hibernation, thought Nico.

"Will Michel be upset that you are not taking him to the Jupiter?"

"Non, he is very happy," said Henri. "He will run the Tea Room kitchens now. I think he has been wanting to get rid of me for years."

"Who can blame him?" Nico winked at him.

"Besides, I have my own manager and sous chef now, don't I?"

"Am I to be both? Am I to be paid two salaries?"

"You will be paid in kisses and affection."

"I prefer cash, you know."

Henri smiled a wicked smile. "Bâtard."

"And will you be bringing David along to the Jupiter?"

"Mon dieu! Don't be ridiculous. He is Michel's problem to

solve now."

"I think David will surprise you one day."

"He could do nothing more but that."

They paused just before the entrance.

"Shall we visit the furnishings department to discuss our order?" asked Henri.

"No," Nico said. "I think we should go home and enjoy a freshly made cocktail from my very gauche but open-minded drinks cart, and sit by the fire."

"Shall we go out for dinner first?"

"Why should I go out for dinner when I live with a renowned chef?"

"I am expected to work at home as well?"

Nico smiled at him. "You will be paid in kisses and affection."

"C'est bon, then I shall take my first payment now."

Henri wrapped his arms around Nico and kissed him sweetly.

Author's Historical Note

The gentle reader will note that the department store featured in this series bears a striking resemblance to a certain infamous institution on Oxford Street, London. And though it was primarily inspired by that noted palace of shopping, my Hartridge & Casas should in no way be understood to be a documentary of that or any other store in whole. Its bones may be based on Oxford Street but I have taken inspiration from and incorporated elements of many of the department stores which existed during the Edwardian Era—from Scotland to France to Chicago and beyond.

Likewise, the idea of blending French and Greek cuisine is inspired by Nikolaos Tselementes, who is considered by some to be the father of modern Greek cooking, and by others a corrupter of tradition. I'll let you decide which one for yourself. So while his moussaka à la béchamel might not have been recorded for a decade to come, and was not invented in the kitchens of a department store tea room late one sultry summer night—at least, not that we know of—I do hope you'll allow me a little leeway in my creation of fiction.

I hope you've enjoyed visiting this department store of my imagination, this Hartridge & Casas, as much as I wish I could actually walk its floors.

About the Author

Joshua Ian can easily be captured by a witty turn of phrase or a low-bottomed electronic bassline. If you manage to combine the two, then you have his heart forever. He lives in New York City and is a keen cinema lover and self-proclaimed Dark Chocolate Expert. When not staring at a blank screen and cursing the futility of life, he can be found watching cozy mystery shows, daydreaming of his future kaftan collection, or scouring used book vendors to accumulate more vintage romances and mysteries than his shelves are actually capable of handling. One day he plans to travel the world – to see what each country has to offer in the way of used books, movie theatres, and dark chocolate, naturally.

Social Media Links:
Website: moodyboxfan.com
Goodreads: goodreads.com/joshuaian
Instagram: instagram.com/moodyboxfan
Twitter: twitter.com/joshuaianauthor
Bookbub: bookbub.com/authors/joshua-ian

www.ingramcontent.com/pod-product-compliance
Lightning Source LLC
Chambersburg PA
CBHW071226210726
48293CB00002B/591